1.7 billion yen in a single hour. A certified marksman and driver who possesses a mysterious sixth sense called the Lion's Nose.

Sophia

A Magistellus contracted with Lily-Kiska. Elf.

Lily-Kiska

A member of Ag Wolves, a group seeking to prevent the Overtrick from falling into the wrong hands and thus maintain the order of *Money (Game) Master*.

MAGISTELLUS BAD TRIP

Kazuma Kamachi

Illustration by **Mahaya**

1

Tselika

The Magistellus contracted with Kaname. A succubus dressed like a pit babe. Wearer of many hats who has high specs, but has hedonistic and decadent tastes that often earn her a swift rebuke from Kaname.

o should we prey on
?"

Midori Hekireki

A girl rumored to be related to the legendary Dealer Criminal AO. Ends up at odds with Kaname and his associates while on a mission to retrieve the Overtrick. However...

MAGISTELLUS BAD TRIP

1

Kazuma Kamachi

Illustration by **Mahaya**

YEN
ON

New York

MAGISTELLUS BAD TRIP
Kazuma Kamachi

Translation by Jake Humphrey
Cover art by Mahaya

MAGISTELLUS BAD TRIP Vol. 1
©Kazuma Kamachi 2019
First published in Japan in 2019 by KADOKAWA CORPORATION, Tokyo.
English translation rights arranged with KADOKAWA CORPORATION, Tokyo, through TUTTLE-MORI AGENCY, INC., Tokyo.

English translation © 2021 by Yen Press, LLC

Yen On
150 West 30th Street, 19th Floor
New York, NY 10001

Visit us at yenpress.com
facebook.com/yenpress
twitter.com/yenpress
yenpress.tumblr.com
instagram.com/yenpress

First Yen On Edition: September 2021

Yen On is an imprint of Yen Press, LLC.
The Yen On name and logo are trademarks of Yen Press, LLC.

Library of Congress Cataloging-in-Publication Data
Names: Kamachi, Kazuma, author. | Mahaya, illustrator. | Humphrey, Jake, translator.
Title: Magistellus bad trip / Kazuma Kamachi ; illustration by Mahaya ; translation by Jake Humphrey.
Description: First Yen On edition. | New York, NY : Yen On, 2021–
Identifiers: LCCN 2021023505 | ISBN 9781975314262 (v. 1 ; trade paperback)
Subjects: CYAC: Science fiction. | Fantasy. | Artificial intelligence—Fiction. |
    Virtual reality—Fiction. | Magic—Fiction.
Classification: LCC PZ7.1.K215 Mag 2021 | DDC [Fic]—dc23
LC record available at https://lccn.loc.gov/2021023505

ISBNs: 978-1-9753-1426-2 (paperback)
       978-1-9753-1427-9 (ebook)

10   9   8   7   6   5   4   3   2   1

LSC-C
Printed in the United States of America

CONTENTS

Prologue

Server name: Alpha Scarlet.
Starting location: Tokonatsu City, Mega-Float II.
Log-in credentials accepted.
Welcome to *Money (Game) Master*, **Kaname Suou.**

The young man saw bright lights and intense colors flashing in his eyes, burning his retinas. He suppressed the knot in the back of his throat, overcome with sudden vertigo and nausea. Eventually, the storm began to quell, giving way to sensations of a new world.

A few seconds later, his vision focused, and he found himself in a low-built right-hand-drive sports car. Neatly contained in the driver's seat of the stationary vehicle, Kaname checked his face in the rearview mirror. A pair of piercing eyes glared back at him, framed by silky black hair. He was wearing a white dress shirt with rolled-up sleeves and a loose red necktie. He looked down at his arms to find a smart watch strapped on one of his wrists. His eyes trailed down his arm to his legs, clothed in a pair of blue pants, attached to which was a small black carrying case.

For a second, he'd been disoriented, but then he settled into his new environment.

This was him now. As for where he was…

He opened the door and stepped out of the car. Beams of sunlight and a clear sky greeted him, and the warm, dry air reminded him of the tropics. He was in a seaside industrial area dominated by asphalt and concrete. The car he now stood outside sat just off the road by the seafront—a small two-seater coupe painted a garish green color, like mint ice cream.

And upon the hood, sprawled out on her front, lay a beautiful woman who oozed sex appeal. Every now and again, she would take a languid sip from a straw stuck into a coconut. It was as though she was relaxing on the beach, sunbathing. Except what she wore wasn't a swimsuit exactly. A white bikini top and a pale-green miniskirt, over which was a cropped jacket trimmed with fur. It seemed to be based on a pit babe's outfit.

ToyDream. MegaloDiver Shipping. Fiamma Securities. Logos traced the seductive curves of her body. They weren't printed on, but rather they scrolled constantly like on an LCD screen or projection mapping.

There was something even more striking about her than the way she dressed. Her long, fluffy hair was dyed a mint green, and a pair of white horns, cowlike, sprouted from the sides of her head. She had bat wings on her back and a tail that extended from her waist, arrow-shaped but forked at the end in a way reminiscent of a bident or a stag beetle's horns.

"Tselika."

"Why, if it isn't you, My Lord. Punctual as ever, I see." The pit babe grinned without changing her posture.

"What exactly are you up to?"

"I was just in the middle of taking a selfie using the dashcam," she said. "After all, it would be blasphemous were we not to preserve such beauty for future generations."

Kaname was about to retort when an electrical sound came from the car on which Tselika was lying. It was gentle, like a cell phone's ringtone. At the same time, lines of text, large and small, began to wrap around the entire frame of the car. They looked like the sponsorship messages on a race car, but that's not what they were. The polished surfaces of the vehicle became a monitor, and a large square window appeared on the side of the car facing Kaname.

A video message started to play, and a timer appeared in one corner of the screen. A short-haired girl popped up on the window, looking around with a somewhat nervous expression. It was as though she was trying to record herself without ever having used a video camera before. To Kaname, her speech sounded different from normal. Stiffer.

"Ahem... How's my dear brother?

"I'm thinking of going to see a movie with my friends Mich and Tanya. It's called Kotemitsu Gold Rush. *It's that one about the Swiss Depression. You know, the one that nearly got out of hand.*

"I wasn't sure how to respond when they asked me, but I don't think it's right for me to stay cooped up in here all the time. I figured this could be a good chance to try to switch it up. Can I go? If it's okay, then please give me permission to leave.

"...Ack, hurry! I don't have a lot of time left!"

There *were* movie theaters here, but the one that Kaname's sister was referring to was in the real world. Kaname moved his gaze around a digital keyboard, typing an e-mail granting her request, and sent it off to his sister's address.

Tselika was stunned. "Rather overprotective, I must say."

"I know how it looks," Kaname said, "but it's what she wants. She gets even worse if I don't pay attention to her, so I have to go along with it. Besides, my stomach is on the line."

"Oh? You make Ayame cook for you?"

"Not really. My parents usually take turns. But when Ayame gets frustrated, she often heads to the kitchen. To 'clear her mind,' she says. I don't know what secret ingredient she uses, but it's enough to ruin supper for the night. So you see, I'd prefer to keep her happy."

Anyway, back to the task at hand. After taking care of business, Kaname checked the time on his smart watch and shifted his focus back to taking stock of the situation.

"I want to know everything that happened while I was away. What's the vehicle's status?"

"Why, everything is as your shopping list demanded. Tank full, tire pressure optimal, all systems are go. Since we've got a job coming up, I also took the pleasure of ensuring it was cleaned inside and out, and I've even included a little drink for when this is over."

"Weapons?"

"A fully stocked short-range sniper rifle in the trunk. However, as requested, there's only one magazine."

"And how are things going with F. Ober Industries?"

As Kaname inquired further, Tselika rolled about on the hood of the car—from her front to her back. She was crushing her wings or bending them out of shape, but it didn't seem to hurt her. As she answered his questions, she continued to show off her body.

Among the strings of characters crawling over her pit-babe outfit, which included a pair of thigh-length boots, F. Ober became particularly prominent. Numbers scrolled horizontally across her. Even the odd graph would surface. Although these logos belonged to companies, they weren't her sponsors. Her clothes were displaying all kinds of information pertaining to the prices of various products and commodities from every company, alongside the trading names of notable stocks and securities, in real time.

Tracing from her chest down to her thigh with her finger, Tselika pointed out one graph that moved across the curve of her body.

"As you can see, they've been in the red for some time now, owing to the sharp increase in the price of rare-earth elements. But if somebody was to give their stalled research a little push in the right direction, I daresay *things could change quite suddenly.*"

"All right," muttered Kaname to himself.

His basketball shoes hit the asphalt as he marched to the rear of the mint-green coupe and raised the trunk door. Just as the demon had said, the weapon was there. Kaname took it out. The short-range sniper rifle Short Spear. Kaname ran his eyes over the characteristic red rubber covering both its grip and collapsible stock.

It would be more accurate to describe it as a large handgun with an added stock and extended barrel, rather than an assault rifle with its best components accentuated. It was even chambered in .45-caliber ammunition instead of rifle rounds. The muzzle velocity was subsonic, so the weapon prioritized stealth over range. The magazine was not located within the grip like a handgun but had a separate slot, like a rifle, and loading a fresh magazine would automatically chamber the first round.

"Get in the car, Tselika," ordered Kaname.

"As you wish, My Lord," she replied.

The two sat down in the coupe, with Kaname taking the driver's seat on the right. As if by magic, the wings on Tselika's back neatly folded themselves away, revealing the smooth skin of her back through her cropped short-sleeve jacket. Since it would be difficult to drive with the weapon, Kaname tossed it into Tselika's lap. After inserting the key and depressing the clutch, he thumbed down the ignition button, and the engine flared to life.

The vehicle roared like some terrible beast. Releasing the hand brake and putting the car into first gear, Kaname nudged the accelerator with his right foot while smoothly taking his left off the clutch. The transmission engaged cleanly, and despite the horsepower of the sports car in which the pair sat, it set off quite gently down the left-hand lane of the road, like a needle settling into the groove of a record.

Tokonatsu City was made up of a peninsula shaped like a shark's tooth, a bunch of islands that extended off the coast, several artificial islands created using industrial flotation systems, and a coral reef, all connected by a huge circular bridge. Kaname and Tselika were currently on the enormous Mega-Float II, which stretched for several kilometers in all directions. Yet even amid this gray world of pipes and factories, other Dealers had noticed him and drew secretly closer.

Here's a question: How can you guarantee a return on investment without taking any risks? There are many ways to do this. One example would be insider trading, where you trade securities with advance knowledge of some large upcoming event between the companies involved. Another would be threatening the director or some big investors to stage a hostile takeover. You could lower a company's value by spreading false rumors or stealing technical information through cyberattacks. If you wanted, you could even choose to induce technological innovation yourself by uploading diagrams of new technologies in an internet video, like a puzzle to be solved, or even blow up trucks and trains containing your rival's newest product.

Of course, some might object to such behaviors in the real world. But here, that wasn't the case. *Money (Game) Master* was a place cut off from the rules of reality, after all.

"Several publications have reported that Asgard Motors, known under brands like Hunts and Arhen, has branched into the defense industry, producing tanks and other armored vehicles. Their AI press secretary has said…"

"The Rainy Girl Study, widely touted as an efficient way to combat poverty and increase production of edible insects, has been called into question recently by information revealing that it has barely any management or regulations…"

"The rumors of internal discord within the management of Rush General Trading Co. was allegedly confirmed several days ago, as the board of directors announced their decision to remove the current sitting president. This has prompted the president to bolster his ranks by recruiting PMCs and Dealers, which has aggravated the…"

In-game broadcasts. All you could hear on the radio was Western music or economic news like this. It signaled the beginning of an event. You could choose to go with the flow or against it, make money sucking up to the big AI companies or even go so far as to destroy them. It was an open-world game with no wrong way to play.

"Remind me of the mission," Kaname instructed.

"We're currently buying up as much aluminum as possible, a metal you might recognize. It's used to produce a one-yen coin in real life. Not much is happening at the moment, but if prices spike within the next hour, our stock will skyrocket, by a factor of up to ten thousand. That will give us the opportunity to sell off the metal we purchased for tens of thousands of *snow* at a price in the hundred millions. In fact, we've already taken steps to do so by making use of a large but declining corporation named F. Ober."

It was tempting to invest in expensive metals like gold or platinum, which cost at least three thousand *snow* per gram, but aluminum, at one *snow* per gram, was the target here. It was easy to buy, and if the per-gram price went up by even a single *snow*, you could double your money.

The coupe sped out of Mega-Float II onto a long highway-like bridge. One side looked out onto the coral sea, the water a greenish shade of blue. Kaname accelerated, weaving between the other cars as he made his way over the gently curving bridge. The speedometer hit two hundred kilometers per hour in an instant, but Kaname didn't feel his life was in danger. It just felt like playing a racing game.

"How can we make that happen?" he asked.

Tselika explained. "F. Ober Industries is an AI business in the camera sector, but it's currently not even in the top ten. It's been difficult for them to obtain semiconductors, thanks to the sharp increase in the price of some particular rare-earth materials: metals the average person has never even seen or heard of called kuchnoids. But there's this new technology that smaller companies have discarded, ignorant of its true value. Once F. Ober gets its hands on it, it'll be able to substitute kuchnoids with regular old aluminum. The company will become a global leader, and the price of this metal we're sitting on will shoot through the roof."

Windows popped up all over the display-like windshield. They showed stock numbers and estimated trading prices of the aluminum that F. Ober would soon need, various routes from the park to the main offices, predicted numbers and strength of enemy Dealers, and the locations of possible attacks.

"So what do we actually need to do?"

"Pick up a briefcase from the park on the peninsula and deliver it to F. Ober headquarters on this landmass. However, this is a big moment in history—a tug-of-war between kuchnoids and aluminum, between tradition and the future. We must handle any opposition that comes our way, or else it's all over."

Money (Game) Master was best thought of as a game of financial dealings where nothing was against the law. The players, called

Dealers, entered a virtual financial district known as Tokonatsu City and competed to see who could grow their seed money the most. There were no levels or experience points. A Dealer's strength could be boosted only by cash, which players used to secure items and equipment. Those reduced to nothing could collect empty cans for change and try to earn it all back, and a serious player could begin to own land and businesses, turn their hand to financial dealing, and even blow up the buildings of enemy Dealers. That was the kind of world this was.

Reaching the end of the long bridge, the car approached the shark's tooth–shaped peninsula. White beaches lined the shores, and palm trees and hibiscus flowers flourished along the roadside and in flower beds. Tall skyscrapers reflected the sunlight like mirrors. A cesspool of money that gobbled up desires and bloated itself on them. Sometimes even the Dealers couldn't control it.

"One last question," said Kaname. "Are you ready?"

"When you are, My Lord," Tselika replied.

The sports car, vibrant like mint ice cream, arrived on the peninsula and headed for the financial district.

Kaname received the silver-paneled briefcase in the park from an AI agent whose smile was just a little *too* perfect and threw it in the trunk. The estimated distance to the F. Ober headquarters was about fifteen kilometers. He turned the vehicle around, brushing dangerously close to a large metal dumpster about the size of a small car. As soon as he left the park, enemy Dealers immediately closed in on him. Kaname shifted gears up and up, quickly manipulating the stick, pushing the car into sixth, then seventh gear, even though he usually stuck to fifth. The needle on the speedometer flew up to three hundred kilometers per hour.

But this was nothing but an ordinary day in Tokonatsu City. The flashy sports car behind Kaname remained visible in his rearview mirror, and although security cameras covered the walls of buildings and streetlights, not a single one of them would bother to report him.

In the passenger seat, Tselika scanned the map that covered the windshield in front of her and spoke in a puzzled voice while turning to her right.

"My Lord? We've veered off our shortest route!"

"If we go that way, we won't stand a chance."

Racing down the main road, Kaname ignored the traffic signals and cut across the curve of the intersection. He forced the gears back down, making them drop speed, and yanked hard on the hand brake to cause the rear wheels to skid. The tires screeched, painting a black crescent on the surface of the road, and he completed the right turn while narrowly avoiding a large truck coming in from the side.

By using the hand brake and gearshift, Kaname was slightly outpacing his pursuer. It didn't look like this was going to be enough to shake them off, though. The roof of the bright-red sports car opened, and a man poked his upper body into view. He was holding something in his hands.

"Submachine gun!" yelled Tselika.

"He'll never hit us when we're moving this fast."

Rat-a-tat! A quick burst of fire sprayed, but just as Kaname said, not a single shot hit the tires or the gas tank. That said, it still wasn't fun to see sparks fly from the asphalt so close.

Tselika began to protest. "He could have a red dot sight that lets him auto-aim or something! It won't matter how fast we're moving if his sights are lined up automatically!"

"Why is an AI-controlled Magistellus so scared of taking a bullet?" he asked.

"Because it still hurts to get shot! And if I take a fatal wound, I get frozen and can't move! But most of all, I couldn't bear the thought of damaging this vehicle that serves as my temple!"

"Why not? It's not like anything would happen to your AI data if they destroyed it."

"And? Do you think the temples and cathedrals of *your* world were only meant to serve a functional purpose? The glory of my vehicle is how I present myself to the other Magistelli! How humiliating! For it to suffer even a single scratch would be like shattering every single window in my bathroom, so the entire street might feast their eyes on me while I'm showering!"

"And that's a big deal because...?"

"Aaargh!"

"Tselika. The auto-aim is especially susceptible to any kind of sudden movement. At this speed, in this wind, there's no way he'll be able to line up a shot."

Kaname appeared unperturbed as he gripped the wheel. Just then, something started to happen in the bright-red sports car behind them. The man, appearing to give up, shrank back down inside the vehicle and reappeared with a new weapon resting on his shoulder.

Tselika's eyes went wide. "Whoa, whoa, whoa. Is that a rocket launcher?!"

"Don't worry. It's not guided. Only a direct hit will deal enough damage to destroy us."

"Are you still counting on the auto-aim?"

"He won't hit us. The most he could do is blow up one of these dumpsters."

"How can you be so sure?!"

"I can smell it. I'm not getting that tingly feeling yet. We're still safe."

"The Lion's Nose, I presume? Listen, how am I supposed to place my trust in something that's not an in-game skill or physical booster?!"

At that moment, he realized something. Scattering 9mm bullets was one thing, but what would happen if a rocket launcher missed and took a piece out of the sidewalk? Of course, these accidents were one of the best parts of *Money (Game) Master*, but in some cruel twist of fate, a hardworking Dealer girl had just so happened to pick that exact spot to set up a fruit stall.

"..."

"My Lord? Are you listening?"

Kaname had a split second to decide. He slammed his foot down on the brake pedal. The coupe suddenly fell back, like it was stopped from advancing by a huge hand. Tselika, apparently too cool for seat belts, flew forward and nearly struck her forehead on the windshield. Then, in what felt exactly like being blasted backward, the vehicle closed in on the red sports car that was approaching from behind. Kaname fell in alongside it, matching speeds. The two men, one driving and one above, looked on, flabbergasted.

Kaname took Short Spear from Tselika's lap and used it to break the glass of the driver's seat window. Without relying on auto-aim, Kaname manually lined up the sights with the driver of the red sports car, focusing on the man's forehead. He pulled the trigger once.

There was no loud gunshot. The barrel sported an integrated silencer. There was only a short metallic ringing sound, like plucking a metal pick. The bullet punched straight through both the other car's window and the driver's skull. The red sports car spun out of control, crashing into a nearby camera-equipped traffic light, the other man still hanging out of the open roof.

Tselika gave an almighty shriek. "Aaaaaaaaarghhhhhh! My vehicle! My temple! What are you doing, My Lord?! Aaaaaaaaaaaaaaaarghhhhh!"

"What? Sorry, I can't hear you over the wind!"

"Don't play dumb with me, My Lord! It's not like that fruit-vending woman is going to thank you, and yet you chose to defile my precious windowpane!"

"Helping others isn't about bragging rights or asking for something in return," Kaname replied offhandedly, hoping to shut Tselika up. At that moment, something else happened.

As if to block the road, a huge tanker broke across the intersection and slammed on the brakes. More cars were closing in from behind. Kaname was trapped.

"What are we going to do, My Lord?!" asked Tselika.

"We get that huge thing out of the way."

"Ha! You sound very confident. And how exactly do you plan to do that?!"

As the wind roared around him, Kaname fiddled with the gun in his hand.

"You mind if I break the front window, too?" he asked.

"ARE. YOU. OUT. OF. YOUR. MIIIIIIIND?!"

Clicking his tongue, Kaname shoved his right arm out the broken

side window and pointed the barrel. Of course, it wasn't like he needed to use the scope at this range, but he would still have to eyeball the aim.

To kill a person, you aimed at the head.

The car equivalent was its gas tank. Hit that weak spot, and it didn't matter how much HP it had. For a tanker, besides the fancy reinforced tank in the trailer, there was a separate square one right below the front tractor.

One shot was all it took. The gas tank exploded with a boom. As heavy as the cylindrical trailer was, the force of the explosion still lifted it a few feet off the ground. Pulling his arm back into the vehicle, Kaname took that moment to speed up as fast as he could toward the opening. The car barely made it through the meter of space before the huge steel maw clamped down behind him. The pursuing vehicles, a second too late, plowed into the tanker with a succession of loud crashes.

As he checked behind them in the rearview mirror, Kaname mumbled to himself, "I think we can relax for now."

"But there's still a bunch more cars coming from down a different road!"

"They're probably just a contingency team. The ones we crushed will have been the elites. These guys are the backup. They won't be as strong. No problem for us."

"How can you sound so sure?"

"We're close to F. Ober headquarters. If we assume that somebody planned this, they should have positioned their main forces closer to the target. I mean, otherwise…"

Kaname didn't finish that thought. After checking the sidewalk was clear, he swerved the coupe right onto it and up an accessibility ramp, launching the carbon frame of the vehicle into the air like a skier making a jump. The car flew past an intersection, over a row of short metal posts, and straight into the F. Ober building. Not the lobby or the parking lot but straight through the glass window of an upper floor.

"Aaaaaaaaaagh!" Tselika screamed from the passenger seat. Kaname ignored her.

The glass shattered everywhere. Kaname yanked on the hand brake and spun the car around ninety degrees, using all four tires to bleed off the vehicle's speed. Tables and chairs were strewn across the space as the car plowed through the meeting room, stopping just centimeters short of crushing the AI employees against the wall.

Meanwhile, Kaname's pursuers tried to stop their momentum, screeching to a halt on the F. Ober grounds.

Then there was a terrifying, mechanical growl. Not from the coupe or the pursuers outside. Out of nowhere appeared several enormous armored vehicles, and attack helicopters rushed between the buildings to join them. The new force opened fire on the intruders.

Kaname looked exasperated.

"...Sounds like the company's PMCs got them. Don't they know it's suicide to go up against AI mercenaries unprepared? What do you think will happen if you try to fight infinite soldiers with only a finite amount of ammunition?"

PMCs protected only the grounds of the companies that contracted them, but they were unmatched on that front. You could have as many Dealers as you wanted, break whatever laws you wanted, have all the money and items you could ever ask for, and they still wouldn't allow you to land so much as a scratch on the company's factories and buildings, much less interfere with their business directly.

...Well, that was what made fighting them so engaging. It was more fun to play smart.

Anyway, now that they were on the grounds, Kaname and Tselika were safe. Not because the mercenaries harbored any particular favor for the two but because they possessed something of great value to the company: the briefcase. The surviving enemy Dealers came to a halt, surveilled by the multiple armored vehicles and gunships of the PMCs. It seemed unlikely that any one of them would be able to set foot on the premises without being blasted in retaliation. The worst thing that Kaname would need to be on the lookout for would be an attack from a sniper, he thought, as he slowly got out of the car.

But for some reason, Tselika didn't seem to want to leave her seat.

"What's wrong? Hurry up, Tselika," Kaname urged.

"Ugh. I hate going onto other people's property. We Magistelli deal in contracts; it's not right for us to touch things that don't belong to us."

Of course, she could still open doors or walk down hallways, but it was beyond her to grab a fire extinguisher and bash somebody over the head with it or to break into a vault and steal wads of cash. Nevertheless, she had no problems taking the wheel of Kaname's car and running over an AI employee or grabbing his rifle and going on a shooting spree. In many ways, the restrictions were rather lax. Perhaps it was supposed to hold Dealers liable for the actions of their Magistelli.

"It's not about whether you like it or not. I need your abilities."

"Bleh."

Tselika reluctantly got out of the car. Kaname gave her a sidelong glance and went to retrieve the briefcase from the trunk. Almost pinned to the wall of the trashed meeting room, the AI-controlled manager responded with a smile that was just a little *too* perfect.

"Thank you kindly. After confirming the success of the mission, we will deposit the funds into your account as per our agreement."

Kaname waved his hand dismissively. It wasn't the reward that interested him. It was his stockpile of aluminum, currently only worth its weight in pebbles.

"Tselika, check the metal trading prices!"

"Yes sirree! Everything has gone according to plan, so I expect we shall see our jump... Aha! In just the last couple of minutes, the price of aluminum has risen from one *snow* per gram to ten thousand! A free market with no trading limits is a force to be reckoned with. We'd better sell immediately or the AI might freeze the market!"

As the demon smiled, graphs scrolled across her green-and-white pit-babe outfit—fur-trimmed jacket, bikini top, miniskirt, gloves, thigh-high boots—detailing the sharp turn in aluminum and kuchnoid trading with F. Ober.

Kaname felt something that wasn't quite a smell. It wasn't a jolt, like electricity, or a numbness. It was an inexplicable sensation that tickled the tip of his nose.

"Not yet," he said. "Ten thousand isn't good enough."

"My Lord...? Didn't you hear what I just said?"

"Wait another five minutes. We're aiming for twenty-five thousand. Hold out until then."

"But if the market gets flooded, our transmission might get jammed, and our orders might not get through! Wait, forget that—if the price rises too much, the buyers will pull out! We're in a good position right now because we have a large stockpile of the stuff, but aluminum itself is everywhere. You can extract it from empty cans, for crying out loud! Once F. Ober finishes its buying frenzy, it'll have plenty of sellers to choose from, and they'll go with the lowest bidder. There's no point in having a mountain of aluminum that nobody wants to buy!"

"Two and a half minutes."

"There's ten thousand transactions being carried out every second! A few seconds is like an eternity in the investment world! Once the peak passes, that's it, and our gold mine will be reduced to worthless rock again!"

"Ninety seconds."

"Grgggh!!!"

"Trust me. I can smell it."

"The Lion's Nose? There are wrinkles all over your forehead!"

Tselika bit her lip, as though she was watching a baby crawl across a rickety rope bridge.

Yet Kaname still waited.

And he waited.

And then…

As the graph on Tselika's bikini top passed a certain threshold, the color changed to a bright red.

"Ah! Threshold passed! That's twenty-five thousand!" Tselika yelled.

"Then sell it all! And don't leave a single gram!"

"Got it! There! Phew, that was a close one."

Numbers raced across her curves.

Besides F. Ober, countless Dealers snapped up the aluminum like a pack of hungry piranhas, hoping to make a quick profit off reselling it. The money came rolling in. Just a second later, the line took a sharp downturn. The bubble had already burst.

The dream had lasted only a few minutes, and aluminum cans had once again become regular old trash. If they had been seconds too late, any hopes of profit would have gone down the drain with it. The weird sensation in Kaname's nose had disappeared as well.

"I estimate our tens of thousands of *snow* worth of aluminum have turned into roughly 1.7 billion, My Lord."

The AI employees continued to observe as though nothing had happened, despite the future of their very company being batted about left and right like a tennis ball. Kaname paid them no mind, either.

"We've completed the first step," he said as he approached the car. "We have enough funds to get started."

"So you're going to use this to secure the Legacy?"

"This is no ordinary mission. We need money if we're to grab their attention."

"I hoped you'd say something like that," Tselika commented as she watched the numbers and graphs float across the windshield, leaning back into the passenger seat. "But are you sure this is what you want to do? The exchange rate for *snow* to yen is one-to-one. You, a high school boy, could have 1.7 billion yen right now if you so wished."

Kaname's response to that was quite short.

"This is more important than that."

04/01/20XX 10:20 AM

Money (Game) Master
Currently the largest online game in the world, *Money (Game) Master* is an open world of financial dealings where nothing is against the law. Compete with other players by dealing in property, futures, and stocks to grow your starting capital. There are no levels or experience points. A Dealer's strength can be boosted only by cash, which players use to secure items and equipment.

Tokonatsu City
The fictional city that serves as the stage for *Money (Game) Master*. A financial district in a tropical environment that comprises a peninsula shaped like a shark's tooth and several islands scattered off the coast, as well as a number of artificial industrial mega-floats, all connected by a huge circular bridge. Guns are legal, steering wheels are on the right, and cars drive on the left side of the street like in Japan. While there are many servers, they all constantly share information, so your experience will be the same regardless of which one you connect to.

Snow
Originally just an in-game currency, *snow* has been growing in value as the in-game population skyrocketed, before stabilizing at a value rivaling the dollar or the yen. It has become a famous example of what is now called "virtual currency." In countries and regions where the exchange rate is unstable, *snow* is often preferred over the local currency, and it has already started to make an impact on continent-wide economies. As a result, the very best players can not only attain personal success but also influence the economy on a global scale. It is said to have been named after the rarity and transience of snowfall in the tropics, but nobody knows for sure.

Dealer
The name given to a player character. Their origins are varied: Some players are casual; others have a professional business background. Some are backed by multiple patrons, while others invest taxpayer money gathered from public services.

Magistellus

A name originally given to a human who made a contract with a succubus. In the game, however, Magistelli are navigators and partners to the player. Although they are capable of conversing like humans, they are in fact tapped into artificial intelligence. There are many theories, but few facts, as to why they are the only fantastical element of the game. Besides succubi, other types such as mermaids and elves have been confirmed to exist. A Magistellus shares attributes with its Dealer such as money, property, and skills, but they cannot even ride a bicycle if it does not belong to them. The exception to this is that if they have a shopping list, they can purchase goods with their Dealer's money.

AI Business (Virtual)

Large in-game companies named after ones in the real world. Every employee, from the CEO to the lowliest intern, is an AI-controlled NPC. The majority of listed companies in the game are virtual, therefore Dealers needn't feel guilty about engaging in unfair business practices such as intimidation, fearmongering, or violence.

PMC

Soldiers that protect the AI companies. They are also controlled by AI but are not part of the companies, since they work on a contract basis. This contract restricts their movements to terms that have already been agreed upon, but they wield unmatched firepower. Ordinary Dealers cannot defeat them in a fair fight, no matter how much equipment they have.

Once upon a time, *Money (Game) Master* was home to a legendary Dealer named Criminal AO.

When he Fell, his equipment was scattered across the land.

In that world, there were no levels or experience points. A Dealer's strength could be boosted only by cash, which players used to secure items and equipment. Even someone who had been playing for only ten minutes could be equal to Criminal AO in power if they possessed his equipment.

This was equipment so heavily customized and strong that it was thought to be a hack. It was the only exception to the gritty realism of the metropolitan crime setting that permeated *Money (Game) Master*. These items were so heavily modded that they had exceeded even the preset physical limits of the world, and the incredibly powerful artifacts were known as the Overtrick—End Magic.

The value of *snow* was currently stable and on par with the yen or the dollar. If you made one thousand *snow* in-game, it was as if you'd been wired one thousand yen. In some places, it was not uncommon for people to store their savings in-game, as property or gemstones, rather than in a bank. And this was not the practice only of a few eccentrics but financial institutions on which entire countries relied.

Controlling the economy of the game meant you could control the economy of the real world.

That was why everyone wanted to get their hands on the Legacies of Criminal AO.

Some, simply to be the most powerful in all of *Money (Game) Master*. Others, to restore order to the game world. Still others wished to throw that same order into chaos and bring turmoil to the businesses and nations of the real world. Each had their own motivations.

The Legacies of Criminal AO had been modified beyond the limits of the game world as if by cheating, each boasting monstrous stats.

As ridiculous as it sounded, if *snow* were a real virtual currency, then so long as humanity remained dependent on the financial institutions of the world, the Legacies were a terrifying weapon on the level of an atomic bomb.

Why?

That depended on how you used them. You could lay waste to the economy of an entire continent, turn a country's banknotes to worthless paper with a flick of your wrist, or put an end to the lives of billions of people.

This is a story about those Legacies.

04/01/20XX 10:20 AM

Legacies
The name given to the equipment wielded by the legendary Dealer Criminal AO. The owner poured mountains of money into them, modifying them beyond recognition, in order to grant them stats higher than those of anything on the market. Their many customizations allow them to exceed the preset physical limits of the world. Their monstrous stats have earned them the somewhat ironic moniker Overtrick (or End Magic) among Dealers.

Fall
The closest thing in the game to a Game Over. When a character dies for any reason, the player is forcibly logged out and prevented from conducting business for twenty-four hours. Usually when logging out, the Magistellus serving as a player's partner is programmed to continue operating automatically, but when you Fall, you don't even have that saving grace, and you're left defenseless and at the mercy of the other Dealers. Even if you're a *snow* billionaire, one Fall is all it takes to plunge players into the deepest depths of debt. In the real world, this can be a fate worse than death.

Down
This happens when a Magistellus such as Tselika suffers a fatal wound. A Downed Magistellus is not erased completely but frozen for a fixed time. They become frozen immediately upon taking lethal damage, and recovery time depends on the severity of the injury. A slit artery will mean a short downtime, while being blown to pieces a longer one. It is not as bad as a Fall, as the downtime ranges from a few minutes to an hour. And since they're controlled by AI, there are some Dealers who use Magistelli as decoys to open an escape route while under heavy fire.

While a Magistellus is Down, you will have no access to features such as navigation, financial news, or programmed buy and sell orders. Keeping in mind that since transactions take place ten thousand times a second, it's best to avoid your Magistellus going Down as much as possible, unless you are skilled enough to perfectly and manually make market predictions while also engaging in gunfights and high-speed pursuits.

Housing

It is possible to purchase land and buildings in *Money (Game) Master.* However, you will mostly deal in stores and warehouses, as there isn't much use in building elaborate mansions. Rather than living in them, it is far more common to remodel such buildings in order to flip them for a profit.

Gemstones

Like housing, it is possible to purchase gemstones to be used as equipment. These are more restrictive in their use, but they can grant rare skills, and certain communities even require the wearing of specific jewels to gain access.

Chapter 1
Land and Sea BGM #01 "Auction & Pirate"

1

Server Name: Theta Yellow.
Starting Location: Tokonatsu City, Peninsula District.
Log-in credentials accepted.
Welcome to *Money (Game) Master*, Kaname Suou.

The spiked peninsula they call the Shark's Tooth is the heart of Tokonatsu City. Stunning tropical beaches, world-class casinos, and a financial metropolis divide the land into three sectors, and the streets are paved with proverbial gold. The palm trees and hibiscus flowers sway in the breeze, and blue butterflies flit alongside birds with feathers of green and scarlet. In stark contrast to this natural beauty, rows of skyscrapers tower overhead, gleaming like mirrored pillars.

There, in a parking lot reserved for beach-going swimmers, sat the mint-green coupe. Kaname stood outside it, leaning against the driver's side door, a bottle of soda touching his lips. He could feel the blistering heat of the sun on his skin, the refreshingly cool bottle, and the drops of condensation that formed across its surface. He felt its weight in his hand, the tingle in his throat as he drank, as if it were all real.

In fact, when was the last time a cheap soda from the real world tasted as good as this one?

Money (Game) Master technically had food and energy gauges, but because the values were reset upon logging out, food items were unnecessary if you were planning on staying for only a couple of hours. On the other hand, logging in for days at a time could lead to malnutrition in the real world. Unless you were one of those people who got addicted to the point of skipping meals, you usually picked a good spot to log out.

The fact that you could taste food and feel full, however, helped aid focus and kept your emotions in check. In addition, since the food was zero calories, it was a dieting hack of sorts.

Meanwhile, Tselika was sunbathing on the hood of the car as usual. She appeared to be trying to take another selfie with the dashcam, but under the searing heat of the sun, she looked not unlike a lamb chop sizzling in a pan of oil.

"Are you okay there?" Kaname asked.

"Of...of course I am. Do I look like anything other than the most elegantly reclining demon you ever did see?"

The loud, booming stereo blared through the car's open window. In *Money (Game) Master*, you could basically either listen to loud Western music or financial news (so there were celebrity guests in the game who commented on these things, like in real life). Sometimes a channel would be flooded with anime songs, so it was easy to guess which sponsors had temporarily bought out the rights to the station.

"White Queen Tourism announced that their owners are moving forward with online meetings to bring together their assets, including their airlines, ships, and hotels. No need to bother with AGMs when you're a massive financial conglomerate, I suppose. The company is calling this the Surf Riding Project, and its advantages are..."

"A follow-up on the satellite industry. Communications across the peninsula are currently handled by undersea cables, but some reports have suggested that these would be replaced by radio base stations. It is

now possible that the information in these reports was fabricated by a group of Dealers. According to the blogs of several AI analysts..."

"Based on official announcements regarding the volume of trading in weapons and ammunition, life insurance companies such as Tokime Life, Mistress Inc., and Tarot Girls 22 are on the rise. Even according to our limited data, the numbers are up massively compared to last week. We could soon be looking at a huge..."

"Boooring." Tselika pouted as she simmered on the hood of the car. The logos and stock prices of White Queen Tourism and various life insurance companies appeared and disappeared across her pit-babe outfit.

"Boring, boring, boring! If you're going to put trash on the air, then have a beautiful woman reading smut out loud! In fact, just whisk me away to Prostitute Island or even just a strip club or *something*! A demon queen needs a little excitement in her life, for crying out loud!"

"Why do you want to look at other nude women? I mean, you're supposed to be a woman yourself."

"Why, simply to capture with my own eyes the beautiful sight of a woman at work! *(Starry-eyed.)*"

"Cut it out. When you take it that far, you sound sarcastic. Are you trying to kill them with kindness?"

"Whoa, is that a trace of classism I hear, My Lord? Dancers and sex workers do perfectly legitimate work, I'll have you know! Prostitution is the world's oldest profession! If you feel pity for them, that's discrimination!"

It's a waste of time to lecture a demon on morality, thought Kaname with a sigh. Magistelli included an auto-investment program that could handle ten thousand transactions a second, trading everything from wheat, to stocks, to gold, to weapons. But they were also meant to provide many other services such as navigation, assisted driving, and combat support—so many powerful features that it could be overwhelming.

While this was going on, the person they were waiting for appeared. Long black hair cascaded down to her waist, and her bangs were swept completely back, held in place by a band made of thin gold, braided into shape. The pair of glasses sitting on her nose added to the determined look in her eyes. She was tall for a woman, buxom, and the holster beneath her arm doubled as a smartphone case and stood out like the suspenders on a waitress's outfit. She wore a stark white blouse and tight black skirt, topped off with a dark tie around her neck. Her slender legs were covered with stockings, and on her feet were a pair of mismatched boots. Overall, she looked not unlike a military officer who had taken off her jacket, sweltering under the sun and northern winds. Her belt was loose at the back, probably for holding an extra weapon.

It wasn't uncommon for players to adopt a more casual look in the game—not to be gratuitously flashy but simply because of the heat. The more conservate Dealers settled for taking off their jackets, while most walked around in swimsuits. Even though the city was nothing more than digital data, in some respects, it could be frustratingly uncompromising. There was even a saying that the best way to sabotage one of the unbeatable PMC armies was to cut off their water and air-conditioning.

"It's time. You must be Kaname Suou, I take it?"

"And you are…?"

"Lily-Kiska of Ag Wolves. And from now on, your teammate. I suppose that means I outrank you, though not by much. In any case, it's nice to meet you."

She extended a hand, and Kaname straightened himself up from the car door and obliged the handshake. However, Lily-Kiska's eyes seemed to focus not on Kaname but on the car. More precisely, on the fact that as soon as Kaname left the vehicle, lines of text large and small streamed across it like racing stickers vanished.

She tilted her head slightly. "What were you doing just now?"

"Oh, just talking to my sister. She went to buy some sleepwear and was asking me whether she should get pajamas or a nightie. In fact, she dragged me into some sort of dress-up pageant video."

"I see… You're an overprotective brother."

"She gets mad if I don't do stuff like this. And when she gets upset, she starts cleaning up the place. A 'change of pace,' she calls it. But it's *my* house, too, and I end up not knowing where anything is."

Anyway, back to the task at hand. Lily-Kiska ran her finger along the arm of her glasses.

"The preparations are complete. Kaname Suou, you are now an official member of Ag Wolves, and as such, we will be working together to obtain the Legacies of Criminal AO."

"There'd have been hell to pay if you'd turned me away after I paid my 1.7 billion *snow*."

"Ha-ha. Well, it was necessary, both as a test and to carry out our plans. Oh, I hope you don't mind, but perhaps we could save the rest for somewhere more private. I don't feel comfortable discussing tactics with those things watching us."

She was probably talking about the security cameras. Several poles lined the beach, atop which sat speakers for use in natural disasters. A perfect spot for a camera. Even from where they sat, you could easily pick out their crude lenses.

"Works for me. You don't have to take your shoes off or anything; I'm not a stickler about what you do in my car," Kaname said as he turned back toward the vehicle.

Lily-Kiska smiled and corrected him. "Oh, no, that's not what I meant. I was saying we should go in *my* car."

"?"

She gestured over her shoulder with her thumb.

There was barely a sound as a luxury car with a black finish glided smoothly over. A hybrid, perhaps? It was totally different from Kaname's coupe. It was long, extremely long. Way too long, like a dachshund that had been stretched on a rack.

It was enough to leave even Kaname puzzled.

"You drive around in a limousine? With all the gunfights and car chases?"

"Oh, it's not as bad as you might think. A large vehicle allows for more armor and a bigger engine." Lily-Kiska gave a sly chuckle and continued. "It's basically a tank. Speed and maneuverability are one thing, but there's a special kind of thrill that comes from having the power to steamroll everything in your path. Haven't you ever wanted to drive around in a huge truck like in an action movie?"

Lily-Kiska was starting to sound very different from the diligent impression she had initially given.

Meanwhile, there was a flash of white skin as what appeared to be another AI-controlled Magistellus slipped her bare legs off the driver's seat of the limousine and exited the vehicle. She was a blond girl with long ears, presumably an elf. She was wearing a dark waistcoat and tight skirt that resembled a dealer at a casino, but the pair of rabbit ears on her shoes and her miniature hat made her look like she was wearing a costume of sorts. Unlike Tselika's outfit, the brand logos that covered it looked out of place. She opened a thick door at the rear of the vehicle.

Lily-Kiska beckoned Kaname toward the girl.

"Any additional questions?" she asked.

"Ah, yeah."

Kaname took a tiny step backward, as though taking in the whole sight again. As his bespectacled partner looked back at him blankly, he asked his question.

"Erm, is that a swimsuit or your underwear?"

"?"

"Well, maybe it's meant to be shown off either way, but it sure is a bright red, don't you think?"

A few seconds passed as the gears in Lily-Kiska's head turned. The bright color of her bra was showing straight through her white blouse.

"Huh? Wh-wh-wh-what?!"

Her whole face turned as red as a beet, and Lily-Kiska panicked, clutching her shoulders with both hands…which produced a strange sound.

A click? A snap? There was the sound of tearing thread, and unable to withstand the sudden strain, the buttons around her chest area popped off in quick succession.

"—???!!!"

With an ultrasonic cry impossible to put into words, Lily-Kiska crouched down where she stood. Even her impenetrable visage had fractured. It reminded Kaname of the time his sister's bathing suit had gotten washed away by the sea. Tselika cackled softly in the background.

Those suspender-like holsters probably weren't helping. As if her top wasn't under enough strain as it was. Crouched on the ground with tears in her eyes, Lily-Kiska, ever prepared, produced a sewing set from her underarm holster.

Kaname asked the question that immediately came to mind.

"Why didn't you buy a different size?"

"The next one up was too big and felt too loose. I'm trying to go for a sniper build, so I can't be dealing with the constant distraction."

That must explain the mismatched boots on each foot as well. Different clothes came with different stats and skills, after all.

There was a brief silence as Lily-Kiska completed her needlework. Then she buttoned her top and slowly stood up straight, stretching as though just waking and curving her back to test the strength of the fix. This of course meant that she was showing off her large breasts right before Kaname's eyes, a fact of which she remained totally unaware.

Humans tended to neglect small details when dealing with the bigger picture.

...The red garment—somewhere between a bra and a bikini top—remained visible through Lily-Kiska's shirt, but Kaname thought it prudent to discuss it no further.

"A-anyway," she said at last. "Let's talk business. (...Geez, why do my buttons always burst off like they're trying to introduce themselves every time I meet somebody new?)"

Kaname was concerned by whatever curse she appeared to be muttering under her breath, but he let it go. As he followed her lead, he turned to Tselika, who was relaxing atop the hood.

"Tselika, wait here."

"Oh, it's ever so dull when there's no one to whom I can show off my body. Do you mind if I go for a little drive?"

"Fine by me—just don't leave it by the side of the road. There's a

rule protecting cars in a designated parking space. It seems friendly enough at first glance, but it's basically giving free rein over a car that's parked illegally. I don't want it stolen or blown up."

"Understood."

"Also, no strip clubs. And no Prostitute Island."

"Whaaaaaaat?! Then what's even the point?!"

"You can go on your own time. I just don't want you drawing attention before we start a job. As a Magistellus, you can't even interact with items that aren't mine anyway. Outside my hideout, it's not like you can so much as buy a drink from a vending machine."

"Ah, so what you're saying is I can still pick up sex workers off the street. They're Dealers, not items, so I'm not breaking any rules!"

"Tselika."

With that warning, Kaname turned away. Lily-Kiska was stroking the arm of her glasses with her finger.

"You two seem to get along well," she noted.

"Is that not what all Magistelli are like?"

"It varies. Anyway, she's got such pale skin. I'm jealous. And this is coming from someone who has to slather on SPF fifty-plus sunscreen every day. This game can be frustratingly unaccommodating at times. Sometimes, the problem is that it's *too* real."

Kaname entered the limousine. The interior was air-conditioned and, of course, quite long and thin. It was probably larger than a single room at a city hotel. A sofa stretched across the walls, with a glass table at the center. There was even a television and mini fridge.

There were about a dozen men and women already inside, presumably other members of Ag Wolves, along with several Magistelli. One, a *yuki-onna*, a ghost woman who appeared only on snowy nights. Another, a dullahan. Lily-Kiska must have used this limousine as a mobile base when she wasn't mowing down pedestrians in it.

Lily-Kiska was the last to enter. She pressed the button on an intercom atop the glass table and spoke to the driver's seat.

"Sophia. Get us onto a main road. And drive safely, okay?"

"*As you wish, Miss Kiska,*" she replied.

A gentle inertial force washed over Kaname, relaxing him, as the limousine pulled out of the beachside parking lot and merged onto the road. Meanwhile, Lily-Kiska addressed the rest of the room, getting straight to the point.

"This is our new friend, Kaname Suou. With the capital he's bringing to the table, I believe we are finally ready to put our plan into motion."

Several windows appeared across the surface of the glass table. Each member was putting in a buy order for *something* for the price of 1.7 billion *snow*. All sitting around this table were on Kaname's level, paying the same amount of money for the same purpose.

"I hardly think I need to reiterate," she said, "but Ag Wolves exist to prevent the Legacies of Criminal AO from falling into the wrong hands, and by so doing, we protect not only the order of *Money (Game) Master* but also the entire world economy. Do you remember the Swiss Depression, Kaname?"

"...More or less." Kaname Suou took a deep breath and explained. "It was a global financial crisis originating in *Money (Game) Master* before spreading to the real world. Same old story: Some Dealers trigger a 'moral hazard,' there's a shortsighted money grab, and before you know it, there's violence in the streets."

"Well, thankfully, it all managed to sort itself out. It could have been much worse. If somebody had the Legacies, they could make that happen again. It would be child's play. Millions of people would lose their jobs. Entire cities and even countries could fall into economic ruin. It'd be bad enough if a malicious actor got their hands on the Legacies, but the worst-case scenario is if they fall into the lap of some clueless rookie. We can't even estimate the scale of the damage that would occur if that was to happen."

"Okay. So?"

"Here's our current target."

An image of a shotgun appeared on the glass table. Except that name didn't quite seem to fit.

The term *cannon* was used to describe a gun with a caliber above a certain size. Armies across the world had different standards of what made a gun a cannon versus a shotgun, but they would all agree on this point: This was not a shotgun but a shot cannon. Its overall shape resembled a revolver-style grenade launcher, a brutal orange weapon whose design defied all notions of sensibility.

"It's known as #tempest.err. One pull of the trigger releases two thousand pellets of buckshot in a sixty-degree angle up to a range of five hundred meters."

"And that's just by default," a large, burly man with a silver crew cut, wearing a tank top and a pair of blue camo-print pants, interjected. "The shot's guided by an under-barrel beam. Anythin' caught in the light gets turned to mincemeat. Now, I know what you're thinking: Sounds just like a big laser pointer. But here's the catch. You can distort light. Reflect it. If you've got a lens, you can focus it all down to a single point. See where I'm goin'? All you need is a disco ball, and you can fill the whole damn room. Doesn't matter if your foe's behind cover—they're toast."

Money (Game) Master was a game that mixed modern-day finance with urban crime, but some aspects of the game defied conventional physics.

For example, the Magistelli.

And the Legacies of Criminal AO, so overpowered they became known as the Overtrick. Weapons so heavily customized, they exceeded even the preset physical limits of the world. Items that, while through legal means, had broken the mechanics of the game so much that using them felt like cheating.

"Just one question," Kaname ventured. "Wouldn't the user be in the crosshairs of the light beam, too? I mean, the only reason you can see walls in the first place is because reflected light from them is hitting your eye."

The man who answered Kaname's question was a nervous, fidgety, slouching man with a backpack and a hoodie with some kind of anime character on it. Kaname thought he'd remembered the character's name was Cyber Rain or something like that. The man looked like he had a room full of posters, light sticks, and figurines.

"Actually, it's the amount of light that determines the effectiveness. The beam gives about three fifty to four hundred lux…about the same as a fluorescent bulb, I suppose. Walls don't reflect much light, so the blast will break it down. For a mirror, or glass, or even water, on the other hand, well, then the reflected light takes priority. I wouldn't want to be in your shoes if you accidentally pulled the trigger in one of those scenarios, especially if it was pointed to a mirror in an indoor fight."

"Anyway," said Lily-Kiska, taking over. "Firing the weapon from on high, like in a helicopter, causes a storm of bullets to rain down, just as the name implies. #tempest.err can massacre everything in sight with just a single pull of the trigger. It's also semiautomatic, giving you free rein to go on the ideal shooting spree... It's such a nasty weapon, you start to think it must be a hack."

The large man with the silver crew cut scratched his head as he joined the conversation. What looked like...dog tags were wrapped around his wrist and appeared to act as a smart health scanner that displayed his vitals like blood pressure and perspiration rate.

"Man, it makes regular guns look stupid," he griped. "It's like a superweapon out of some cheesy space movie."

"If this weapon gets out there," warned Lily-Kiska, "the balance of the game will be in tatters, make no mistake... And yet, despite that, we've got some idiot auctioning it off to make a quick cash grab."

She looked down at the glass table, controlling it with her gaze, and an image appeared of a beautiful woman in a green dress. Her long black hair was held at the back by a pair of ribbons that stuck up like rabbit ears. She looked heavily made up, and the slits in her revealing clothes offered glimpses of her chest and thighs. She gave the impression of being out of her depth, a little insecure, still a rookie.

The man with the crew cut looked displeased and slapped his head a few times. Perhaps he'd chosen that hairstyle because he liked the way it felt more than the way it looked. Kaname got the impression the player might be a woman in the real world.

"The chick's name is Pavilion," he explained. "She shouldn't give us any trouble. It's the auction site itself that's the problem."

"True," replied Lily-Kiska.

The next image was not of a building but a large ship.

"This is the cruise liner *Tropical Lady*. Owned by the AI conglomerate White Queen Tourism, it has a two-thousand-person staff and a maximum displacement of one hundred thousand tons. It's powered by four diesel engines...but I suppose the specs aren't what's of interest. The important thing is that while it's at sea, it's out of the reach of us land dwellers."

"A-and that's not all." Shrinking himself up even in the large limousine interior, the man with the backpack and hair over his eyes slipped into the conversation. He was covered in anime buttons and pins that rattled as he spoke. "The *Tropical Lady* is escorted by an army of AI-controlled PMCs. God, even if we had a helicopter or a submarine to get on board, they'd fill us full of holes. Going up against them will only turn out very, very badly for us."

"We'll be blown to bits before we even get close, with mines or something," the crew-cut man concluded. "White Queen Tourism is an AI conglomerate. There's no chance in hell they'd ever employ an actual human... Seems to me like they must have taken on this Pavilion chick as an external contractor. That would make the *Tropical Lady* just another toy they've given her to play with."

Conglomerates differed from ordinary companies in that all the top jobs were filled by family members. The concept of an AI conglomerate, then, might sound a bit odd, but basically, they could be thought of as run by a group of NPCs who didn't follow normal protocol. Obviously, human players should not be able to get a job at an AI company. It would be a boring game if the only way to rise to the top was to get a cushy job and work for some company.

Which is all to say how exceptional this treatment was. Lily-Kiska took a quiet breath and spoke up.

"To the AI management, Pavilion is like a hunting dog. She has a skill they don't—a flexible mind—and that's why they need her, which makes her a Dealer backed by the power of an AI conglomerate. She's in a fragile position, though; one wrong move and they'll cut her loose. As long as she continues to prove herself worthy, however, she'll be able to enjoy a position of relative authority."

One mistake and you got the sack. Talk about high risk. Perhaps there were game-related factors at play. It was more fun to keep the players moving around, like a round of musical chairs.

The backpack man spoke next. "It seems that White Queen Tourism has simply drawn up a list of the biggest transactions and is reaching out to the Dealers involved one by one. They're at about 1.7 billion per person, s-so if Pavilion loses her seat, they might contact one of us Ag Wolves next."

A troublesome opponent indeed. She would also be authorized to give orders to the AI PMCs. Of course, their activity would be limited to the territory of the AI conglomerate itself, but it would still be extremely powerful to command a force designed to indiscriminately slaughter any and all intruders.

Kaname tilted his head slightly. "So then *those things* we bought?"

"Right," said Lily-Kiska. "We can't fight them head-on, but we can take the PMCs out of the picture entirely by exploiting their weakness. Work smarter, not harder. Such is the way of the Dealer, is it not?"

"..."

"The 1.7 billion *snow* we've all contributed will not go to waste. It is merely an investment required to take even more valuable steps." Lily-Kiska flashed a sly grin and once again operated the glass table without touching it. "There's only one way we can get onto the *Tropical Lady*. Hard Engage Bridge. It's the sole place the ship can return to port here on the peninsula from the open sea. There's no other point along the ring road capable of accommodating a ship that size. They will, of course, be expecting attacks from atop the bridge, which means there's one more thing we need to do."

Lily-Kiska continued to explain her tactic, though at this point it was more like filling in the gaps. Afterward, she had one last piece of information to share.

"Now, this is all unconfirmed, but we have identified a Dealer who may be related to Criminal AO."

"..."

At Kaname's silence, Lily-Kiska continued. A photo appeared on the glass table and expanded to fill the whole surface. It looked like it was taken with a telephoto lens.

"Her name is Midori. We know nothing about how strong she is or even what she wants #tempest.err for. But given that she's related in some way to Criminal AO, we ought to consider her a dangerous opponent both in terms of strategy and power. In fact, considering this is all the information we have even after our tireless research, we ought to be on maximum alert."

From the pictures, she just looked like a cute little girl. Long black hair with even bangs, pale skin, and twin tails. She wore a black bikini top that covered her flat chest and a matching miniskirt, both adorned with frills. A pair of short gloves covered her hands to the wrist, and black socks extended up past her knees. On her head, she wore a head-dress decorated with blue roses. The white lace everywhere lent the ensemble a very gothic-lolita feel.

However...

"If she's related to Criminal AO, she may know more about the Legacies than anyone else. Perhaps she's even familiar with #tempest.err. Worst case, she could be the one controlling Pavilion from behind the scenes."

The girl, the ultimate wild card, sat astride a large motorcycle painted bright red with a pattern of autumn leaves. The gloomy shadows of that one photo taken in a brick-lined back alley told Kaname all he needed to know about the world she inhabited.

"Should we run into her, deal with her as you would an enemy. That way, she can't shoot us in the back."

Their path was clear. Kaname looked around at the faces of everybody in the limousine. He had just one question.

"When do we start?"

"Immediately."

2

I apologize for making you put up with this. Well, I suppose I shouldn't treat you like a stranger.

I bought this snowman-themed letter-writing set on a whim, because it looked so cute, but it has more envelopes here than I expected, so all my letters are going to look like this for a while. I know texts and social media are so much faster these days, but I prefer this. Analog, not digital. They say that even the act of putting a stamp on an envelope and placing it in the mailbox will soon be a thing of the past. I just want us to keep trading letters for as long as possible.

Today, I looked up how to grow a melon.

Whenever I eat grapes or watermelon, I always hold on to the seeds instead of throwing them away. It's an old habit of mine. I know it's a lot of effort to grow them until they're edible, but I can't help it.

Do you have any strange habits?

I eagerly await your response.

3

After disembarking the dachshund-like black limo, Kaname spent some time leaning against a large metal dumpster as he waited for Tselika to return with the mint-green coupe. Now he was back behind the wheel, having booted the demon pit babe from the driver's seat.

"The merger of the century is approaching. The family behind the AI conglomerate known as White Queen Tourism is proceeding with its online meetings to unify its five partner companies. This merger, known as the Surf Riding Project, could result in White Queen Tourism becoming the second-largest tourism company in the world…"

"Hard Engage Bridge is a famous landmark in the financial district, but concerns have been raised over its condition. Several construction firms such as Satsuki Construction and Alice Manufactories have offered to conduct maintenance efforts on the bridge, but contract negotiations are expected to continue for some time…"

"The radio shows are boring me to death, as usual." Tselika sounded extremely uninterested. "Conglomerates, construction companies… How am I supposed to get excited if I can't see any of the dirty details? Ahhh, just lock me in a hotel and let me browse the pay-per-view all day. Or hand me a telephone and let me bring over a few call girls."

"Is it just me or is your IQ lower than usual today, Tselika?"

Tselika stretched upward, almost able to press her palms against the low roof. "Hng!"

"Tse— You idiot! Get your wings out of the way while I'm trying to drive! I can't see!"

The car scraped against something as it swerved across the road. Kaname somehow managed to regain control of the vehicle and reached over, grabbing the cowlike horns atop Tselika's head and shaking them in punishment.

"And I know it takes a whole lot of money to find a way into those places. What's next, you're going to ask me to front you the cash? That's a *Money (Game) Master* strategy if ever I heard one."

"*Gulp.* Aaah! I'm sorry! I'm so sorry, My Lord! Please forgive me!"

"Wings. Now."

"Okay, okay!! I'm retracting them!! I won't bother you while driving again, I promise!!"

A conglomerate relied on family. That might sound irrelevant when talking about AIs, but it actually affected how the business operated in quite a few ways. They sold shares on the market without giving shareholders a say in how to run the business. That was enough to give a glimpse into the kind of tin-pot dictatorship they had going on. They couldn't even make red-bean buns unless the water, eggs, yeast, and red bean were all produced in-house. If you didn't agree with them, then you could go somewhere else.

You could also see their unique style of governance in how they cut their "outsider" contractors loose after a single mistake.

"You know, I haven't had a red-bean bun in a while."

"Now that you mention it, I could go for that myself, My Lord. Let us pick up a few along with some milk later."

As Kaname headed to Hard Engage Bridge, he met up with sports cars and 4WDs of all colors. They clearly belonged to the other members of Ag Wolves, not because they had stickers or any other markings to distinguish them but because it would be hard to attribute the army vehicle with the military camo and the car covered in anime girls to anybody else.

In the confines of the passenger seat, Tselika reached up with both hands and arched her body, stretching her limbs. The names of several construction firms vying for the bridge contract scrolled along the curve of her body as she showed off her breasts. It looked like she was trying to wake herself up and clear her mind.

"I suppose it's finally time to begin," said Tselika, as if asking for confirmation.

"Good. I'm tired of waiting."

"Are you sure about this? I wouldn't be surprised if the path you chose turned out to be more dangerous than you anticipated, hmm?"

"…"

Several windows appeared on the windshield: a simplified map of the city, a graph of gold prices, a flowchart detailing the newest fads, and a chat window that resembled an instant-messaging service. The chat requests were all labeled "Ag Wolves." When Kaname accepted, lines of text about one hundred characters long scrolled by in quick succession.

Lily-Kiska: Sorry about the quick start. We'll have your welcoming party when we go for congratulatory drinks afterward.

Hazard: Which means if we fail, you can kiss it bye-bye. If you want that drink, then eyes on the prize, new guy.

M-Scope: I would think the "prize" here is us not all Falling and going into tons of debt, personally.

Zaurus: Hey, keep trying to jinx us before a job, and I'll kill you myself!

Titan: If you wanna fight, see who can get the most kills on the job or somethin'. We gotta stay productive.

It was impossible to put all the names to faces, but Kaname could sort of identify some of them from the way they spoke.

Zaurus: So where are we holding the after-party?

Lily-Kiska: The usual spot, I guess. There's a bunch of Italian places on Third Avenue on the peninsula.

Titan: That's no fun! I'm tired of hamburgers and rib eye steaks. Let's go somewhere like Coconut Isle or Diver Isle; the menus are absolutely insane there.

M-Scope: But those places just boil whatever they can find in coconut milk and call it a day. Like bats and crabs and stuff.

Hazard: Let's stop talking about all this in front of the new guy. Don't want to scare him off.

As much as they seemed able to keep the conversation flowing by themselves, they might get the wrong idea if Kaname's only response was silence, and that would be annoying to deal with. Kaname operated the digital keyboard on the windshield with his gaze and tried typing out a few sentences in response.

Kaname: So how did you guys manage to put together the 1.7 billion? I would have thought you'd all be stepping on one another's toes if you'd been upsetting the market in some way.

Titan: You ain't gotta start a war to make money in this game. I've been tradin' food futures, myself. It's pretty easy 'cause typhoons and whatever are announced beforehand as "events," unlike in the real world.

Zaurus: You mean cyclones, Titan. But yeah, it's pretty easy to calculate. You can even get a program to do it for you. Not many people know that one.

M-Scope: Just think about the origin of our name, and you'll see how we made our money. Ag Wolves. Silver Wolves. Get it?

Lily-Kiska: How is he going to get that? It's basically because wolves have evolved to hunt in packs. We're the same, only we use money instead of fangs. That's what it's supposed to mean.

As the very casual job orientation unfolded, they approached the huge bridge.

Hard Engage Bridge stood around five hundred meters long, with a maximum height above sea level of thirty meters, but the largest cruise liners could barely pass under it. It stretched out over the sea, just one part of the large circular road that connected the peninsula to the surrounding islands. Therefore, although there was a company that owned it, it was considered neutral ground.

Kaname parked his car midway along the bridge and stepped onto the asphalt. Even after rolling up his sleeves, he was sweating. As he gazed out over the green sea, the woman with swept-back hair and glasses, Lily-Kiska, walked up next to him. She held in each hand a freshly cooled glass, perhaps produced from somewhere within the limousine. Each was filled with a translucent blue liquid, giving Kaname absolutely no idea how it might taste.

"It's amazing," mused Lily-Kiska as she placed the glasses down on the railing, offering one to Kaname. The hibiscus flowers decorating the rim of the glass swayed in the sea breeze.

"I wonder how many computations are going on in this one glass," she said, wiping away a drop that clung to the outside with a thin fingertip. "The gravity, the temperature, the humidity, the water droplets formed when the air cools, not to mention the fluid dynamics, the light refraction, the friction between the bottom of the glass and the railing, even the taste, the smell, the feel... This is all over the city, from coast to coast. It's impossible to understand how this is all free to play."

Her voice was soft as she stared out over the sea just like the young boy next to her.

"Did you know? This game supposedly has anywhere between fifty million to 0.2 billion Dealers playing in a space the size of a city-state. And that's only counting active accounts."

"Well, it would be pretty foolish to go inactive and leave your affairs to your Magistellus in a game this grueling," Kaname replied. "You might as well post your bank details online for everyone to see."

"Oh, but there *are* people who leave everything they own in the hands of shady online banks, aren't there? Anyway, what I'm trying to say is, open world or not, it's just one city. How do they fit everyone in here?"

"..."

Both of them sipped their blue drinks. Kaname didn't taste any alcohol. It was just like a carbonated energy drink. He felt a warmth in the center of his chest.

Lily-Kiska continued. "But this game affects more than just those fifty million to 0.2 billion people. One hundred thirty million people use yen, and 320 million people use the dollar, but just as those currencies directly affect the lives of all seven billion people, so too has *snow* covered the entire globe. In fact, estimates say there's over a billion people worldwide who don't use banks at all and instead rely entirely on *snow*. The whole world depends on this game, and nobody even knows who developed it, who runs it, or where the servers are based."

Indeed. Even "just" those who completely relied on it numbered one billion. When services appeared that would convert the local currency to *snow* solely for the benefit of such people, governments looked the other way. They were "illegal" in name only.

Whether it was in the asset management of investment funds or large corporations, the financial management of the banks themselves, or the tax funding of nationwide public services, the virtual currency affected anything that involved money, large or small.

"The Legacies of Criminal AO could destroy it all," spoke Lily-Kiska bitterly as she gazed out over the sea. "We're past the stage where you can say it's all just a game. Past the stage where it's all just for fun. I mean, *we* can play around a bit without thinking of the consequences, and it's all a bit of fun, but the Legacies don't have the word *restraint* in their dictionary. If some clueless rookie gets their hands on them, you'll see what I mean. We won't be talking about just another Swiss Depression, that's for sure. It'll destabilize the game immediately. One by one, the weak will end up in debt, and we'll see countries going bankrupt left and right. It's no joke."

To think a game could destroy the world. They lived in a time when an imaginary war could decide the fates of not only people but entire nations. It was the elephant in the room that nobody wanted to acknowledge.

"...We have to do something," Lily-Kiska muttered as she stared out over her glass at the sea. "We have to regain control of *Money (Game) Master* at all costs."

"I agree," said Kaname. "#tempest.err is the first step. We have to get to it before it falls into the wrong hands."

"That's right. That's the first step." Lily-Kiska turned away from the sea to face Kaname and smiled. "I hope this serves to bring us closer together as well. It wouldn't be a bad idea to forge some strong friendships on the battlefield. As Titan would say, it's productive."

Just then, Tselika leaned out of the passenger-side window of the mint-green coupe and called to him.

"It's almost time, My Lord. I can see the ship approaching."

Kaname's and Lily-Kiska's expressions changed to ones of urgency.

"It's almost time for our secret weapon to get here, too. I'll go get armed. I'll need some skills as well. Sophia! Bring me my jewelry box! I want to swap out my accessories!"

"I'll support. Its range is short, but I have a sniper rifle."

Lily-Kiska opened something that looked like a tackle box and started trying on accessories of various colors. It was like her mismatched boots were for skill or stat reasons. Kaname gave her a sidelong glance and went to fetch Short Spear from Tselika.

Their enemy was a group of lowlifes attempting to auction off #tempest.err, a monster shotgun and one of the Legacies of Criminal AO, also known as the Overtrick.

The site was the *Tropical Lady*, a cruise liner untouchable from land. Once they managed to get aboard, they would have to deal with a swarm of AI PMCs, enemies against whom a front-on assault was all but useless.

But Ag Wolves did not flinch.

Kaname stood among them, atop Hard Engage Bridge, awaiting the sordid vessel.

4

Ta-daa!

Did you notice the stamp affixed to this letter? It's a special stamp celebrating the anniversary of commercial space travel! I know you're supposed to keep them as memorabilia, but I really wanted to show them to you, so I had to use just one.

Hmm, I don't really think it matches the snowman envelope. Besides, collecting stamps was always more my brother's thing. With me, I collect all sorts, like seeds. The kids in my class keep calling me a squirrel. Sad face. I've kept every letter you've ever sent me, of course. I love rereading the old ones.

Writing is so powerful—the warmth of a line of handwriting, the emotions put into every stroke. I hope this letter makes you feel the same way.

I eagerly await your response.

5

The deck of the *Tropical Lady* contained a large swimming pool, a place for swimsuit-clad partygoers to stand and eat, and most importantly, an auction house where staggering amounts of money changed hands.

In the center of it all stood the girl known as Pavilion, wearing a purple dress, her long black hair tied and secured by a pair of ribbons that stood up like rabbit ears. She looked about sixteen or seventeen years old. The touch of innocence about her voluptuous body only amplified the lasciviousness of her exposed cleavage and thighs.

She was the sole external contractor to the AI conglomerate White Queen Tourism. Just a hound, to be cut loose upon making a single mistake, yet hers was a significant position nonetheless.

Money (Game) Master was a game of financial dealings where nothing was against the law, not even gunfights or car chases. But at sea, there was nothing to fear from the guns and cars back on land. Especially not when you possessed the legendary #tempest.err.

The guests here were true VIPs, hoping to enjoy some high-risk gambling in a low-risk location. Since virtual *snow* was more or less equivalent to physical yen, a list of the highest-ranking players could just as well serve as a list of the most influential people in the world.

They had no need for the large sums of money they could get from selling #tempest.err. That's why this auction had *charity* in the title. It didn't matter who took home the mountain of cash. That wasn't important. What was important was making connections with the people who had enough wealth enough to afford it. Spending time with them. Obtaining that list of the most influential people in the world. Upon completing that, it was like you'd already eaten your fill of the main course.

The important thing about money wasn't how much of it you had lying in your vaults. It was how much of it you were making right that second. Did you have the power necessary to create wealth? Money changed hands all the time, and power wasn't in stopping it but in allowing it to do so. Anyone who survived in this business realized that eventually.

Money came from connections. And it was *who* you connected with that determined how much money you could make. An engine didn't run without burning a little gas. But at the same time, an engine did nothing if it wasn't connected to anything. In the same way, you got nothing from brownnosing the unwashed masses. There were only so many hours in the day, which is why it was best to get all the most powerful people in one place and network as hard as you could. It was only natural to focus on what would net you the greatest return. That was just good investment practice.

Life was a finite resource. How were you getting the most out of it? Who would net you the greatest return? That was what Pavilion was here to learn.

And then...if she was successful...

Surely, a certain someone will be pleased with me.

One of the PMCs waiting nearby spoke up. "It's time, ma'am."

Indeed. Pavilion nodded, her rabbit-ear ribbon bobbing.

The auction would soon begin. Some lucky buyer would win #tempest.err, the shotgun without peer, and Pavilion, the girl who made it happen, would obtain a list of the most powerful people in the world. Whatever happened after that was none of her concern. The Overtrick could break the game balance and send every person and nation into ruin. The world could be plunged into a second Swiss Depression. As long as she went up in the world, Pavilion didn't care about any of that one bit.

Pavilion tapped her mic and addressed the floor.

"Ladies and gentlemen, thank you for your patience!" She beamed brilliantly. *"We're about to start the main event, the charity auction! I*

think everyone might already know what we'll be bidding for tonight, but here it is! One of the famous Legacies of Criminal AO, #tempest. err!"

Like the sounding of a death knell.

6

The cruise liner approached the bridge.

Kaname, now a member of Ag Wolves, glanced toward the hood of the mint-green coupe. Several windows were spread across its surface. There at the eleventh hour, Lily-Kiska was fiddling with the parts of a bolt-action sniper rifle. When she suddenly looked over at the windows on Kaname's car, what she saw was not weapon specs or cruise liner blueprints but...

Bro.
Dad's supposed to be making dinner tonight, but he's running late. Should we sort out dinner ourselves? I can't decide whether to order soba or go out for beef bowls, though. Pizza's a bit expensive, I guess. I'm also a little worried about trusting those delivery boys on their bikes using their phones to navigate. Do you have any other suggestions?

"...What are you doing over there?"

"My sister sent me a text, so I'm just replying to her. I need to write back something, doesn't matter what, within three minutes or else she gets mad."

"I'm shocked... You're an overprotective one."

"It's for my own good. Or else she'll do some 'renovating' and drill a bunch of holes in the wall again. Last time, it was the bathroom wall. Can you believe that?"

Perhaps that's what she did to collect her thoughts, Lily-Kiska mused to herself, tapping a small piercing in one of her ears to check the aim-steadying skill she would need for long-distance sniping.

It was finally time.

7

Of course, it wasn't as though Pavilion hadn't assessed the risks. Hard Engage Bridge was the choke point, after all.

Boom! There was an explosion a little way away, and orange sparks scattered across the deck of the ship. As soon as one of the AI attendants realized this was merely to calibrate the range and not a missed shot, a well-placed sniper bullet flew cleanly through its head.

Inside the ship, the auction floor buzzed with commotion, but atop the stage, Pavilion kept her cool. Her heels clicked as she addressed the crowd, microphone in hand in a manner that seemed to say *all is well*.

"I see twenty from number fifteen. Sitting at twenty, any advance on— Yes! Twenty-three from number fifty-nine! Twenty-five from number forty! Twenty-eight from seventy-two! Any advance on twenty-eight?"

The minimum bid was 100 million *snow*, which meant that bidding was currently sitting at 2.8 billion, but it was still early days. The shotgun #tempest.err was a nightmarish master key with which you could destroy any individual, business, or nation you chose. It was more useful than a nuclear bomb, and it didn't produce fallout. It was a devastating economic cyberweapon, capable of ejecting a person from society entirely, while allowing you to seize their assets, rights, and properties intact. And not just once but any number of times... Even 10 billion would be a small price to pay for that kind of power.

But money was not the end goal for Pavilion, who had infiltrated the management ranks of an AI conglomerate as their pet Dealer, even knowing that she would be cut loose if she made one wrong step. She was after connections with people who could pull veritable mountains of cash out of their backsides. *That would surely please a certain someone.*

"There we are! One hundred! Number seven takes it right to one hundred!! And I see two hundred from number thirteen! Going once, this is your last chance! The perfect opportunity to get your hands on the master key of the world! There, I see three hundred from number ninety-nine! Sitting pretty at three hundred!"

The world's most powerful people were looking upon the machinery of the global economy and fighting over the power to control it. It was a war in all but name. There was no time to worry about taking a bullet. Besides, anyone who turned tail and fled didn't deserve to be on Pavilion's list.

Of course, owing to a comprehensive risk assessment, the VIPs had gathered in a place inaccessible to sniper fire from atop the bridge. The *Tropical Lady* would soon be passing directly under it.

The bridge stood approximately thirty meters above sea level, but given that there were three floors of cabins above the deck, piled up like a staircase, it was a tight squeeze. Across the entire circular bridge that connected the peninsula to the surrounding islands, this was the only place high enough for the ship to pass through.

"*Any more? Remember, there's only one hundred and twenty seconds on the clock! And it looks like it's going to number ninety—Yes, number twenty, three hundred and one! Three-oh-one from number twenty! What are we going to do, ladies and gentlemen? Are we going to keep creeping up or is someone going to leap ahead?!*"

As her auctioneering performance loosened the buyers' purse strings, Pavilion chuckled to herself. *Now, are they going to leap off the bridge, vehicles and all? There are a thousand PMCs on this boat; we'll blow them to pieces as soon as they land!*

Just as she thought that, something happened on Hard Engage Bridge.

A truck atop the bridge lurched violently toward the barrier and toppled over the edge backward like a seesaw. But instead of falling, it simply hung down vertically, clinging to the side of the bridge by some unseen force, and stopped.

Is there a wire or winch or something?

Then the doors of the truck's trailer burst open, and what had been hiding inside began to fall.

Is that an anti-ship missile?!

8

Lily-Kiska moved her bespectacled eyes away from her sniper scope and sighed. She seemed to have turned off her smart glasses. Perhaps they weren't compatible with the scope.

"Two hundred million a pop," she said. "It's highway robbery, I tell you."

"It works, though," Kaname observed, standing beside her. Although he held his short-range sniper rifle, his role this time was that of spotter. "Now we just need to launch *the rest of them.*"

It wasn't only one truck strung up with a wire off the railing of the bridge. To the side, there was a whole line of them. In one fell swoop, a row of SSM68F anti-ship missiles fell from their trailers and rushed toward the sea.

9

Pavilion's heart sank, if you could say such a thing of a virtual avatar. A dull, tight pain spread throughout her body as the row of anti-ship missiles dropped down from the bridge overhead like the blade of a guillotine.

"…!!!!!"

Aren't they after #tempest.err? Don't they care if it gets destroyed?!

As the first missile hit the water's surface, it produced a huge spray that reached as high as the ship's observation deck.

One direct hit would mean the ship's utter destruction, and if it landed on the deck, then it was likely that all the VIPs would Fall in the explosion, the girl in the purple dress with them.

It was like Niagara Falls in reverse. The fearsome curtain of water obscured everyone's vision, and the shock waves from the explosions obstructed their hearing. Everything disappeared as the ship entered a world of silence.

But despite this…

Despite this…

"I apologize for the inconvenience."

Pavilion was still onstage. The explosions, and the curtain of water, disappeared. The ship was unharmed, with not a single scratch. It had threaded the needle, avoiding every last blast.

The VIPs found themselves still in the land of the living. Although they were frightened, they had no intention of fleeing. Not even to duck down, cradling their heads in terror. They suppressed the primal fear welling up in them with all their might. The look in their eyes said, *Now is not the time. We're dealing with something much more important.*

They were in possession of something very special. It wasn't logic that let them win. They knew that if you pushed your luck far enough, reason would back off. That's why they wouldn't die. That's why they wouldn't Fall. They had *luck*, the mark of a winner. They could face a million anti-ship missiles, and the result would be the same. Luck would see them through!

As the PMC guards sprang into action, the girl in the purple dress and bunny-eared ribbon ordered them about with one hand. As presumptuous as it would be to guess at her wishes, at the very least, Pavilion *knew the beautiful girl didn't want this.*

Her demeanor on the stage showed that she was seeing the same thing as the VIPs, that this was proof she could not be disposed of so easily. Pavilion smiled. What didn't kill you made you stronger, after all.

"*Let's get back to the auction! Currently, we're on three hundred and one from number twenty. We'll start the countdown again; in one hundred and twenty seconds—that's one hundred and twenty seconds— number twenty will win #tempest.err! If you don't like it, then let's see numbers in the air! Let's go!!*"

Pavilion realized her words could return the world to normal. She took back command of the room, snatched up her fate, and decimated any hope those petty thieves once had.

Winners always won.

She had entered a new world. A world inhabited by VIPs. A place for people who took whatever they wanted whenever they wanted it. She wasn't scared. No one could stand in her way on the path to success.

Until the auction was over and Pavilion obtained the list of truly powerful people, until she made *her young mistress* proud, Pavilion's machinery would never break down. Anyone who got in her way would simply be caught in the gears. She was confident of that. She was an oracle. A true prophet.

The *Tropical Lady* had now put the bridge behind it. With the missiles all gone, there came the roaring sound from above of a number of engines revving up. The attackers were probably switching to a more desperate tactic, planning to launch their vehicles off the side of the bridge and land atop the roof of the third-floor cabins.

But Pavilion and the VIPs were in the zone. There was no way they could lose now. They could just sit back and let the droves of PMCs do their thing.

Even now, she's somewhere here, watching me. I will bring her victory.

"Four hundred from number five!" Pavilion shouted. *"What a lead, ladies and gentlemen! Four hundred!!"*

A mint-green coupe. A sky-blue convertible. Vehicles fell toward the ship. It would be impressive if they could even land without taking serious damage, but they wouldn't get anything more than a gold star for effort.

Pavilion chuckled to herself as she took her gavel in hand.

"Any advance on four hundred? Going once, going twice…"

She lifted her hand gently. The thousand-strong army of PMCs raised their rifles skyward. The girl with a hint of innocence moved to close the sale.

"Sold, to number five! Everyone give a round of applause!"

She pounded the gavel against the round plate atop her podium. That was the signal for the PMCs to open fire.

10

And so their fate was sealed.

11

"   "
…

Kaname and the rest of Ag Wolves landed upon the topmost roof of the *Tropical Lady.* He got out of the car. Countless PMCs, armed to the teeth and packed tightly like soldier ants, swarmed the lower decks, the areas around the cabins, and even the same roof upon which Kaname stood. But none of them—not Lily-Kiska, with her swept-back hair and glasses; not Titan, the huge man with the crew cut; and not

even M-Scope, the slouched man with the merch-covered backpack—
showed the slightest sign of fear. That was because…

With the rattling sound of metal, the PMCs cleanly turned around
and pointed their weapons at Pavilion and the VIPs.

"Wh-what…?"
The short girl in the purple dress that was too large for her was
confused. What had happened? Why were the AI PMCs, the most
powerful force imaginable, turning their guns on their own external
contractor?
"Why are you…? Hurry up and deal with the intruders! What are
you doing?!"
The PMCs did not respond. It was Kaname, standing atop the roof,
who answered.
"I wouldn't if I were you. Any sudden movements and they'll gun
you down where you stand. They're under our control now."
A chilling unease spread throughout the crowd. It sounded preposterous, but staring down the barrels of a thousand rifles, nobody
wanted to test Kaname's claim. The heavy silence only served to
drive the point home. In stark contrast to those quivering motion-
lessly on the deck of the ship, Ag Wolves leisurely descended from
the rooftop. Taking the cabin floors one at a time, they arrived at the
auction floor.
"What's going on…? Have you hacked the PMCs to take control of
them or something?"
"If it were that easy, there's no way *snow* would be anywhere near as
valuable as the yen or the dollar. There's never been a single successful
cyberattack in the entire history of this game. That's what makes this
world so powerful."
Then how…? Pavilion groaned, and it was Lily-Kiska, her breasts
pushed together by her underarm holsters, who answered, giving a
derisive snort.
"First, keep in mind who has been protecting you here. The
PMCs are controlled by AI, and they're programmed to distinguish

between friend and foe based only on the contract they have with their client."

Next to speak was the slouching, backpacked M-Scope, clad in a hoodie with an anime character on the front.

"Second, there's this rather interesting development that White Queen Tourism, the owners of this vessel, has been undertaking: the Surf Riding Project. It seeks to unify all branches of the AI conglomerate—flights, ships, hotels—under a single entity. I-in fact, the online meetings have already reached the final stages."

Titan fiddled with the dog tag–shaped device wrapped around his wrist.

"Third, well, what if we interrupted those all-important online meetings? The group would be split, and no one would know shit about who's in charge of what, including this very ship."

"Ah!!" cried Pavilion at last.

"Fourth, the missiles weren't aiming for the ship. We set a delayed fuse. We simply needed a guided weapon that could withstand the pressure of the water." Kaname completed the explanation, his black hair swaying in the sea breeze. "They were aiming for the undersea cables. Vital infrastructure for communicating with the peninsula district and, recently, the subject of a huge debate over whether to replace them with satellite communications. The whole reason we dropped them vertically instead of firing them was to hit those cables. By tearing them up, we were able to put a stop to the online meetings that were instrumental to the advancement of the Surf Riding Project—"

"...Wait," interrupted Pavilion. "So what if you put a stop to it? It's just about bringing all the airline, passenger shipping, and hotel companies under the control of the AI conglomerate!"

As the blood drained from Pavilion's face, Kaname picked up the thing leaning against the podium atop the stage. It was one of the Legacies of Criminal AO, the Overtrick. The shotgun #tempest.err. Giving the orange gun barrel a theatrical kiss, he replied:

"You're an external contractor, Pavilion. Just a skilled hound in the employ of an AI conglomerate, because you have the flexibility they don't. What would they think, then, if you were unable to prevent the disruption of their precious online meetings, despite being right there when it happened? Though it may only be to ensure the game runs smoothly, you're in a position where one mistake earns you the sack, and apparently your AI boss chooses who to recruit next based on a list of Dealers with the most expensive transactions. Incidentally, we're all worth 1.7 billion each. I wouldn't be surprised if one of us got the position after you lost the job."

"Crap…"

The reason Pavilion could control the *Tropical Lady* and the AI PMCs was because she was an external contractor for White Queen Tourism. What if a mistake happened before her very eyes that took all of that away from her? And what if, after that, the next appointee automatically chosen by HR just so happened to be one of the very Ag Wolves she now faced?

Lily-Kiska smirked. "The background checks your company runs are all automatic, aren't they? As long as we keep up appearances, they'll never discover the connections that run deeper. So we've kept a member on standby, just waiting for the call."

A company fully staffed by AI would never employ a human, even as the lowliest intern. The fact that Pavilion had made it onto the payroll of an AI conglomerate at all was an anomaly. One mistake and she'd be out the door. Faced with such a cutthroat contract, it was hard to make an appeal.

Kaname made his declaration. "Now it's time to turn the tables. That's what *Money (Game) Master* is all about. If you want to slowly but surely make a living, then join a company in real life. Here, it's all about high risk, high reward."

12

I apologize in advance for ranting in this letter.

Also, I ran out of snowman envelopes, so I'm sorry it looks so sterile.

I know I was the one who kept talking about how handwriting conveys our emotions…but there's something I have to put into words. Something I can't discuss with my friends at school.

I don't like my older brother.

He dumped everything on me. I can't believe I'm related to him.

But there's still a part of me that believes in him. And even though I say nasty things about him, I can't bear to hear those same things come out of other people's mouths.

I'm so selfish.

I'm such an awful person.

I don't even know whether I should send this letter. If you're reading this, then it means I was weakhearted enough to put a stamp on it and drop it in the mailbox.

I'm so sorry.

I don't know what to do.

13

"Phew…"

The one Ag Wolves member who remained on the bridge was a young girl with her hair in a long braid, Zaurus. She was relaxing in the driver's seat of her four-wheel drive, wearing a netted tank top and a pair of dangerously short shorts. Her long limbs, covered by an animal-print hoodie, and pair of catlike eyes that you only get in games, contributed to her wild look.

While lightly snacking on a portion of fries resting on the dashboard, the girl with pale-pink hair gazed at several windows scattered across the windshield. Thanks to the interference of Ag Wolves, the Surf Riding Project was spinning its wheels. The AI conglomerate was frantically searching for alternatives to the undersea fiber-optic network to reestablish communications with the outside world, but it wouldn't be easy. The downtime might last only about four and a half minutes, but that was plenty of time.

After all, the plan wasn't to drive White Queen into bankruptcy. It was to give HR a wake-up call, have them investigate Pavilion, and give her the sack. One point seven billion. The size of their transactions would put Ag Wolves at the head of the list, and the recruitment e-mail would simply fall into their laps.

And the secret ingredients were those anti-ship missiles. If all you wanted to do was cut some wires at the bottom of the sea, then a simple torpedo would do the job for a fraction of the price. Even a diver equipped with bolt cutters would suffice. So why did Ag Wolves settle on a set of anti-ship missiles for 2 billion apiece? The answer was simple.

"Hee-hee-hee, I wonder what White Queen will think once they find out that the missiles that shut off their communications were produced at one of their very own airplane manufacturing plants. Probably that their external contractor, Pavilion, was lying about the attack on the ship and the cause of the communications failure, that she'd been the one to take weapons from their own warehouses and turn them against their assets."

In general, forces owned by a company, such as PMCs, could only be used in defense of that company's own property. However, it was always possible for a stray bullet intended for a VIP to hit an innocent Dealer. In the same way, weapons produced by an AI conglomerate could destroy communications infrastructure if, say, a load of anti-ship missiles was to miss their target and rupture a bundle of undersea cables.

That made her seem maximally suspicious.

Ping. An electric sound rang, indicating a received message. It was the recruitment e-mail transferring all power from Pavilion to Ag Wolves.

"Now I'm White Queen Tourism's external contractor... So that ship is ours."

The auction house and #tempest.err had been out of their reach. In that case, why not take the whole ship? What's more, while Ag Wolves now held the incredibly fragile position of external contractor, they now held command over the thousand PMC guards who were bound by their contract.

A single SSM68F anti-ship missile cost 2 billion *snow*. The ten participants of Ag Wolves each contributed 1.7 billion, but that money didn't all go toward missiles. Over 80 percent of it was spent on financial trading, moving vast amounts of wealth through the markets. This was all in order to shoot to the top of White Queen's list.

Zaurus cracked her neck, and her feet, clad in a pair of monochromatic boots, rested heavily on her steering wheel.

"Once we get our hands on #tempest.err, I'm gonna wash my hands of this boring external contractor post...but I wonder if they'll at least let us hold the after-party on this ship. We could use the hot tubs and pools... Awww man, there's even a bunch of five-star French restaurants on board!!"

14

I wonder. Would you still be my friend if you knew I was an AI Dropout?

[The rest of this letter is tearstained and illegible.]

15

The battle was over. One wrong step, and Pavilion and the other VIPs would Fall as a thousand PMCs gunned them down. They could barely breathe, let alone stage a counterattack. The members of Ag Wolves who now occupied the cruise liner assembled on the poolside stage.

With her sniper rifle clipped to a belt on her back, freeing up her hands, Lily-Kiska gulped. "So this is the Overtrick...#tempest.err. Can I hold it?"

"Me too," said Titan.

"Me three...," added M-Scope. "After everyone else has had a go, that is."

All wanting to be part of the legend, the members passed #tempest. err's crude frame among themselves, fawning over it and taking photos. When it made it back to Kaname, Lily-Kiska spoke to him as he fiddled with its parts.

"Well, now we have to figure out how to get out of here. It won't be long before people start to realize what happened. We might even run into other Dealers who've heard the news and come to steal #tempest. err for themselves. Let's see…"

"Oh, that is important. But first, I have something I want to ask you."

"What is it?"

Having gotten her permission, Kaname continued—just as instructed by that familiar yet strange sensation that tickled the tip of his nose.

"When are you going to kill me so you can have #tempest.err to yourself?"

Grrrrr-gr! The sound of grinding metal filled the air. On one side, Kaname held the revolver-style grenade launcher #tempest.err. On the other, Lily-Kiska had unfastened the sniper rifle from her back and wielded it, surrounded by the other Ag Wolves and the thousand PMCs under their control.

Anyone could see that this standoff was absurd. Facing down over a thousand gun barrels out on the open poolside with no cover to speak of, there was no way that Kaname could win.

However, he held one of the Legacies of Criminal AO. This was no ordinary gun restricted to firing upon a single point but a monster shotgun like something out of a cheesy space movie. One pull of the trigger of this brutal orange-colored weapon would release two thousand pellets into the area dictated by its fan-shaped light, killing anyone and everyone unlucky enough to be caught inside. It was one of the Overtrick, a weapon so monstrously powerful that it couldn't possibly be legitimate.

With just a couple of shots, everyone standing there would be dead. For Ag Wolves, it all came down to whether or not they gave Kaname the chance to do that.

The giant with the crew cut, Titan, roared ferociously, brandishing in each hand a ridiculous full-auto magnum pistol with a stupidly long magazine. "I told ya, Lily-Kiska! We shoulda gotten rid of him earlier!!"

"Shut up, Titan. This is my jurisdiction!!" She barked back.

"…You planned to shoot me in the back all along once we got #tempest.err."

"You misunderstand," Lily-Kiska replied.

"It was never about securing the peace and order of *Money (Game) Master*. You just wanted the Legacies all to yourselves. And something tells me this isn't your first time. You're hiding more of the Legacies somewhere, aren't you?"

"We *are* going to restore order! We just need a deterrent, that's all! If we never have to use it, so much the better!"

Kaname's black hair swung as he softly shook his head. "This is going nowhere."

"Negotiations have failed, then."

The tingly scent of danger prickled Kaname's nose. Tension was high. If so much as a pin dropped, all hell would break loose.

"Tell me," offered Lily-Kiska. "What made you choose to do this? Do you really want to Fall so badly?"

"Well, lots of reasons. But the main one is simple." Kaname spat out his words. "Helping others isn't about bragging rights or asking for something in return. You made your mission sound noble, but that's exactly why it seemed so suspicious. You talked as though you were expecting a reward for saving the world."

But something happened before he could finish.

Bam! There was the faint sound of a gunshot, and a dark-red hole appeared in Kaname's right arm.

"…???!!!"

The shot came from off to the side. An intense heat and pain spread from the wound across Kaname's entire body. Of course, since Kaname had never been shot in real life, he had nothing to compare it to, but pain flashed in his mind. Perhaps triggered by his pulse or blood pressure, the smart watch on his wrist let out a warning sound. #tempest.err fell to his feet.

But it wasn't any of Ag Wolves or the PMCs under their control who had fired the shot. It was someone among the crowd of cowering civilians—a fair-skinned girl with her black hair tied up in twin tails. A pair of black gloves and thigh-high stockings matched her frilly bikini and miniskirt combo, with a headdress adorned with blue roses and white lace that contributed to her gothic-lolita image. The unknown variable. The wild card.

The giant with the crew cut, Titan, bellowed and the dog tag–shaped health scanner wrapped around his wrist emitted a beeping sound, indicating his agitation.

"It's Midori!! The Dealer related to Criminal AO!! I knew she was the one pullin' Pavilion's strings!"

Just then, Kaname did something unthinkable. With his foot, he kicked #tempest.err away. And not because he feared Ag Wolves would pick it up. As the orange-colored Legacy skimmed across the floor of the poolside deck, a slender hand reached out to pick it up. But surrounded by countless PMCs, Pavilion suddenly panicked and pulled her hand back. Somebody had stopped her.

"Don't do it, ma'am!! Stay out of this!"

The one who feared for the safety of the girl in the purple dress was not Midori. It was a girl clad in what looked like a tennis outfit, with medium-length hair, yet below whose waist a large snake body slithered on the ground: a lamia Magistellus.

That's Pavilion's mistress?! Is she so addicted to this game that she is serving her own Magistellus?! The queen wasn't Midori after all. I thought she was with Criminal AO. If not, why is she on the ship...?!

As Lily-Kiska's head reeled with possibilities, the situation continued to unfold. #tempest.err skated across the poolside deck. It was headed straight for Midori. Of course, the PMCs wouldn't let that happen. The lamia Magistellus might have stopped Pavilion before she could do anything, but if she had so much as touched the Legacy, they would have considered her an enemy of Ag Wolves and moved to protect the interests of their "employer." As those hundreds of barrels turned to face Midori, Kaname raised his free left arm.

He held the short-range sniper rifle Short Spear. Firing it with one hand, he shot one of the AI PMCs to aggro them. "Get inside!! Tselika!!"

As soon as the AI's priority switched to Kaname, the petite girl named Midori scooped up #tempest.err in both hands and made a break for the watertight bulkhead door of the passenger compartment. At that moment, Kaname's mint-green coupe came falling down from the sky, crashing through the members of Ag Wolves and sending them sprawling across the floor. The PMCs began their assault in earnest. The car interposed itself as Kaname's shield, but in the blink of an eye, it was painted with orange sparks.

"Aaaagh! They'll blow us up!" Tselika shrieked from the driver's seat. "My temple's health is plummeting!"

"It's fine! We need to go after Midori!"

"Argh! Get off my back! You know I'm not comfortable being on other people's property!"

"Don't worry—we may be in the midst of a brief falling-out, but it's still our team that controls this ship."

There was no time to switch seats. With Kaname clinging to the outside, both arms wrapped around the driver's seat's open window, the mint-green coupe set off for the interior of the ship. The bleeding from his right arm only worsened, but it was better than staying here and becoming Swiss cheese.

A vast space extended within the ship. It served as a terminal to reach other locations such as casinos and shopping malls, but it could also probably serve as a dance hall for events.

"What a sorry state, My Lord. We'll have to take it in for repairs as soon as we get back. *As soon as we get back!!*"

"We have to get out of here first."

In just a matter of seconds, the gleaming sports car had become destined for the junkyard. It was a wonder the engine was still running. Tselika backed the car up against the double doors through which the pair had entered. That would stop anyone coming into the space for now, but once their pursuers found another way around, they were doomed.

"Goodness, My Lord, both you and my vehicle are full of holes! Let me see it, you oaf!! You're lucky the bullet passed straight through!!"

Tselika hurried from the car and reached beneath the miniskirt of her pit-babe outfit, bringing out a small device that looked like a can of hair spray that had been strapped to her outer thigh. It was a powdered blood coagulant. She sprayed it liberally over Kaname's arm wound. It was more effective than wrapping it in Kaname's red necktie.

Ker-chik. A loud noise echoed through the room. Midori stepped out from behind a large piano and pointed #tempest.err in their direction.

"Put down your weapons and step away from each other!" she shouted with open hostility. "I'll never hand over my brother's Legacy! It needs to be destroyed!!"

"I agree. Let's talk it over."

"Shut up!"

As Kaname attempted to open a discussion, his hands raised, standing beside the mint-green coupe, Midori shouted him down. But Kaname didn't comply.

"How do you destroy the Legacies exactly? Do they just break if you slam them on the ground enough times? We probably have about ten minutes before Ag Wolves and their PMC buddies get here. If we don't figure out a way by then, #tempest.err will fall right back into their hands."

"...!!" The twin-tailed girl chewed her lip in a way that suggested she had already tried that. "Then...then run it over with that car! Do it or I'll shoot!!"

"I guess it's as good a plan as any."

Keeping his hands raised, Kaname sat down on the hood of the coupe. "But are you sure you can shoot?" he asked, attempting to hide his pain. "That shotgun you've got can't take precise shots, and as you can see from the state it's in, my car's HP is close to 0. If you shoot me now, it'll go down with me, and so will any chance you have of destroying the Legacy. Besides, the reflective surface of the car could cause the beam of light to reflect back. And given all the sharp bits poking out of its bullet holes now, I'd be extra careful about that."

"Wh-wh-wh-wha…?"

Still pointing #tempest.err, Midori's eyes darted about in confusion. She wasn't paying attention to Tselika screeching, "Whose fault do you think *that* is?!"

"As I said, we've got ten minutes. If we can't come to an agreement in that time, we'll be left with the worst-case scenario. Ag Wolves will take the Legacy, turn all the other Dealers into mincemeat, and send a bunch of real-world companies into bankruptcy. Now, time is on our side. Do you want to talk or not?"

"…???!!!" Midori looked as though she wanted to stamp her feet in frustration, but there was no other way. The fact she held such an overwhelmingly powerful weapon made it all the more powerless right now. No tool was effective in every single situation.

"Besides, even if you weren't holding #tempest.err, you wouldn't shoot me. You couldn't make someone Fall."

"Couldn't I?"

"When I'm in a dangerous spot, my nose tingles. I'm not getting any of that from you. I'm not sure what you meant to gain by catching me off guard and acting so tough." Kaname relaxed. "As Criminal AO's sister, you know more than anyone else what a Fall does to a person. That's why you can't do it. And that's why you aimed at my arm the last time."

Midori choked back her words. Hanging her head, with lips tightly pursed, she spat out only a single line: "…You know nothing about me."

Her voice took on a dark, heavy tone completely at odds with her appearance. A voice dripping with resentment.

"*Money (Game) Master*? This stupid game loaded my brother with tons of debt in twenty-four hours, just for making one little mistake! It put a burden on our whole family!! And then he disappeared!! We don't even know if he's dead or alive!! He just ran away and left us to deal with his debt!!"

Disappeared. Ran away.

The venom with which she coated those words was born of hate, not concern.

"And on top of that...on top of that, they say there's still a load of unexploded bombs in this world! They call them Legacies and tell me they're dangerous things that can send even more people into debt or even destroy countries on the other side of the world! Someone I don't even know could be made to feel this pain, this confusion, that I feel right now!!"

"..."

"I can't let that idiot's Legacies continue to exist. People pick on me at school. I can't even walk down the street. Every time the phone or the doorbell rings, I nearly jump out of my skin... I wouldn't wish that on anybody. I have to get rid of everything he left behind. Remove all traces that he ever existed! That's the only way to bring the world back to normal!!"

It was impossible for Kaname to truly understand what kind of world Midori lived in. Perhaps something had caused her to turn hate upon her own family.

But...

Despite all that...

"You're wrong."

"About what...?"

"Takamasa didn't deserve to be called an idiot."

"What do you know about...?!" Midori began to yell but stopped herself as she realized. As she pointed her brother's shotgun, her face took on a puzzled expression.

"How did you know his name...?"

"..."

"Did you know him? Had you met him? Fought here alongside him?"

"He did tell me he had a sister. We used to complain about our lives to each other. This is our first time *meeting for real*, though. But anyway, it sounds like it was only recently that you decided to do something about the Legacies—is that right?"

Midori didn't answer the question. Biting her lip, she responded with one of her own. "Then you know, don't you? People put him on a pedestal, called him a legendary Dealer, but it's not like he was that skilled. All he could do was customize. His strength was solely in the weapons he made."

"Yeah, he was definitely more of an ideas guy. *I* actually got a higher score using his weapons than he did."

"But he got too big for his boots, ended up in a battle he couldn't win, and was completely slaughtered!! Then he Fell, saddled us with his debt, and scattered his Legacies across this world!! ...Why'd *he* have to be my brother? It wouldn't have been so bad if he had been some complete stranger, but he had to go and bring Mom, Dad, and me down to rock bottom with him...!"

Kaname's eyes narrowed slightly—as though he was trying to endure a pain much, much worse than that in his arm.

"I'm sorry."

"?"

"It's me you should be saying that to. Takamasa took the fall for us. He was our hero. Your grievances are with me. Please, I don't want to hear his own sister talk about him like that."

"What did he do...?" A drop of blood formed on Midori's lip as she clenched her teeth. She screamed as though her underdeveloped chest might burst. "What did he do except make other people's lives miserable?!"

Kaname looked like a ghost, but his reply was immediate.

"He risked his life to save my sister."

In an instant, Midori lost her train of thought.

"He saved us. It was supposed to be my sister and me who Fell."

He knew. Kaname Suou always knew.

He knew what Criminal AO was really like. He knew what Midori was feeling, how she was suffering. This may have been *their first time meeting in person*, but the two had been exchanging letters for a long time.

On pale-blue writing paper. Envelopes decorated with snowmen.

Midori could never forgive her brother for what he did, but somewhere in her heart, she still believed in him. Even as she placed that barely legible tearstained letter into the mailbox. That's how important she was to him. It wasn't so black-and-white that she could just throw him away. Even now, after jumping into *Money (Game) Master* and obtaining one of the monstrous Legacies. Even now, as she screamed her lungs out. Even now, deep down within her small chest, her wounded soul was weeping.

But he had stolen him. Whatever the reason, however it had happened, Kaname had stolen her brother from her. Stolen something so precious for his own benefit. So...

Don't run away.

Kaname took a deep breath. More than any firefight, more than any car chase, more than any market prediction.

Don't run away from what you did.

The tension in the air was suffocating, but Kaname kept looking right into Midori's eyes.

"Perhaps you've heard about the Swiss Depression on TV, or perhaps you've seen the movie *Kotemitsu Gold Rush*. It was a huge plot to make seventy million people across the world lose their jobs and concentrate the wealth into just a handful of people's bank accounts. My sister and I went to the conspirators' den to try to stop them before they threw the switch, but they were too strong for us."

That's the Second Great Depression that never happened, Midori thought. *The economists on TV kept saying it was on the way. So it was all planned in secret?*

Problems didn't spring into existence for no reason, and they didn't disappear without a reason, either.

A secret battle, and the Dealers who fought knowing that they would receive no recognition of their efforts.

"We stopped their plan, and all was going well, except we overextended ourselves and took too long to escape. Those Dealers were powerful and out for blood, and we were hopelessly outnumbered and outmatched. We took refuge in an abandoned building, but it was obvious we were trapped. We were just waiting to Fall. My sister was contacting everyone she knew, begging for help, but I was sure that nobody was going to put their necks on the line for us, no matter how much we could pay. I guess it was like being pinned down, screaming for help, even if we knew nobody was coming to save us."

"…"

"But he did come to save us."

Kaname remembered that day. In that abandoned house lit by moonlight, in the deepest pits of despair, the doors flying open and him standing there. He remembered the face of his friend, who did what no one else in the world could, and without hesitation.

"He was carrying every weapon he owned. And although he was useless in a firefight, he was grinning, desperately trying to hide the fact that his knees were knocking against each other. He had come running and broken the siege, told us everything was okay. He didn't come for the money or to show off. He came only to rescue us because we were in danger."

It was him who came to mind when Kaname imagined the word *hero*. Even if he hadn't been all that strong. Even if he hadn't been all that smart. That image had burned itself into Kaname's mind, giving him a brand-new goal in life.

"But even then, it wasn't enough to save us all. At the very end, an enemy Dealer fired at my little sister, and he took the bullet. He Fell protecting her. It should have been me saving my sister's life, but I was too in shock to do anything, and so he did it for me."

The incident left such a mark on Kaname's sister that she had deleted "Ayame" and given up the game for good. That was certainly one way of dealing with it.

But Criminal AO was never coming back. This world had no levels, no experience points. A Dealer's strength could be boosted only by cash, which players used to secure items and equipment. Without money, it was nearly impossible to stage a comeback once you racked up a large-enough debt. You couldn't even delete your old avatar and start afresh. Top-class Dealers earned the ire of everyone around them, so as soon as they found themselves vulnerable, everyone would gang up on them before they could even stand back up and properly equip themselves, and they would Fall once more. They would be unable to make a single move, a condition known as "Dead."

And so Kaname, the only one left, decided to do something about the Legacies of Criminal AO, so that the sister of the man who had saved his life didn't need to risk her own.

Fearfully, cautiously, with trembling lips, Midori asked, "So he wasn't a detestable human being...?"

"No."

"He Fell saving the world, protecting his friends, things to be proud of?"

"Yeah, he did."

But there was something else Kaname needed to say to her. Kaname desperately continued to weave together his words, bringing his own crimes to light.

"It's all because of us that you and your family are living in such poverty, so I'm in no position to act all high and mighty. You can hate me. In fact, I expect you already do."

He had to say this:

"But Takamasa, your brother, is a hero who did what nobody else could. He saved us. Saved our lives. Our dignity. My family... My only sister in the whole world. Please remember that. It's not him who's a detestable human being. He's not the coward who survived due to his own weakness, who froze in the moment and couldn't even save his own sister. I am."

That was all she could take. #tempest.err fell from Midori's hands and hit the ground with a clatter. No matter how much she bit her lip, the tears streaming down the young girl's face did not stop. They fell in huge droplets until ultimately she opened her mouth wide and began sobbing loudly like a baby. She was finally released from having to harbor such animosity toward her own family.

"He never told us any of that..."

"I bet."

"We shouted at him, hurled abuse at him. And he never tried to argue it, not even once! He just went and disappeared!!"

"That's why he was our hero."

Perhaps she wanted him to have argued back, to offer a reason why the brother she looked up to had become such a burden on the family. Perhaps she wanted to be told that there was more to it than that.

Nobody knew why Criminal AO, why Takamasa, had run away from his family. Maybe he wasn't a perfect person and just wanted to get away from the jeers and the situation he had caused. That was certainly a possibility, but it didn't sit right with Kaname. He couldn't help but think it all came back to Ayame and himself. They were the cause behind his massive debt. If his family ever discovered that, they would turn their hatred upon the two siblings.

And he couldn't bear that.

To the very end, Takamasa was covering for them. Even after being locked out of the game world, he was a hero in the real world, too. What if he hadn't been so brave? What if he hadn't cared about Kaname and Ayame and responded, even as a reflex, to his sister or his family? Perhaps that would have changed the way this young girl saw her big brother. In fact, it might be more appropriate to say that she would have continued to see him the way she always had, as good an older brother as he had been before his Fall.

In one way, Kaname had said all he had to say. But he couldn't just let it end here. This wasn't about money; it was about honor. That was one thing that Kaname would never let go of. His life had been saved. Kaname knew what that meant, and he would repay it, even if it took everything he had.

"...So this time it's my turn."

Kaname slowly walked toward the sobbing girl. Right toward the symbol of his own sin.

"It's time for me to protect his family, just as he protected mine."

"Ooohhh."

"I'll protect you, even if it kills me."

"Oooohhh!!"

As he made his declaration, Kaname planted both hands on the girl's small shoulders, crouching down to look her in the eye. Midori sniffled as she listed her demands.

"You'll help me look for my brother's Legacies?"

"Yeah."

"I don't want anyone to lose their life because of the things my brother left behind. Will you help?"

"That's a small price to pay."

Kaname had been willing to die—ever since a true hero had saved the life of his family.

"One more thing," he added. "I can't afford to let you Fall at the hands of Ag Wolves or whoever else we might encounter. So please, Midori... Order me to protect you."

"..." Midori relentlessly rubbed her eyes, which were bright red, though the tears did not stop flowing. She continued to sob heavily, her breath ragged. Eventually she stopped trying to hold it back. She spoke with a face filled with emotion, the sobs interrupting her speech like hiccups.

"I... I order you...," she started, in shambles. Then her lips formed these words:

"I order you to p-pwotect me! Swear on your life!"

At last. In that moment, the gears all clicked into place.

Ah.

At last. Kaname could now start on equal footing with him. That much was clear.

Takamasa. Is it okay?

At last. For the first time in a long while, Kaname Suou felt that his mask of ice was beginning to thaw.

Am I allowed to have the chance to get my life back?

Suddenly, like the flame from a single cigarette burning an entire prairie to ash, the scent of danger caressed the tip of Kaname's nose.

Most likely, they were already surrounded. Unless they did something, Ag Wolves would burst through that door at any moment. There was no point in staying here a second longer.

There was no fortune to be made by helping Midori. And Kaname wouldn't get to keep any Legacies they managed to scrape together;

the whole point was to destroy them. In fact, Kaname would be putting his life and livelihood on the line, investing mountains of his own money, to fend off any Dealers who stood in their way.

But that was exactly why Kaname didn't hesitate. He knew there was no profit to be made. And that, he felt, led him to make up his mind.

Because helping others wasn't about bragging rights or asking for something in return.

16

On the other side of the doors, where the pool and auction house were set up, Lily-Kiska was standing on the deck with the hunched backpack man, M-Scope. For reasons they did not know, the front doors refused to open, and so Lily-Kiska had ordered the PMCs to explore the interior of the ship and find another way into the hall.

"I hope they haven't already destroyed #tempest.err," whimpered M-Scope. "Perhaps we should help find another way inside."

"If they use that shotgun in an enclosed space, it'll be impossible for us to dodge. The fact they haven't already thrown it into the sea gives us reason to believe they're looking for a way to destroy it completely, which means they'll have to wait until they're back on land."

Lily-Kiska gave her reply while going through different accessories to wear in her ears. As her mismatched boots showed, she didn't choose her clothes based on fashion. She was re-speccing from a long-range sniper build to something better suited to close-quarter combat. She thought as she peered through her rifle scope.

#tempest.err might have been one of the Overtrick, but it wasn't omnipotent. If you had a mirrored shield or a silver catsuit, you could reflect the guiding light. In the right situation, you could counter it with nothing more than the sheet of foil from a sandwich picked out at a buffet.

…However, it was a different story entirely to have the courage to actually face #tempest.err with such a makeshift weapon. It was impossible to predict where the two thousand pellets would go, especially in a small room with lots of windows and mirrors. And once you factored in that a single error would result in your Fall, it was hard to make such a risky gamble. Money was something you didn't appreciate until it was gone. Only then did you feel the dread working its way into your bones.

"Isn't there something else you should be more worried about?" she asked. "Like the number of shots #tempest.err has?"

"Based on when I held it, I'd say it's about ten shots," said Titan. According to the numbers displayed on the dog tags wrapped around his wrist, he had calmed down.

Lily-Kiska made that her target.

"Then let's send our PMCs at them and force them to waste all their ammo. They won't be able to buy or make any more right now. After the AIs have had the stuffing beaten out of them, we can just waltz in and collect the prize once they're exhausted."

Ag Wolves had a thousand PMCs on their side, and they were at sea, with nowhere for their foes to run. Their enemies were desperate, but as long as they didn't allow the cornered rats to bite back, they could win without taking any losses.

Wary of #tempest.err possibly being able to break through the door, Lily-Kiska pressed herself up against the thick walls and shouted through to the other side.

"You know you've got no way out of here, don't you? Hand over #tempest.err and we'll spare your lives. We don't care about Midori! Just give us #tempest.err so we can restore order, and we will end this without you two having to Fall!!"

It didn't matter if they responded or not. This was their final warning. But sure enough, a voice responded through the sealed door.

"We're not handing over #tempest.err to you. And we also need to take back all the Legacies you already have. So the negotiations are over, Lily-Kiska."

"It makes no difference to us. That just means you two will have to Fall for us to restore order to *Money (Game) Master* and the real world. It's a pointless waste of your lives, in my opinion, but good-bye."

"Oh, I wonder about that."

"You still think there's a way out? You're up against the best of Ag Wolves, backed by a thousand PMCs. Besides, we're at sea. There's nowhere to run."

"Oh, it's a tough situation for sure. I can feel the tingle on the tip of my nose," the man on the other side of the door acknowledged. "But I have the Lion's Nose. Any other Dealer would pull out once they knew when to quit. But that's not how I do things. I know exactly how thick the wall is, and that's why I'm going to break through it."

"…?"

"Listen. This isn't an island or a mega-float; it's a ship. And I think you were so wrapped up in the ecstasy of stealing it, winning the PMCs' contract, and becoming more disposable than the merchandise from last year's World Cup that you forgot one thing. As we speak, the ship has been working its way across the waves."

W-wait…!

"No… It can't be!!"

Lily-Kiska's words came a moment too late.

Kaboom! A dreadful sound, like an explosion, rocked the ship. The cruise liner, continuing along its path, had collided with the wharf ahead.

There was a big difference between those who had predicted it and those who had not. Lily-Kiska, M-Scope, Titan, Pavilion, and the countless PMCs stationed in the area were thrown to the floor as the ship lurched. In the middle of it all, there was the roaring sound of an engine revving up. The double doors burst outward, and the mint-green coupe came rolling out back-first onto the deck. In the driver's seat of the battered vehicle sat Kaname, while Tselika and Midori sat in the passenger seat, wrapped in each other's arms.

"…Grrr!"

At short range, it was easier to aim based on the support provided by Lily-Kiska's smart glasses than to use the scope. She quickly leveled the rifle in Kaname's direction, but it was too late. Even though she had changed her accessories to be more suited to close-quarter combat, she was still using a sniper rifle. It was impossible to cover all one's bases.

While she tried in vain to line up a shot, the sports car spun a clean one-eighty by the poolside, as if mocking her. Without losing momentum, the vehicle swept across the deck with a roar before breaking through the railing and off the bow of the ship. The main road of the peninsula district stretched beyond the grounded cruise liner.

"...!!!"

Midori screamed as they entered free fall, and a strange sensation gripped her stomach, as if it were being lifted out of her body. Tselika clamped her hand over the girl's small mouth, probably less out of consideration for her biting her tongue and more simply to muffle the awful racket.

They were about three stories up in the air, and Kaname obviously wasn't following the traffic signals.

The bottom of the car scraped the asphalt, tossing out a slew of orange sparks as it touched down with a *thud*. Kaname pulled on the steering wheel as he landed, narrowly avoiding a large oncoming bus, and lightly tapped the brakes to regain control of the coupe, somehow rejoining the flow of traffic.

"Bwa! Wh-what are we going to do now?" Midori asked.

"Look for Criminal AO's...I mean, Takamasa's Legacies. It's unclear how far they've spread, but at the very least, we know where one of them is."

Kaname, his black hair slick with sweat from his brow, steered the car with only his left hand as he answered.

"Ag Wolves... We find out what they're hiding and where, and we destroy it all."

Just then, wrapped in Tselika's arms in the passenger seat, Midori noticed something strange.

Kaname had taken it upon himself to deal with the Legacies of Criminal AO, as well as his sister, Midori. He had even put himself up against the formidable Ag Wolves. If word got out that they were in search of the Legacies, who knew just how many more people would get involved?

And yet, through his pained expression, Midori could see that Kaname's lips were turned up in a ferocious smile.

"That's My Lord for you," whispered Tselika as she clung to Midori's side. It was as though they were both gazing upon something blindingly bright. "He's had to deal with all this Criminal AO business, and he's been worrying about your well-being, too. But My Lord always loved *Money (Game) Master* more than anyone else."

"Huh?"

This filthy, dirty, rotten, unfair game. Here was a man who ate it all up with pleasure.

A true fighter.

"The immediate danger has passed, and he's done mourning. That means My Lord can have fun again. He'll have his fill until there's naught left but bones. You're lucky, Midori. You're about to find out firsthand what it means to really play *Money (Game) Master*."

With one hand on the wheel, Kaname was thinking about something. When he and Lily-Kiska had been waiting on Hard Engage Bridge, she had said something like, "*...That's the first step. I hope this serves to bring us closer together as well.*"

"Sheesh."

"?"

As Midori gave Kaname a puzzled look, the mint-green coupe sped off into the city.

04/01/20XX 10:20 AM

Event
Strictly speaking, there are no fixed events or quests in the open-world format of *Money (Game) Master*. The story is not written beforehand by the developers but by the actions of the many Dealers as they play the game. The events described on the car stereo are mostly large actions taken by AI businesses that are easy for many Dealers to get involved with.

The Concept of Food
Food and stamina do exist, but the values are reset upon logging out, so they are irrelevant unless you plan on playing for more than a few hours at a time. However, food continues to taste and fill you up like it does in the real world, so many Dealers insist on having meals to concentrate better and keep their emotions in check. Needless to say, it requires a lot of focus to simultaneously handle shoot-outs, car chases, and market speculation.

The Stability of Snow
The reason that *snow* possesses a value on par with that of the yen or the dollar is that it is impossible to tamper with *Money (Game) Master* through hacking or other cyberattacks. This also means that there is no need to run any kind of regular maintenance such as encrypted security checks for users.

Ag Wolves
A group of Dealers seeking to reunite the Legacies of Criminal AO and restore order to *Money (Game) Master*. Or at least, so they claimed. They turned out to be seeking the Legacies for their own gain. The core of the group consists of about a dozen members, including Lily-Kiska. It is highly likely that they possess one or more of the Legacies already.

AI Conglomerate
A conglomerate is a method of organizing a business that puts management into the hands of a single family. In the case of an AI business, it is a large company with very few points of contact with the outside world. However, they also indulge in some odd practices, such as subcontracting Dealers to serve as their lap dogs. In a world where

most AI businesses never employ humans, even as interns, this behavior is very peculiar indeed.

Avatar

A Dealer's embodiment in the game world. Since there are no level-ups and everyone starts out with the same abilities, it might seem beneficial to choose an extremely large or extremely small body. In practice, however, players tend to gravitate toward a form they find aesthetically pleasing.

Dead

If you are unfortunate enough to attract the attention of other prominent Dealers, then the moment you become vulnerable, such as if you Fall and become overwhelmed with debt or try to create a new avatar, you can get trapped in a vicious cycle of Falling and respawning from which there is no escape. The state of being subjected to such nasty pile-on behavior is known as being Dead.

Chapter 2

Land and Air BGM #02 "Dive to Freedom"

1

Something had to be done about the mint-green coupe. It was looking less like a car and more like some kind of abstract modern-art piece. Smoke was rising from the hood, which noisily rattled on its hinges, swinging open and shut like a clamshell. It was more beaten up than the rusted old dumpsters that could be found in the back alleys of the city.

Midori lay in the passenger seat atop Tselika, who was looking rather pale, her mouth agape as though her soul were attempting to escape her body through it. It certainly didn't look like a comfortable arrangement.

"Mrrrghhh. Mmmrrrmrmrmmmgggghhh."

"What's come over you, Tselika? You were fine a moment ago."

"Hmph. It's much worse when nobody looking on this mess knows what happened. What a disgrace it is to be driven about like this! Sure, it still runs fine, but people are going to make assumptions based on how it looks. You don't understand, My Lord. This is like a beautiful girl being forced to walk down the street in front of all her friends while wearing nothing but an apron made of dirty old newspapers!"

"Oh. I thought it was something important."

"One of these days, I'm really going to beat you up, My Lord!"

Midori looked uneasy. "H-hey, those guys are pretty high up in White Queen Tourism, aren't they? Won't they just send their AI soldier buddies into the city to take care of us?"

"They're external contractors, and their 'soldier buddies' are PMCs. I'm 99.9 percent sure that won't happen," Kaname replied.

"How come?"

"Well, for one, companies can only use AI PMCs to protect their own property. They're not a private army."

"But they're external contractors, right? They could still order the soldiers to protect them."

"I'm getting to that. I doubt it would be worth it. Being an external contractor has its perks, but it still puts you in service to the company. That restricts your freedom. Only a little, but it makes it difficult to engage in economic activities. Now that they've missed their chance to claim the Legacy, they might as well cut themselves loose so they can do what they want again."

Kaname himself had already severed his connections with White Queen Tourism when he left Ag Wolves. He was now a free agent. Freedom came first. The immediate monetary benefits that came with associating with a large AI company simply didn't compare.

Midori was stunned anew by this insight into the mind of a frontline Dealer. But her daze was short-lived, for once she saw the mint-green coupe drive straight past a repair shop, she spun her head around, watching it slip away behind them.

"Aren't we stopping to fix the car?" she asked.

"If we stop now, Ag Wolves will catch up to us. We'll have to go farther afield, perhaps even off the peninsula. By the way, Tselika, how are you doing on that analysis I asked for?"

"Changing the subject, are we, My Lord? Well, hmm…"

The demon pit babe and Midori were both squeezed into the space of the passenger seat. The two girls were dressed lightly, but especially Midori, who had nothing more than her black, frilly miniskirt and bikini to cover the slight curves of her chest and butt. One wrong move could mean a serious wardrobe malfunction.

However, Tselika didn't seem too concerned about this possibility, instead turning #tempest.err over in her gloved hands.

"These are just my first thoughts, but I think even if we physically destroyed it, you'd still be able to glean some useful information from it. I don't know how skilled our foes are, but if we want to eradicate the possibility of someone making their own knockoff Legacies, we'll need some special disassembly tools."

"You're as vague as ever…"

"Well, perhaps I'm a little distracted, seeing as how my beautiful temple is currently riddled with holes!"

"Let's solve two problems at once, then. We'll go hide on Mega-Float III."

The two seemed to have come to a decision without consulting Midori. The twin-tailed girl looked from one to the other anxiously.

"…Wait, my vehicle is still in the peninsula district parking lot! What should I do?"

"Can't you let your Magistellus bring it over?" Tselika asked. Midori choked at the question, suddenly looking embarrassed.

"Erm…that's not going to work…"

"Then we'll figure something out. We can't waste any time," said Kaname, controlling the front windshield with his eyes.

First, they had to leave the peninsula; then they would take the large circular bridge that encompassed the area of Tokonatsu City, taking them out onto the sea. Kaname smiled as he thought of passing over Hard Engage Bridge again. He was going back and forth today. Of course, Zaurus was likely to still be on the bridge, but she didn't seem like the kind of girl to stage an attack unassisted.

Midori was fidgeting uncomfortably—perhaps because she was in an unfamiliar vehicle or perhaps because Tselika was poised above her on all fours as if pinning her to a bed. Tselika, meanwhile, spoke without reservation, looking Midori straight in the eye, while she poked at the buttons on the car radio with her split tail, looking for a music station.

"So how are you enjoying the ride in my temple? Are you finding it uncomfortable to be surrounded by such extravagance after becoming accustomed to a life of poverty? I'd wager you've grown to think of luxury as the enemy."

"Urk."

"Tselika." Kaname issued a swift rebuke from the driver's seat, but Tselika ignored him. She gave a seductive smile as she leaned over the girl.

"Once the issue of the Legacies is resolved, My Lord will teach you how to generate all the scraps of paper you could ever need, but first, you must get rid of that pathetic servile demeanor of yours. It may be true that your life is currently one of poverty, but this is through no fault of your own, is it? This is just a momentary setback, a tiny abnormality. It does nothing to negate your own existence, your own worth."

"...What do *you* know?" Midori replied in a voice barely above a whisper. "A Magistellus, talking as though you know anything about the real world..."

"True. I don't know. But real people still have pride and dignity. Money may be among the most important things in the world, but there are some things that money can't buy. What if My Lord snapped his fingers and freed you from your debt right now? Would you say, *Oh, thank you. You're my hero. I love you so much, and I'll be your little heart-eyed servant forever* and sell your soul into a life of menial servitude? I doubt it. What about, *I'm the victim here, and I need more compensation, now, now, now, and oh wow, what a convenient lifestyle, I'll never need to lift a finger again, and I can just leech off this guy forever*? I don't think so, either. So take pride in yourself. Be the best you can be. Start being someone who helps other people instead of always being helped. If you don't, you'll be putting My Lord's efforts to waste, even after he swore to atone for his sins by putting his life on the line for you. He didn't have to do that, you know?"

This is never going to end, thought Kaname with a sigh. He cringed slightly, wishing that Tselika wouldn't put words in other people's mouths. Since when was he the savior looking down on Midori? If anything, he should be apologizing profusely to her and her family for putting them in that situation in the first place.

...So without further deliberation, Kaname reached his free hand over and grabbed Tselika's squirming tail out of the air, directly before where the two ends forked.

"Tselika. I mean it."

"Hyah?! Stop that! Can't a girl get away with saying something cool once in a while?! You spout that crap twenty-four seven, with your damn good looks, throwing your signature pose! *Oh, hello! I'm Kaname Suou!*"

"Now you've done it."

"Ee-gyaaaa?!"

Kaname squeezed her tail a little harder, and Tselika's backside vibrated in a rather unnatural manner.

"..." Midori, doing her best to keep up with all the new developments, finally realized something.

This was what normal felt like.

Midori became aware that her stomach had been freed of a heavy weight, and her head was no longer plagued by negativity. It wasn't about getting out of poverty or reclaiming her social standing. It was about something everyone had, even Midori, somewhere deep inside. Something Kaname and Tselika were trying their hardest to bring back. They weren't like some disgusting philanthropists who dropped a load of cash and walked off, feeling satisfied because, *Well, I did my bit*. They were committed to seeing it through to the end, until Midori could once again stand on *her own two legs*. And it was clear from Kaname's words—he knew that rounding up and destroying the immense power of the Legacies would only be the first step.

"Atone for his sins," they had said. For the Fall of Criminal AO—of Midori's brother. To protect that man's sister, as he had protected Kaname's. But just how far did that "protection" extend? And on the other side of the scales, just how much had her brother "saved" Kaname's sister?

Perhaps Kaname's behavior reminded Midori of how she had seen her brother, back when she'd innocently followed in his footsteps. Perhaps she was ready to accept that her brother had also jumped into his car, pointed his guns, and thrown his life away to save someone.

And maybe, just maybe, they had already returned to Midori something that money couldn't buy, something they had taught her, not with words but by putting their very lives on the line.

"Hmm? What's wrong, Midori?"

"N-nothing..."

"Excuse Tselika for her insensitive comments. Despite her high processing power, she can still be a bit dumb sometimes."

"My Lord, I can't tell if you're complimenting me or insulting me."

"See? You might follow the conversation, but you can't read between the lines."

Midori relaxed a little as she listened to the exchange. It was silly to close herself off and do nothing. She realized that now.

Passing through the many scattered islands, they soon arrived at the large, square floating structure Mega-Float III.

"This is my first time coming here... What a place."

While holding Tselika like a large stuffed toy, Midori slowly peered out the window.

"It's so...brown."

She was not wrong. Compared to the standardized industrial complex of Mega-Float II, III was a disorganized mess. Rusted old huts of corrugated iron were packed together in the tens and hundreds, piled up like building blocks and even stretching out overhead. The road itself seemed more like a serendipitous gap in the chaos than anything else, and although the whole thing appeared to be constructed out of waste materials, it did not feel very environmentally friendly at all.

"Apparently, this whole place used to be an airport," Kaname explained, navigating with noticeable familiarity. "After they built a new one on the peninsula, this place fell out of favor. The airline

companies that had backed it all went bankrupt, and it became a
breeding ground for small workshops."

Kaname must have been a regular around these parts, appearing to
know exactly where he was going, as he drove up to one of the rusted
iron huts and passed through the open shutter.

Seeing Kaname exit the vehicle, Midori made to follow suit but was
halted by Tselika, who squeezed her arms tightly around her. Tselika
smiled coyly, her forehead pressed to Midori's.

"There's no hurry. You wait right there."

"Hng?" Midori flinched, not at Tselika's words but at the long,
seductive breath that issued from her lips.

Meanwhile, Kaname had finished his discussion with the mechanic.
He took the opportunity to wrap a handkerchief around his arm
wound, which had previously only been crudely sprayed over. Then
he took out a few bills and picked up a ragged old backpack that was
hanging on the wall. He threw it into the car through the open window. Tselika carefully placed #tempest.err inside it before getting out
of the vehicle. Midori followed her, confused.

"Hey! Where are you taking the Le—?!"

Before she could say the word *Legacy*, Kaname placed his finger to
her lips.

*Th-they're both overly friendly! I do have someone who writes me
beautiful letters, you know!*

As much as she wanted to deny it, Midori had been feeling a little
hot under the collar for a while now. Did this man always act like
this, or was it just when he was in the game? She blushed. Waving her
hands as if to bat away her unseemly thoughts, she attempted to steer
the conversation elsewhere.

"L-let's just destroy it right here!"

"If that's all you want to do, then we can do it right now," said Kaname. "Just run it over in the car."

"Okay, then…!"

"However, that still leaves the risk that someone could extract
data from it. There's no point in destroying it if someone can copy it

afterward. If we really want to leave no trace, we have to use special tools. And we need to do it somewhere that everyone can see, to leave no room for any unwarranted theories to crop up in the future."

Midori grumbled. Tselika, meanwhile, was standing in front of the car staring at the damage. She gripped her head in both hands and did some kind of strange dance, frantically scratching her scalp as though she was tearing her own hair out.

"Ooh... Ooohhh... Oooooooooohhhhh... This is the worst...the absolute worst..."

"Yeah, the guy said the repairs will take five hours. And this bill... It almost would have been cheaper to buy a new car secondhand. This arm wound will take a while to heal, as well. Perhaps it's worth logging off for a bit and making our money back."

"Abulabrefurghah?! H-how dare you say such a thing about my temple! This all only happened because you went and got yourself in trouble, and I had to be a hero and come to your rescue! If you're going to be so dramatic about Criminal AO, then why don't you spare a tear for me, as well?! Come on, out with it! Let's see those waterworks!"

"Bragging about your achievements? That's why you'll never be a hero."

Despite what he had said, Kaname couldn't log out no matter how much he fiddled with the smart watch on his wrist. He had no choice but to wait for the repairs to finish.

There were only two ways to log out in *Money (Game) Master*. The first was to get inside a vehicle you own, park it, and wait for at least five minutes. If your vehicle was destroyed or stolen, that could make things quite difficult. You first had to either recover your vehicle or buy a new one.

Otherwise, you had to rely on the second method: put a gun to your temple and blow your brains out.

Kaname had Short Spear with which to defend himself, but it was still unsettling having no wheels in the motorized society of Tokonatsu City. And #tempest.err didn't make him feel any safer. In fact, if word got out that he had it, crowds of people would descend greedily upon him. It was for that reason that he had chosen a ragged old backpack to store it in. Walking around with a safe strapped to him would only attract unwanted attention.

Tselika side-eyed the mechanic, predictably frustrated at the sight of this strange man fiddling with the coupe.

"So, My Lord. Where do we begin?"

"We have several things to do. First, we need to retrieve Midori's vehicle from the peninsula district. Second, we need to find the special tools required to take that thing apart. And third, we need to come up with some way to waste five hours."

"...Do you really hate spending time with me so badly, My Lord?"

"I hate spending time doing nothing. Time is money, you know."

"Then let's set sail for Prostitute Island! If you're there with me, I'll be able to eat and drink as much as I want, get as *hands-on* as I want! Why, My Lord, pleasure awaits us! One hundred years won't be enough to experience it all! *(Starry-eyed. ☆)*"

"And how are we supposed to get there? Also, you really want to take Midori, too...?"

Kaname retorted with derision, but his words did little to soothe Midori. When she heard, she suddenly put herself at a distance and averted her eyes, as if engrossed by a strange bug or some such.

"I see, so that's what you'd get up to if I wasn't around, hmmmm?"

"Uh-oh."

"Utter trash. This is why I hate digital relationships. Everyone is so vulgar and direct. Ulterior motives are obvious, there's no emotion, no reading between the lines. It's crass and obscene! Aaargh, I just want to go home and write a letter..."

"The darkness is flowing out of Midori uninhibited! Tselika, back me up! Help me settle this misunderstanding!"

"On it, My Lord! Okay, Midori, you've got your hands on your hips and leaning closer to us, looking ready to give us the scolding of a lifetime."

"S-so?"

"Well, what do you think the camera aboard my temple-car behind you is seeing right now, as you sway your hips from side to side?"

"Huh? Hwah! Aaaaaaah?!"

The girl's face turned bright red, and she jumped up and leaped about, placing both hands over her small bottom as though blasted by an invisible water gun. Obviously, despite the miniskirt of her frilly black bikini partially blocking the view, it was embarrassing to be spied on so directly. With teary eyes, she gnashed her teeth.

"Grrrr! This is why you can't let your guard down around digitalites…!"

"Tselika! Are your subroutines loopy? Why are you throwing oil on the fire?!"

"'Twas a jest, My Lord. You really think I'd turn on the dashcam for this weed of a girl? That device is exclusively for images of my gorgeous self. Ahem. Anyway, it was that Criminal AO guy who was always more into places like that, not us. All we did was show up on occasion. For every good place we found, he'd been to ninety-nine more."

"???!!!" Midori's face instantly boiled over. Her Takamasa stock levels had been on a downward trend all day.

"Tselika! You haven't cleared up anything at all! You're just fanning the flames! And you *conveniently* neglected to mention that Takamasa only sent us *coordinates*! It wasn't until we got there that we realized where he'd sent us!"

"And so My Lord throws his best friend under the bus. But truly, the instincts of a woman are the one thing my subroutines can't calculate."

"Wh-what's that supposed to mean…?"

"…I've been getting a lot of questioning texts from your sister. Reading the subject lines, I thought for certain that they were spam and classified them as such. What do you think—shall we have a read through them? I just wonder how she heard our conversation without an account. How *does* she do it…???"

"Oh God!"

Ag Wolves would be desperately combing the main peninsula financial district for any trace of Kaname and the two girls. Kaname really didn't want to go near the place, but neither could he abandon Midori's vehicle. Without it, she wouldn't be able to log out. She'd be trapped in the game. After thinking for a while (perhaps still reeling from the psychic damage dealt by the streams of abuse within his sister's messages), he spoke:

"L-let's start with finding Midori's vehicle."

"Huh?" Midori was puzzled. "After we finally made our way here, you want to go back?"

"We don't need to go anywhere. We can have an AI truck pick it up."

"B-but…" Midori put her doubts aside for the moment. "…Argh, I know where it is, but…I don't remember the name. It's coin-operated, but I made sure it was a proper garage. They have a barrier that prevents the vehicle from being damaged or stolen, right?"

"First things first. The vehicle you're using is that large motorcycle, right? The red one decorated with autumn leaves."

"Huh?"

Before Midori could ask, *How did you know that?* Kaname continued. "That vehicle uses the Odin Navigation System, Version 4.0. That comes with a security alarm. I'm paying some freelancers to carry out attacks in the area. When your phone gets a GPS alert, we'll know we've hit the money. We can pin down the exact name and number of the place that way."

"You're hiring other Dealers…real people for this?"

"Don't worry. Even if they hit the place your bike is stored, it won't take so much as a scratch. Then, if we buy out the garage, it'll change the settings and overwrite the rule that treats it as neutral ground. It won't count as a garage anymore. Then we just call an AI truck to go and bring it here. Tselika?"

"Given my vehicle is in tatters, this is all I can show you at the moment."

The demon pit babe put both hands behind her head, displaying her body in a most provocative manner. Alphanumeric characters scrolled across her bright green-and-white bikini top and miniskirt, and Kaname controlled them with his eyes to proceed with the purchase of the land.

"I don't think money is everything," Kaname clarified as he worked, "but money gives you options. You can do so much more when you're rich, see the world in a completely different light. There are few things that money can't buy, few things more important than money. Not as much as the movies would have you believe anyway. But that just means when you do find something that important, you shouldn't hesitate to splurge."

"..."

In that moment, Midori looked at Kaname's face in profile. Was that how he saw her? Or was he talking about Criminal AO—about her missing brother?

"All right. I've requested the truck. Ag Wolves don't seem to be on to us. Tselika, the parking garage is of no further use to us. Sell it. Immediately. I don't care if the price has changed."

"Surely, you must know we're not breaking even on this, My Lord. This is a big loss. We're almost flat broke! What are we going to do?" Tselika then lowered her voice, talking under her breath. "...Come to think of it, we still have to pay for the repairs. I told him cash on completion, but we don't even have enough!"

"We started off with three objectives. We've just ticked off one of them."

"And?"

"Now we have to obtain the special tools and kill five hours. There's a way to fulfill both objectives, and it's right here on Mega-Float III."

Kaname wagged his finger.

"We'll make it all back at the casino. That's the quickest way."

2

Leaving the wreck of the mint-green coupe at the repair shop, Kaname walked through the cityscape of rusted brown sheet metal.

"Huh, there sure are a lot of bargains around here," he observed. "Looks like they're selling plenty of used cars at those garages, too."

"My Lord, don't..."

"If we don't want to pay the repair fee, we could always just buy one of these and have you transfer your contract to it, right, Tselika? What do you think?"

"N-never! Not on my life!"

"I didn't say we'd have to sell our old one. Just have some dirt-cheap car to ride around in while the other one is being repaired. Our second car! It'd mean I could log out, as well."

"I'll never accept it, My Lord. My vehicle is my temple."

"But it doesn't make sense to have only one vehicle in your inventory. It's a good idea to buy a cheap secondhand vehicle and keep it in your hideout in case the main one gets destroyed. I mean, what would you do if that coupe got blown up? You can only drive cars I own, remember?"

"It's about love! Being unfaithful will only lead to you neglecting your precious vehicles as soon as you get a couple more! Once you think, *Oh, I have a spare*, you'll go crashing off walls because it doesn't matter anymore! Some *promiscuous* Magistelli out there may have dozens, switching among them on the daily, but I'll never be like them! It's a mistake to relocate my temple without the consideration it deserves! It'll lead to nothing but discomfort and a guilty conscience! And don't even bother bringing out the puppy-dog eyes because it won't work this time!!"

"None of these words mean anything to me."

"Okay, well, imagine you had a royal four-poster bed, My Lord. Would you be happy sleeping on a fraying straw mat next to it? You can have the fluffiest pillows, diffuse the sweetest oils, and change into the silkiest see-through nightie, but if it's wrong, it's wrong!"

"What are you talking about?"

"Grblebrglewagbrch! Ah! Aaah! Aaaangolmois!"

"You say that, but once we fix it up, it'll be like a whole new vehicle."

"Guh! Bleh! The core will be the same! There's only one temple for me, My Lord! Besides, we're going up against Ag Wolves. Are you really about to entrust your life to some half-tuned sloppy seconds?!"

You know as well as I do that it's common practice to focus your cash injections. It's obvious no good will come of splitting our growth plan in two!"

"Come on, Tselika."

"No!"

As their conversation continued, Midori started to wonder. There wasn't any sign of anything that could be called a casino. Perhaps there might be some people squatting between the buildings, shuffling cards or tossing dice...but an actual, *proper* casino, with gaudy lights and rows upon rows of tables decked out with cards and cocktails... That was hard to imagine. She voiced her doubts to Kaname.

"Casinos are everywhere," he replied simply. "We're in *Money (Game) Master*, after all."

"But there's nothing here but some rusty old shacks, and there's no space for an underground gambling den on a mega-float."

"Midori, don't you remember what I said this place used to be?"

"?"

"An airport, abandoned after financial ruin. There's an exclusive area for VIPs there."

Kaname rounded a corner, and there it was. A huge, partially disassembled passenger plane, sitting on the runway.

"Wow," gasped Midori. "Is this what you meant?"

"First class has been converted into a casino. Economy is a movie theater, and business class is a luxury restaurant, if I remember correctly."

"Hee-hee!" Tselika giggled. "I hear that some rather raunchy activity goes on beneath the tables and behind the partitions of that restaurant. Massages and more... Not a place for good little kids."

"*(Glare.)*"

"Please don't start that again, Tselika. Spare a thought for the beating my poor foot is taking right now."

The mobile loading ramp didn't look like it had moved for quite a while. Kaname climbed the stairs to the fuselage, where a man in a black suit and tie greeted him. In a place like this, you'd usually expect to have to jump through hoops to gain entry, but...

"*Welcome back*, Mr. Suou."

"Yeah."

"And how might you be today? Could I interest you in an overview of our current prizes?"

"I think my chips are going to expire soon. Could you retrieve them for me?"

"In cash?"

"No. I'd like to play for a while, if that's all right. I assume the *cheating* tables are in the same location?"

Kaname, with his wounded arm, and the newcomer Midori, who had wounded it, were not subjected to a search or metal detector. Kaname must have spent a lot of money in this place to have gained that much trust, Midori assumed. But there were a few other things on her mind as well. As they walked through the plane, listening to the classy music playing in the background, Midori pursed her lips and asked:

"What did he mean, 'Welcome back'...?"

"What else could it mean?"

"What are those 'prizes' he mentioned?"

"This place partners with a bunch of pawnshops in the area. When you trade in chips here, you trade them for goods, like weapons and gems, not cash. If you want money, you can take the prizes to those pawnshops and sell them. The merchandise all circulates back around, so the casino isn't losing anything. It's the same concept they use in pachinko parlors... You know what? Maybe that's where the idea came from."

"What are the cheating tables?"

"Special tables where both the guests and the casino are allowed to cheat."

With just a brief look around, the twin-tailed girl could see all sorts of games. Even the relatively common card games of poker, blackjack, and baccarat made her head spin. And that was to say nothing of the more obscure games like Red Dog and whatever else, which left her entirely confused.

As for non-card games, slot machines and poker machines lined the walls, and at special tables, people were throwing dice, playing... craps, was the game called? Midori knew the name, but which numbers were good and which were bad? Last but not least was that iconic wheel, plastered in little red and black markings. Roulette. It looked very pretty, Midori thought, but the game stirred up no further emotions in her. To her, it was a game where players slam down large towers of small toylike chips, and the dealer uses his little rake to move them around.

"So, My Lord. Where shall we begin?"

"Check the list. Right at the top. It's just what we need."

"Oh-ho, a woman, you mean? Well then, let me pick!"

"*(GLARE.)*"

"Please be serious, Tselika. *Someone* is pinching me on the butt."

"*Fine*," Tselika whined as she switched to serious mode. Information scrolled across her curves, and she dropped her gaze down to her chest.

"You mean this? Acid D? A delicate mixture, the perfect balance of strong acids. It's supposedly able to melt anything, even pure gold."

"That's the stuff. It was originally used by thieves to break into safes. It should be perfect for taking care of our little problem as well. Midori, you can... Midori?"

The girl had disappeared. Looking around, Kaname spotted her a little way back. She stood still, staring absentmindedly at a waitress who was carrying a tray of drinks. The waitress wore a bunny suit, and Midori gawked as though she had never seen such a thing before. Tselika smiled a malicious smile.

"...See something you like?"

"?!" Midori jumped and spun around, but Tselika didn't stop there. She chuckled, putting her hand to her mouth.

"Heh-heh. And here I thought you were just a little prude. Turns out all that bluff and bluster was to detract from your true nature, was it not? Hmm, yes, I see. So the blood of Criminal AO really *does* run through your veins! Come now, Little Miss Perfect—there's no need to hold back! Tell us what you really feel! Can't you see how wonderful life can be when you let go of your inhibitions?"

"Tselika, please explain to me why the little girl is trying to beat *me* up when *you're* the one messing about."

Eyes tightly shut, face red, and arms flailing like a spoiled child, Midori shook her fists in Kaname's direction. Kaname grabbed them with both arms and then jerked his chin in the direction of the game he wanted to play.

"That one over there should do," he said.

"Huh? Roulette...?" Midori frowned.

A woman was already sitting at the table. She wore a tight skirt that revealed her bare legs and a gorgeous party dress in lavender and white. She was tilting a cocktail glass in her hand, and her eyes followed a small spherical die that spun around the inner rim of the roulette wheel.

Cheating was supposedly allowed at these tables. But unlike card games where you could choose to change your hand, roulette was based on pure luck. Was there really a way to cheat at such a game?

Midori turned to ask Kaname, who responded nonchalantly.

"If there wasn't, there's no way that woman would be on such a winning streak."

"Everyone has their own way of making money," said Tselika, "and for some people, that's gambling."

When the game ended, Kaname noted the pile of chips awarded to the woman in the party dress with deep-blue hair resting on her shoulders before casually walking over and taking a seat. The lady flashed him a surprised look as he entered the game. Towers of gambling chips surrounded her like a fortress as she peered at him through the pair of glasses that rested on her nose.

"Do you understand the rules of this game?" she asked.

"More or less."

"Then I'll have you know you don't stand a chance here. Please don't come to the cheating tables if all you're going to do is copy my bets exactly."

The bunny-girl croupier took the handles extending out from the top of the roulette wheel and gave it a spin. In the opposite direction, she threw in the small spherical die. The numbers on the board ranged from 0 to 36, but the woman in the lavender dress placed it all on the black 18.

"The Dealer's name is Laplacian," Tselika whispered, wrapping her arms around Midori and effectively stopping her from wandering toward the table. "I think her smart glasses are a bluff, as is the Magistellus in the kimono who's casually turning around behind My Lord. I believe she's making use of Laplace's Demon, just as her name suggests."

Tselika's hot breath made Midori squirm.

"La…what?" Midori asked.

"Laplace's Demon," Tselika whispered. "There's no such thing as chance in *Money (Game) Master*. You can calculate anything given the right information. Even something as simple as throwing a basketball through a hoop entails hundreds of different calculations. What if you could do those same calculations yourself?"

"Wha—?"

"That lady has not once let go of her glass, and it's covered in condensation. Just by flicking a few drops onto the wheel at the right time, she can alter the course of the die, even down to what number will come up."

Preposterous, Midori thought. How could that be possible? She gulped, but Tselika showed no signs of fear. Her silence told Midori that even this was nothing to be surprised by.

"But," she said, "that means…"

What was Kaname going to do? Laplacian, the woman in the lavender dress, could control the result entirely. If they agreed not to bet on the same number, then he would just keep losing as long as she was at the table.

As Midori was thinking, something incredible happened.

Thud! Kaname placed all his chips on the number 0. Obviously, this was not the same as Laplace's 18. At this rate, he would lose his entire stock.

"…Might you be misunderstanding something?" asked Laplacian.

"I'm just betting on what I think will win. That a problem?"

Their gazes clashed like blades. What Kaname was saying, his face calm despite his wound, was this: *I'm going to change the winning number and throw a wrench in your cheating mechanism. You're going to lose all your chips, and I'm going to make back thirty-six times my bet.*

The woman in the lavender dress peered at Kaname from behind her glasses, gently rocking her cocktail glass in her hand.

"Impossible."

With one hand resting on the table and his chin in the other, Kaname replied coolly. "Not necessarily."

All the while, the tiny spherical die continued to race around the rim of the roulette wheel. When it finally stopped, it would come to rest in one of the thirty-seven numbered pockets, and the game would be over.

"Now's your last chance to change your mind, young man. I'd prefer you not to double up on my black eighteen, but I'll be generous and allow you to bet on something else. Red or black, perhaps, or odd or even?"

"No need. It won't be any of those. The result will be the green number zero. Coming out on top today will be green—*green like a Midori Sour.*"

"That will never happen. Not a chance."

"The nose knows. I'm not getting that stinging, fuzzy feeling from you. There's nothing I need to do, nothing I have to fear."

There was a small clatter. The ball had lost its momentum and dropped into one of the pockets below. The bunny girl reached out to grab the wheel, to stop its movement and reveal the result. Midori looked down at the pocket corresponding to Laplacian's bet, black 18.

But there was nothing there.

"Wha—?!"

The woman in the lavender party dress appeared to panic and lose track of the small die entirely. Clutching her glasses, she staggered like she was dizzy. Midori gulped as she looked across the wheel to a different pocket.

Neither red nor black but the sole green. The die had landed cleanly in the space marked 0.

"...I-impossible," Laplacian stammered, her cocktail glass trembling in her hand. "This is impossible!"

"Surely, you should expect something like this to happen when you play at the cheating tables?"

"Are you colluding with the croupier? Trying to get me to leave because I'm winning too much?!"

"Maybe. Maybe not. You can think what you want to think. That *would* be allowed at the cheating tables, after all." Kaname spoke only the facts, with a totally straight face despite the pain in his arm. "Well? If you can't take it, perhaps you'd be better off moving to a different table."

"—Ngh!"

His words were unnecessarily confrontational...but Kaname was well aware of that. The woman in the party dress downed her drink, disheveled her deep-blue hair, and grabbed another from the tray of a nearby waitress before sitting herself back down at the table. The bunny-girl croupier spun the wheel and tossed in the die.

"Red twenty-five. I've got you this time!"

"Sorry, it's zero again. Lady Luck is on my side tonight."

Kaname must have been cheating somehow to win a 100 percent controlled game. But unlike Laplacian, he wasn't wearing a pair of smart glasses. Nor did he appear to be tampering with the wheel or the die. Just how was he influencing the outcome?

The one who answered Midori's questions was Tselika, hugging her from behind.

"Remember how I told you she's using the droplets from her glass to affect the outcome by altering the coefficient of friction of the wheel?" Tselika whispered.

"What? So..."

"So let that happen. Consider the wind from the air-conditioning, for example. My Lord's posture, where he places his arms, what he does with his fingers... All that affects the airflow, however slightly. Makes the droplets evaporate faster or slower. What do you suppose would happen then? Do you think the outcome would match up with Laplacian's intentions?"

"...?!" Midori turned to Kaname, astonished.

He hadn't just exposed her cheating; he had hijacked it, milked it dry. And he had done it without tools, but simply by sitting down at the table.

"No way... Is that even possible? I knew he was a good Dealer, but I didn't know equipment skills and Magistelli could allow you to reach such a high level of precision!"

"Well yes, but it's not about what equipment he's wearing. Even if he had none of that, he'd find out the answer some way."

"Huh? So...how did he know—?"

"Silly girl. In *Money (Game) Master*, your life is constantly on the line. You can't simply give up when something seems impossible. If you try, you must succeed. Do some mental math or build an abacus out of marbles you scraped together if you must."

This time, Midori felt like her breath was taken from her.

...Were Ag Wolves aboard the cruise liner like this as well?

Midori gulped. She finally realized just how dangerous it had been, walking into a place like that unprepared. What a burden she had been on Kaname, who had protected her after she rushed in in anger, convinced that she could do anything.

It wasn't like taking cover to wait out a storm of bullets or using both hands to aim a gun carefully. The tactics the top Dealers had to resort to were on a whole new level.

Just how many mind games were going on back there every second...?

3

Server Name: Gamma Orange.
   Final Location: Tokonatsu City, Mega-Float III.
   Log-out successful.
   Thank you for playing, Midori Hekireki.

"Phew..."

The long-haired girl slowly opened her eyes, and she was in a rectangular room with pink wallpaper. The sensation of the smooth cloth of her black dress came back to her like a memory, and the phone in her hand was warm from being plugged in to the wall.

Money (Game) Master was a totally immersive online experience, but that didn't mean you had to latch some strange device on your head or go into some sort of cold-sleep pod. All you needed was a smartphone. By firing a burst of colored lights into the eyes, it pulled the user's consciousness into a virtual world. It was sort of like hypnosis or mental suggestion, but not quite.

Representational markers, was it?

By rapidly stimulating the brain with symbolic information, a combined image could be built up in the subject's mind. This was called a "representation." It may have sounded like some strange form of mind control, but the theory was actually quite simple.

"Red." "Round." "Sweet." "About the size of a baseball." "Fruit." "Used in juice and pies." Given all this information, a person would typically respond "apple." By taking these representational markers and firing them from a phone screen at 120 frames per second, a so-called "high representation" could be produced that blanked out the user's senses. From there, it was possible to "draw" whatever experience was required directly into the mind itself.

After all, nothing can be more realistic than the image created by the human brain, and even if there was, it wouldn't matter, since no human could perceive that level of detail. It was just like a TV with a ridiculously high resolution or refresh rate. It was no wonder that people felt exhausted after expending all their efforts on what was supposed to be fun.

Since human eyes were not designed to be used like this, some people experienced motion sickness or painful dry eyes. Fortunately, the girl suffered no such symptoms.

She did, however, feel a little tired—listless, depressed, once again cognizant of the weight of reality, like a child who has been playing outside all evening, only to return home and remember that they have homework due the next day.

Brother...

A life of poverty.

It wasn't as if debt collectors were breaking down the door. Midori wasn't auctioning off her organs or selling herself on the streets. Her room had TV. It had air-conditioning. She could eat three meals a day and even go to school.

But there were two things she didn't have. One, her brother, who had disappeared into thin air. A missing person report had been in vain, and if the police couldn't find him, then how could she? It still irritated her, however, how quick they had been to say, "Ah, makes sense," upon learning the reason for his disappearance.

And the second thing…

"Hmm."

Her smartphone's in-box was full of messages. They were all from AI businesses.

We write to confirm this month's payment as of April 11, 20XX. Head company, Absurd Pharmaceuticals. Correspondent, xxxxxx. Please check your account balance and avoid living wastefully.

" … "

In today's modern utopia, living in poverty didn't have to mean starvation. The AI businesses detected such people and extended their benevolent arms.

They were on the TV.

"AI doesn't mean they have wills of their own. All they are doing is using their algorithms to react to the situation. They can carry out work faster, more efficiently, and on a larger scale than humans. It's a new kind of work for the modern era."

And in promotional ads.

"Once AI businesses are the norm, humanity will be free from the yoke of labor. With that time sink gone, we will be able to spend our lives on more meaningful personal development."

The technology that had once been the exclusive province of call centers and assembly lines was spreading, bringing every last industry into the fold one by one. Just a walk downtown revealed that businesses were now automating street cleaning and serving customers in a restaurant. Most part-time jobs were gone, and even many full-time workers were finding themselves replaced. More and more employers were turning to AI workers instead of humans to keep labor costs low: 30 to 40 percent of jobs were now performed by AI, and that figure was only expected to grow over the next ten years to 60 or 70 percent.

Now AI businesses were cropping up, where everything from the bottom to the top was completely controlled via AI. Data flowed from machine to machine, with no human in the loop whatsoever, and it was said 48 percent of all electronic financial transactions were being carried out entirely by computers.

Humans didn't control computers. Computers controlled humans. They pulled the strings of the world economy, and the humans could merely dance like their puppets. It no longer even mattered whether an AI was sentient or not, for in nothing more than the pursuit of efficiency, they had allowed themselves to be controlled, and as the profit rolled in, they told themselves that they were winners, and it was our smart choices that had led them here.

It was a very convenient world, but something about it felt wrong.

It was a very comfortable world, but it seemed too good to be true.

The world was full of uncertainties.

Perhaps that was why.

Although the *needs* of Midori's family were completely met by AI businesses, *they were treated as second-class citizens wherever they went. Even though they lived in comfort. Even though from time to time, she could wear gorgeous dresses and go to parties.*

"..."

She unconsciously let out a heavy sigh. Although the girl was being protected from dying of starvation, it was gnawing at her from within. It was no surprise that people saw her the way they did.

AI Dropouts, they called them.

And the more comfortable a life she led, the more she thought.

It's like there's an invisible wire at the back of my neck.

It's like I'm a slave to the AI businesses. They send me signals like "Comfort" and "Satisfaction," and my arms and legs move like some sort of human-shaped robot.

My thoughts seem like my own, but am I really thinking any of them?

These vague fears and anxieties were eating her up inside.

There's nothing I can do about it.

Even though it was clear what was happening, there was no easy way out. Everyone went with the flow, even as the world slowly began to drift somewhere unpleasant. It couldn't be stopped. Those were just the times they were living in.

And now, a hypothetical. There were Dealers in *Money (Game) Master* making millions off their mastery of the game. Kaname Suou was one of them. If Midori threw herself at his feet and begged him to pay off her debt, would she finally be able to satisfy her psychological needs as well as her physiological ones?

The answer was no. The debt would be gone, sure, but the stigma would remain. She wouldn't be considered on the same level as those who earned their own livings. Not just by society and its prejudices but by herself. Besides, this was all hypothetical. Midori didn't even know if the system would let her use a third party's money to remove the shackle of being an AI Dropout.

So there was no use looking to others. If she wanted to claw her way back up out of the protection of the AI businesses, it would have to be under her own power. Her parents didn't understand the game, and her absent brother was Dead, which meant he wouldn't be logging back into *Money (Game) Master* from wherever he was living these days. There was only one recourse left... Midori herself would have to fight to protect her family.

Don't be silly... How could I do that?

As she did almost instinctively whenever she felt down, Midori reached into the drawer of her desk. She pulled out several sheets of pastel-colored writing paper and a few pens. Her letter-writing set.

Her interest originally stemmed from a love for the retro, but to her now, it was her one small way of fighting back against the life of an AI Dropout, against a life dominated and dictated by digital data. Of course, should they so wish, the AI could flagrantly disregard the confidentiality of the mail and read the contents of those letters. They controlled the mail sorting and delivery, after all.

But her emotions were contained within her handwriting, and no machine could detect that.

What should I write today?

Granted, things hadn't been going so well recently, but Midori couldn't help but feel that she had been overly negative in her recent letters and probably worried her pen pal. It wasn't right to unload so much on others.

She wanted her letters to be happy, fun, she thought, as she fiddled with her colored pens.

4

Server Name: Theta Yellow.
Final Location: Tokonatsu City, Mega-Float III.
Log-out successful.
Thank you for playing, Kaname Suou.

After the repairs on the mint-green coupe were completed and the young man could finally log out using the correct procedure from the driver's seat of his car, he was confronted with the reflection of his face in the dark screen of his smartphone. An average face with casually trimmed black hair and no particularly noteworthy features. He was wearing a set of gray pajamas, perfect for napping on the bed or milling about the house. He suddenly remembered he'd been wearing his contacts when he logged in, so his eyes were even drier than usual.

He clenched his fist and released it. He'd logged out, of course, so his wound was gone.

April 11, showed his phone. The temperature was a little chilly. It was abundantly clear that he was no longer on the golden shores of Tokonatsu City.

The young man gently shook his head, and reality came back to him like an image settling into focus. He took his eyes away from the screen and looked at the picture frame on his desk. Contained within was not a photo but a single postage stamp. It celebrated the anniversary of commercial space travel—a gift from a pen pal using the dying art of snail mail. He gently traced his fingers over the protective glass before leaving the room.

His sister was reclining on the apartment's living room sofa, dressed casually in an oversize pale-pink sweatshirt and pair of short pants, her shoulder-length hair free. On her chest was an image of a cartoon pig, perhaps a character from somewhere. The loose fit of the top around her collar occasionally afforded some pretty risqué views, but she didn't seem to mind too much. She spoke as she watched TV, a pair of black straps visible on her shoulders. A string was tied around her ankle, perhaps some sort of fad.

"I ended up going with that soba place for takeout. Their curry is the best thing on the menu, though."

"Hmm."

He cast a glance over to the kitchen, and sure enough, there were several large plates covered in plastic wrap. The smell of spices and soba broth wafted over: a very Japanese smell. She must have chosen curry instead of soba so that it wouldn't go soggy, since she wouldn't have known when he would log out. The rice and the curry and the roux were all on their own separate plates, too. Perhaps she'd specified that on the phone. It may have looked like a token effort from the outside, but it was obvious to him that his sister had put a lot of thought into it.

He threw the meal in the microwave and sat down to eat at the living room table. His sister had in her hand a glass of milk, and she had added a soft-boiled egg into her curry. Clearly, she was not a fan of spicy foods, but she had compromised for his sake.

"How did it go?" she asked, but not in a nosy manner, as she crushed the egg beneath her spoon.

"Meh. Good enough."

On the TV, comedians were being humiliated by obvious trick questions.

When the siblings spoke, they would be like machine guns or bombs, but when they were silent, they were dead silent. It wasn't an uncomfortable silence, either. Unlike at school or on the internet, these two didn't need to mince words around each other.

"I'm just going to take a break and have a bath, and then I'll log back in. If you have homework or something else to show me, now's your chance."

"It was fine today."

"Oh, also, do you know where the eye drops are? The strong ones. My eyes hurt, so I want to put some in before I go back."

"Awww…" His sister sounded troubled, her spoon held in midair. Her hair fluttered gently around her shoulders as she slightly averted her gaze. At his puzzled expression, she confessed. "Sorry, they're at the secret base."

"Man, how long ago was that? You still using that place?"

"It's on the way to school, so it's perfect for taking a break. You'll never find another place like the abandoned planetarium near the park. It's sturdy. It'll last for another ten years if kept clean."

"You like those ruins? Even though you never know when somebody else could intrude?"

"I could put a big, scary chain and padlock on the front door. They'd be all like, *Oh no! The management companies have their eye on this place!* and scamper off."

"Either way, you never know what could happen out there, so don't leave anything you wouldn't want to lose."

"Okaaay."

"And don't fall asleep there. Someone could always wander in."

"Yeeeahhh."

It was hard to tell whether she was agreeing or just trying to end the conversation.

An ordinary apartment. An ordinary walk to school. This was what Criminal AO had given his livelihood to protect. A life not as an AI Dropout but supported by one's own two legs and carving out a living with one's own two hands.

Nobody knew who had made *Money (Game) Master*, and nobody knew where its servers were based, but with it, Kaname could make millions in a single night whenever he wanted. AI Dropouts, however, temporarily gave up their rights to own property. It was a prerequisite for filing for bankruptcy. That meant that even if someone was willing to donate to them, they had no way to accept. No matter how much Kaname wanted to send Midori money, he couldn't. There was only one way out. The debt that the AI company shouldered had to be paid off in full by the AI Dropout. There was zero interest, so even a little at a time would work.

But even if it were possible to pay off the debts of the AI Dropouts, would that really count as *saving* them? You could send them as much money as you wanted, but you couldn't buy back their *pride*. Whether it was an AI business or a human friend keeping the life support turned on, the mental burden would be the same. In fact, if they took the help, then their relationship as friends, as equals, would be gone.

Perhaps her parents, who didn't fully understand the workings of the game, would be happy, at least for a while. But in the end, it wouldn't matter. Once the novelty wore off, the darkness would begin to claw away from within as they realized they were being kept alive by someone else, that they would need to be thankful to someone else, for the rest of their days. That would be all his money had bought.

I have to do something, he thought as he scooped up a spoonful of curry, a totally normal act in his totally normal life.

For his pen pal who still valued the dying art of writing letters.

For the girl he'd met in *Money (Game) Master*.

For the sister of Criminal AO, of Takamasa.

I need something more substantial. I need a way that will truly pay him back.

5

Server Name: Mu Green.
   Final Location: Tokonatsu City, Peninsula District.
   Log-out successful.
   Thank you for playing, Lily-Kiska Sweetmare.

"Dammit!" the girl screamed as she logged out, no longer within earshot of the other Ag Wolves. She wore nothing but a dress shirt a size too large for her. The most successful Dealers were like world-class poker players: They didn't reveal their feelings, even to their closest allies.

Her room was large but sterile, as if no one had been living there at all. It was like an entire floor of an old office building: dark, cold, and filled with LCD monitors. Some on desks, others hanging from the ceiling, mounted on arms. They covered everything regarding exchange rates and the prices of stocks and commodities such as oil, food, precious gems, gold, and platinum, plus any news that might influence them.

And not just within *Money (Game) Master*. The monitors showed all the money-related data she could find.

Even now, all over the planet, huge deals worth billions were taking place ten thousand times a second. The movement of that data, the money changing hands, was what made the world go round. The demand for autonomous investment programs had increased, and that propelled AI to the forefront. Perhaps the other Ag Wolves were on the opposite side of that data, and perhaps they weren't. After all, they didn't even know one another's real names or faces. It was entirely possible that their programs were fighting one another, and they wouldn't even know it.

In the real world, she wore the oversize dress shirt day in and day out, never venturing outside. She didn't wear a bra, either, for her chest was rather modest. But it wasn't like she knew nothing of the outside world. On the contrary, she had tasted all life's pleasures. People liked to claim that there were things money couldn't buy, but if they meant love, then that was the first thing she had bought. Then she had moved on to art and then to music, then antiques, collectibles, food, travel, a social life, charity, sports, and cameras and trains and history and *anything*. Lately, she had even been buying trouble. But she was sick of it all. She was reaching the end of what the world could offer her.

She could see that this was all life had to it.

So she had nothing left to look forward to. She had amassed a large fortune, done everything that could be done, and had run out of ideas on how to spend her money. Nothing surprised her anymore, and the dull, colorless days gradually stripped away her soul. There was no place left for her in the real world.

The only way to stay human was to give up on the real world entirely and throw herself fully into something like *Money (Game) Master*. And when she had, she had met a man who shook up her soul so much, it made her skin prickle.

Kaname Suou.

Why had he betrayed Ag Wolves and taken #tempest.err?

If he was a member, why was he so strongly opposed to letting us have the Legacy back there? she thought, grinding her teeth. *We must have rushed the initiation. He didn't feel like he was one of us, and that's why he backed out at the last minute...! It's true what they say. The child is father to the man. And now I've failed again!*

She ran her fingers through her long black hair. She was unmatched when it came to numbers and data, but she could never understand the machinery of people's emotions. You might say she had been raised not needing to. If she ever got on the wrong side of somebody, a billion was usually enough to smooth things over.

But...

But this time, it hadn't gone that way. Her opponent was a Dealer of equal caliber: Kaname Suou.

I knew it...

It certainly stung seeing the Overtrick stolen before her very eyes, but there was an even stronger emotion welling up inside her.

There was something else in this world that was not so easy to obtain.

Yes. Beyond this soulless world of gray, devoid of any remaining dregs of color, a thrill yet waited that set her heart ablaze. She remembered Kaname's words. The ones that had so conclusively set them on different paths.

"Helping others isn't about bragging rights or *asking for something in return."*

Incomprehensible. She didn't get it. That was exactly why it stuck with her. That one single phrase. As it burned inside her mind, she muttered something.

"...Then what are you saying I should do?"

6

Server name: Psi Indigo.
Starting location: Tokonatsu City, Mangrove Island.
Log-in credentials accepted.
Welcome to *Money (Game) Master*, Kaname Suou.

Accompanied by a brief spell of dizziness, Kaname was back in Tokonatsu City. He was sitting behind the wheel of the mint-green coupe, which was parked neatly inside a garage attached to a log cabin. And since logging in reset all nonfatal wounds, his arm was as good as new.

For a few moments, he sat back in his seat until the motion sickness passed. When he got out of the car, he was in the open space of the garage. Also parked there was a large bright-red motorcycle decorated with autumn leaves. It seemed he had a visitor. But it was the sound he could hear outside that interested him. A constant, faint, muddy sound.

"?" Frowning, Kaname opened the garage door. It rattled loudly and violently as a powerful storm rocked the building. "Whoa!"

Fine sand had mixed with a deluge of water to create a raging river, and the palm trees were making a very unsettling noise. Strong winds and heavy, angled rain assaulted him. It was difficult to even stay upright, and it seemed the flailing garage door could strike Kaname at any moment.

"A cyclone... Dammit, did I forget to check the event reports...?"

Kaname squinted back at the mint-green coupe, or rather, at the car stereo, but it was too late now. He steeled himself and stepped outside. It was only a short distance to the door of the log cabin, but by the time Kaname reached it, his clothes and hair were soaking wet.

Inside were Midori and Tselika, who had made themselves comfortable in the kitchen. The pit babe's bright-teal hair and the young girl's skin around her black bikini top and miniskirt were completely dry. Perhaps they'd set up before the cyclone hit, or perhaps they had simply been in here long enough to dry out. It was also possible they'd used the shower already.

A large two-handed pot was sitting on the dining room table. Kaname could see vegetables and sausages, and it appeared to be some sort of stew. Presumably the ingredients came from the refrigerator or the underfloor storage of the cabin.

"Nice location you have here," commented Midori, showing none of the restraint of a guest at somebody else's place...or perhaps it had been Tselika who roped her into doing the cooking.

Still feeling a bit dazed, Kaname decided against cooking. He had just been eating takeout with his sister and was not too keen on the idea of food right now.

"Well, when you log in, you can choose between your last vehicle's current position or the garage of your hideout," he replied, grabbing a towel and rubbing himself down. "I figured I'd build my garage as far away from the crossfire of the financial district as possible. It gives me more options."

"It's small, but it's in good shape," noted Midori. "It looks expensive."

"That's so I can sell it quickly if I ever need to."

Even Kaname didn't understand why Tselika, an AI Magistellus, needed to eat, but she stood and stuffed her cheeks with thick sausage like a squirrel. Her two-pronged tail swished back and forth, likely indicative of her good mood.

"*Om-nom.* This stuff isn't half bad, My Lord!"

"I can see that," said Kaname. "It looks like it came out well."

It wasn't entirely a compliment on their cooking abilities, because Midori hadn't peeled the vegetables herself and made the whole stew from scratch, with its carrots, radishes, onions, and cabbage, boiled with pork and sausage in a chicken bouillon broth. She was simply combining insta-meals and microwaveable pouches to create a whole new dish.

"I've always been good at bringing out the best with what I've got," said Midori.

"Ahhh," sighed Kaname. "I bet you're the type of person who sees a million possibilities in a packet of good mushroom soup."

"Aren't those the best? If it were up to me, I'd award it a Nobel Prize."

Anything that could suppress Tselika's normally selfish and whimsical mood was a good thing in Kaname's book. And indeed, she eagerly wolfed down Midori's cooking despite her usual aversion to anything not under his possession. That was certainly a curious point, but Kaname supposed that since the ingredients were originally from his hideout, it must technically count as his.

"Still, My Lord, Midori's been fiddling with that thing in her hands the whole time. She oughtn't be distracting herself! If she focused on the food, I'd wager it'd taste much better! Not that it's unappetizing, but just imagine what could have been!"

"'That thing'?" repeated Kaname. "You mean her phone? Was she looking up a recipe?"

"I-it's nothing, I said!" Midori called out. She was hiding both hands behind her back, looking very embarrassed. It must have been her phone. In *Money (Game) Master*, one's Magistellus usually played the role of secretary, executing calculations at high speed and displaying the results on the car windshield or the like. This meant that mobile phones were more or less obsolete.

But it didn't look like that was what Tselika was referring to.

"She was scribbling down notes for some letter or something," she clarified. "I don't see why she couldn't just send the message as-is, though."

"W-wait, when did you look at it?! Anyway, it's none of your business! I know it's an old person's hobby, but I have someone to share it with, and I won't let you make fun of it! A handwritten letter clues the other person into what's in your heart!"

"Oh!" Tselika happily replied. "I don't get it!"

"...Don't make fun of my hobby with such a big smile on your face..."

Seeing Midori's frustrations, Kaname allowed his lips to crack into a small smile. Noticing this, Midori turned to him.

"What?"

"Nothing."

There was no deeper implication. This was her hobby, an eccentricity, the most fleeting part of her personality.

"Anyway, My Lord. What are we going to do next?"

"What do you mean?"

"Our target right now is Ag Wolves. However, until we find out where they're hiding, we don't know their numbers or their firepower. And even if we stage an assault, we don't know which Legacy they have or where they're keeping it."

Kaname wasn't the next one to speak. It was Midori. However, it wasn't to reveal some sort of grand plan she had prepared.

"Ag Wolves... They're a strange bunch, that's for sure. They've got all sorts: a sniper, a melee expert, a trap master... But it doesn't seem like they were trying to cover one another's weaknesses. It's more like just a group of the best Dealers in each field, all in one place." Midori spoke almost to herself, but Kaname and Tselika had turned toward her in rapt attention.

"Wh-what? Why so quiet?" Midori shot back, growing flustered.

"You know their load outs?!" asked Kaname.

If you knew what weapons your opponents were using, like sniper rifles or machine guns, you could guess at their tactics. But that wasn't exactly what Midori was saying.

"Huh? I mean..."

Without realizing the value of her words, she continued:

"Can't you tell just by getting a feel for it? I don't mean knowing if it's partywear or streetwear but like, *the purpose behind their outfit or, like, their intentions for that day. Money (Game) Master* doesn't have experience points or levels, so your stats only exist as a combination of your weapons and equipment, right? That means you can deduce what someone's role is by the vibe of their outfit, can't you?"

"My, my. Is she saying what I think she's saying, My Lord?"

"Tselika. Scan our dashcam footage for any images of Lily-Kiska's attire you can find. Have Midori draw up a list and see how many we can identify."

"...Wow. I only got about forty percent, but I think with what Midori just said, we may even bring it up to one hundred percent, My Lord."

"She and Takamasa really are siblings. The things that come out of their mouths would put a professional scout with a million-dollar camera to shame..."

If you could find out in advance what your enemy's optimal range and tactics were, then you could come up with a strategy specifically to beat them.

People often tried to deduce such things using their skills or their Magistellus's support, but these analyses were flawed at best. They were nothing more than guesses. Players took great pains to prevent their appearance from giving them away—either by hiding their necklace beneath a scarf or deliberately wearing a knockoff bag with the same design. But none of this fooled Midori. Even the mighty wolf pack would be stripped bare before her discerning eye.

"????" Midori simply cocked her head in puzzlement, unaware of the rarity of her gift, like Cinderella before she met her fairy godmother.

Kaname had Midori write down as much as she could about the features of Ag Wolves members. As she did, he thought.

We have many reasons to oppose Ag Wolves.

First, the obvious one. To steal the Legacy, which Ag Wolves control and use for personal gain.

Second, Midori is in their sights. If we ignore them, they could come after her or perhaps find out that she's related to Criminal AO. There's no telling what they'd do if they were to capture her if they thought she could teach them about the Legacies.

That was reason enough. He had sworn to protect Takamasa's sister, just as Takamasa had once protected his.

The immediate concern was locating the Ag Wolves' base.

"…I actually have some thoughts on that," Kaname declared. Tselika and Midori both turned and looked at him. Kaname approached the dining room table.

"If we can't go to them, we'll make them come to us. They mentioned that to raise the money to pay for those missiles, they've been trading futures in the food market. Many things that would be natural disasters or poor crop seasons in the real world are announced beforehand as events here. That means it's a lot lower risk, since you don't have to worry about irregularities messing with the prices."

"So what are we going to do with the food market?" Midori asked as Tselika presented her empty soup bowl to her and asked for a refill.

Kaname nodded. "Food doesn't mean much if you're only staying in *Money (Game) Master* for a few hours. It all gets reset when you log out, so to normal players, it doesn't matter if you don't eat. But despite this, many Dealers eat because it helps them control their emotions or keeps them focused in the face of difficult market predictions or sharpshooting tasks, as well as because they just like the taste, of course. If this is the market that Ag Wolves are making a killing on, then the solution is simple."

There was a momentary silence. Kaname, the man who walked alongside a demon, concluded as follows:

"We'll destroy their source of income entirely. When they tire of waiting and come out to find us, that's when we'll trace their movements backward to pinpoint the location of their base."

7

They had decided what to do. There was just one thing to confirm. Kaname looked out the window of the rain-beaten log cabin.

"I wanted to use that Acid D we got at the casino to destroy #tempest.err," he revealed, "but this cyclone is making that difficult…"

"You did say that there's no point in destroying it if nobody sees it, didn't you?" asked Midori.

Kaname nodded. "The reputation of the Overtrick is massive. It doesn't matter if we destroy it if nobody believes us. They'd think we're lying, that we're still hiding it. As long as they live in fear of the Legacies, they'll never break free of their spell."

"Which means they'll just keep on thinking we have it forever," Tselika extrapolated.

"Or people could claim to have stolen it from me. We'll have no means by which to disprove any conspiracy theories that might arise. Dealers won't even need to use the Legacy; they can just prey on the fear that it might still exist in order to control people."

"…And people will continue to be hurt by what my brother left behind," added Midori.

"That's why we have to destroy it in a way that nobody can refute. And even video evidence can be faked. We might just have to put on a show right in the middle of the financial district. That way anyone can record and upload it."

"But this cyclone means that…" Tselika trailed off.

"Yeah. Nobody's going to come outside and watch in this rain. We'll just have to wait until it passes."

Midori let out a heavy sigh. It was understandable, as she wanted the thing gone as soon as possible. And Kaname didn't plan to hold on to it for any longer than he had to, either. #tempest.err was the source of all their problems.

"That's why we should focus on Ag Wolves for now," said Kaname. "Tselika, have you finished that job I gave you? All the materials should be on the shopping list I prepared."

"You sure like to work me to the bone, My Lord… Making me grind down all those aluminum cans into little pieces using a blender; trawl the beaches with a magnet for iron sand, as well as get all sorts of other secret ingredients; and fill a bunch of cans with the stuff…"

"?" Midori had on a puzzled look. Tselika had been quite busy before she came to help with the stew, it seemed.

Tselika opened a briefcase and revealed the fruits of her labors.

"Voilà! One hundred thermite incendiary grenades! What do you have to say to that, My Lord?!"

Midori was struck speechless by the incredible reveal.

Thermite was a special mixture of aluminum and iron oxide that underwent a violent chemical reaction when ignited, capable of reaching over thousands of degrees. Given that the melting point of iron was only 1,500 degrees Celsius, even a metal wall provided little protection against this kind of weapon.

And a hundred of them?

"Wh-what are you planning on doing?! Declaring war?!"

"Well, what do you expect? We're taking on Ag Wolves," Kaname answered as though it was the most natural thing in the world. "We've seen about a dozen of them out in the open, but you can bet for sure there's going to be more hiding in reserve, supporting them. If each one has ten people behind them, then that means we're dealing with over a hundred in total. If each one has a hundred, then that's a thousand. If that's not war, then I don't know what is."

"Powerful teams always have plenty of backers," said Tselika. "After all, if you can entrust your fortune to them and have it multiplied without you having to lift a finger, why wouldn't you do it and put your feet up?"

"..."

Midori was once again floored by the enormity of the problem they faced. They had taken on a thousand PMCs on the cruise liner, but this was a whole other level. No matter how strong they were, the PMCs could protect only the territory dictated by their contract. A human opponent, however, was one whose movements you could never quite predict. They were free agents. You never knew where and when they might strike.

Midori hadn't been able to do a thing on her own. Yet Kaname hadn't wavered. He had stridden right into danger and held out his hand.

"But there's still a way," declared Kaname. "Let's get started."

"Huh? Huh?"

Midori, flustered, could do nothing but follow. Another short distance back to the garage through the pouring rain, and Kaname tossed #tempest.err along with the briefcase full of incendiary grenades into the trunk of the mint-green coupe.

"Tselika. How are the tires?"

"Hmm. It looks like we might run into trouble, so I filled them with foam."

"Foam?" Midori looked confused.

Kaname answered. "Tires are usually filled with air, but they can also be filled with resin. It means that even if they take a bullet, they don't puncture, and you can keep on driving."

"I hear that in the real world, they use it on presidential vehicles," Tselika added.

"That sounds useful. Would it work on my motorcycle as well?"

Kaname and Tselika proceeded to replace the tires of Midori's autumn-leaf-patterned bright-red motorcycle.

Midori, still dripping wet, bent over and watched on with interest, once again ignorantly pointing her bikini-clad backside toward the dashcam of the coupe. Of course, there was no point in recording the inside of a garage, so the dashcam was off, but still, in many ways, the girl was not very aware of her surroundings. And so it was Kaname who fretted all the more over the sister of his dear old friend.

"But if it's that good, then how come everyone doesn't use this foam stuff?" she asked.

"Well, it's easy to put in, but taking it out is a different matter. It's a lot rougher on the tires, too. A long, hard car chase will wear them out entirely."

"What?! Why didn't you tell me that before?!"

It was too late. The inner tube was already filled with the special resin.

"It doesn't matter now," assured Kaname. "Let's just get moving; we need to be on the road."

"H-hold up, My Lord! Wipe yourself off before you get behind the wheel! Those seats are real leather, you know!"

Ignoring Tselika's protests, Kaname opened the door and sat right down in the driver's seat, sopping wet. Beside him, Midori straddled her bright-red motorcycle. Obviously, she wasn't going to wear a helmet in a video game, but it seemed like it would be painful nonetheless to be pelted by the torrential rain as she rode.

"Come on out, Meiki. Hold on. Meiki?!"

The girl screamed at empty space for a while until, finally, as though she had waited long enough, a beautiful young woman emerged from the back seat. Meiki—Midori's Magistellus, presumably. Her elegant black hair came down to her shoulders, and a pair of horns sprouted from her head, while between them was a paper talisman. As for her clothes, she wore a rather seductively short cheongsam, bright-red and trimmed with fur around the neck, that daringly teased glimpses of her bare skin along both of her sides. She was quite tall, but her breasts were even smaller than Midori's. All over the surface of her cheongsam, just like with Tselika, the logos of prominent companies, as well as measures of their reputation, stock prices, revenue and expenses, employee counts, and more streamed in and out of view.

And from time to time, her body would flicker with some sort of gray noise. Not the monitor-like dress but the demon lady herself. Sitting in the driver's seat, Kaname appeared uncharacteristically surprised.

"What is that? ...It can't be a bug, can it? Not in *Money (Game) Master.*"

"Perhaps they're not too compatible with each other. I know if it were me, I couldn't abide a lowly *two-wheeled* vehicle. On the other hand, you, My Lord, are far more to my liking."

"Shut up, you," snapped Midori. "A Magistellus's job is to help their Dealer. If anything, *you* should change to suit *us*. I should count myself lucky she showed up at all. When she doesn't, not even bashing the bike will make her come out." Midori pouted.

Kaname used the remote to open the garage door, and they departed. Kaname's wipers were working full blast. Putting the wind- and rain-swept Mangrove Island behind them, the two vehicles joined onto the massive four-lane circular bridge. Even on a day like this, there was quite a lot of traffic, and the radio continued to report.

"Cyclone Elizabeth is expected to continue in full force for the rest of the afternoon. All harbors and airports have closed, and the resulting shortages have caused the prices of..."

"The group of skydivers calling themselves the Skychasers who cross from building to building have become more active recently. According to an online video announcement, they were not about to let this favorable wind pass them by. Anyone out and about in the financial district should take care not to be struck by falling persons. Now, on to our next segment..."

"The Transaction of Pivotal Calculator stock price index, TroPiCal, is sitting at 24,900, up 250 points from yesterday's figures. In anticipation of Cyclone Elizabeth, several insurance companies have seen a sharp increase in their share price, including Early States General, Golden Luxury, and Karen Insurance..."

While idly listening to the event announcements, Kaname fired up a chat window with the old IM aesthetic and sent a request to Midori, who was riding alongside him. She quickly accepted the connection.

Midori: We're heading to the peninsula district, right?

Kaname: Yeah. That's where we'll destroy Ag Wolves' source of income. That should draw them out of the woodwork.

Midori: You mean their..."food futures"? Erm...so we're going to do something to them?

On reading the message, Kaname frowned. He turned to look at the bright-red bike driving alongside him and saw a somewhat uneasy look upon Midori's face.

Kaname: Hold on... You do know what futures are, right? How can you live in Money (Game) Master and not know that?!

Midori: Oh, lay off it! I'm only here to destroy my brother's Legacies!

Kaname groaned. Tselika gave a shrill cackle. What Midori had just said was like playing a fighting game without knowing about the health bar. It was a wonder she hadn't Fallen already.

Kaname: A futures contract is an agreement whereby you pay now and receive the goods at a later date. This span of time can range anywhere from a few months to several years.

At Kaname's words, the company logos covering Tselika's fur-trimmed pit-babe outfit disappeared and were replaced with something else: the names and prices of futures contracts for rice, wheat, beans, and so on.

Midori: Sounds complicated. Why can't they just give it to you right away?

Kaname: What if the price of cider goes from one hundred snow per bottle in the winter to one thousand in the summer? By taking advantage of the change in price, you can turn a profit when the time comes by simply selling the goods on.

Futures trading was everything on the agricultural market. These were no small contracts; the volume of wheat or corn in a single trade was to the tune of many tons.

Midori: So the guys after the Legacies have been raising funds using those futures contracts? But what if hundred-yen soda drops to one yen instead? They'd make a huge loss, wouldn't they? I mean, iced coffee or tea could start trending or something.

Kaname: Of course. And usually there'd be nothing you could do about that. But they'll be using a dirty trick to get around it.

Midori: How?

Kaname: It's easy to make the price of something rise. Just blow up the freight trains or ships carrying the product to create a scarcity. It's like how certain kinds of candy go up in price once they're no longer produced. If they cause the price of a bottle of cider to shoot up, they can cover their losses that way.

In the real world, that would be a textbook case of terrorism, but in here, it was simply par for the course. Kaname continued typing with his eyes on the windshield as the rain struck against it in large droplets.

Kaname: But that's the sort of thing any Dealer can do. Ag Wolves will be going one step further. They don't just make the price go up when it seems like they're about to make a loss, but they can also make the price of a specific stock go down.

Midori: ??? Why would they do that? How do you make money if the price goes down?

Kaname: Let's say Ag Wolves want to make a profit on wheat. It's not just the state of wheat itself that affects the price. If the prices of rice or corn fluctuate, that'll have a domino effect on wheat, as well. By controlling both a positive and a negative, you can effectively make the price whatever you want.

You could also use this to correct the price range if you destroyed too many freight trains or ships. After all, if the price was too high, nobody would buy. Being able to tweak the dial in both directions made it impossible to go wrong.

Futures trading was a method for making profit over the course of a few months or years, but Ag Wolves had raised the money for buying the anti-ship missiles and influencing the cruise liner company in just a short time.

It would have been impossible to put together such a fortune in just a few days without using a powerful means of control.

Midori: But what are they doing specifically? I can imagine attacking boats or trains to destroy the supply, but how do they do the opposite and flood the city with it?

Kaname: We're going to find that out right now and put a stop to it.

8

Server name: Sigma Blue.
Starting location: Tokonatsu City, Peninsula District.
Log-in credentials accepted.
Welcome to *Money (Game) Master*, Lily-Kiska Sweetmare.

Within the dachshund of a black limo, the girl with swept-back hair and glasses seethed. Crossing her mismatched boots, she folded her arms moodily, pushing up breasts that were already emphasized by a pair of underarm holsters.

As soon as she had arrived, the glass table in the center of the room was filled with all sorts of bad news. Several windows opened as reports continued to stream in from the other Ag Wolves. She didn't want to use her smart glasses and have it all get in the way of her vision.

"Crap, crap, crap, crap! I don't know how, but they worked it out! They're coming after our controls!"

A bunch of red crosses were marked on her map around the financial district area. They showed the locations of the control stock Ag Wolves used to influence the prices of their futures contracts, but anyone who saw the actual locations would probably be pretty confused. After all, there weren't any buildings, just large, rusted metal dumpsters.

However...

It's the incubators! They're coming after the incubators that we disguised as commercial waste containers! They're using some kind of incendiary grenades to destroy them!

There were two ways to control the prices of futures contracts.

First, you could blow up the freighters and prevent the goods from reaching the city. That would cause the price to go up as supply fell.

Then, the second way: prepare a large quantity of goods in secret, as Ag Wolves were doing now using nutrients and ultraviolet light. Then, when the time was right, flood the market with an overwhelming supply, tanking the price.

A positive and a negative. By covering both sides, Ag Wolves had created for themselves a situation where they couldn't lose. Or so they thought.

"Those bastards... There! I see them! Their mint-green coupe! I'm gonna go make mincemeat out of 'em!"

"Titan! Stand down! Wait for reinforcements to—"

Lily-Kiska yelled into her communication device, but it was too late. The line had already gone dead. It took her a while to realize what had just happened, but before long, the cruel reality sank in.

"...No... No way..."

9

Server name: Omega Purple.
   Final location: Tokonatsu City, Peninsula District.
   Fall confirmed.
   Titan will be logged out for twenty-four hours.

10

The mint-green coupe came to a halt in the pouring rain. Kaname, still holding Short Spear through the open driver's seat window, clicked his tongue.

"Damn. Killed him. We won't get anything out of him now."

The storm had already drenched his hair, and the wind was so loud, it was impossible to even hold a conversation. Tselika's eyes narrowed as she thought about the poor leather seats. Midori pulled up beside him astride her large motorcycle and fired off another chat message.

Midori: How did you know about the dumpsters?

Kaname: Think about it from another angle. Money is everything in Money (Game) Master. Anything that can be turned into cash is something worth fighting over. If they had a single factory producing enough crops to influence the price of all their futures contracts, it'd be asking for trouble. The thicker you make the walls, the more it makes Dealers think there's something inside worth having.

Midori: So...

Kaname: Keep it in something that looks totally worthless, and nobody will think twice. Even a metal canister can become cash in this city, but nobody would ever pay attention to a large dumpster that's just used to store food waste. And there are hundreds of them all around the city. If they lose one, it's no big deal. And most importantly...

Kaname pointed out his window with his gun barrel, indicating the large dumpster that was sitting there. Or more precisely, the thin cable that ran out of the metal container and along the side of the building. It was connected to an outlet designed for decorative outdoor lighting.

Kaname: What sort of food waste dumpster requires electricity? There aren't batteries strong enough to keep the UV lamps burning day and night without needing to be replaced all the time, and of course, solar power is no use when you're in a back alley. They probably only did it because they had no other choice, but luckily for us, it means we can easily tell the real ones from the fakes.

The car's wipers swept back and forth at a steady pace across the windshield. Kaname's eyes raced about as he typed his response.

At the same time, he brought the short-range sniper rifle back inside and took out one of his incendiary grenades, pulling the pin with his teeth before hurling it through the window. The bomb, no larger than a spray can, rolled cleanly into the narrow opening beneath the car-size dumpster. There was a flash of white light, as bright as a welding torch, as the incubator was engulfed in flames hot enough to melt steel. Closing the electric window, Kaname typed up another message.

Kaname: Let's move on to the next one. The closer we tighten around their necks, the more they panic and give themselves away.

Midori: Right.

Midori was taken aback but managed to type out a response.

Midori: But are you sure about this? Didn't you say there were going to be hundreds, if not thousands of investors backing them?

Kaname: That's exactly why they're scared.

Midori: ?

Kaname: They're only borrowing that money. It's not theirs. Those patrons entrusted their capital to Ag Wolves because they guaranteed a return on investment. Now, what if they lose it all? It won't just be us they'll be pointing their pitchforks at.

The boy let out a quiet sigh.

Kaname: It's not like Ag Wolves are making amazing market predictions. It's more like they're playing poker with a couple of extra wild cards in their hand. So what if you take those away? The trading doesn't just stop. It can't. Once they veer off course, the losses will start piling up. Like they would have done all along.

Midori: Today's ally is tomorrow's enemy, I suppose...

Kaname: Futures trading is a tough business. Nobody wins 100 percent of the time.

The pair set off for their next target, leaving behind the charred remains of the incubator and Titan's convertible, wrapped around a traffic light.

Then Tselika, who was tapping buttons on the radio, bored, switching through the channels, suddenly hit upon something.

"This has been an update to the bounty program. A new bounty has been posted. A reward of fifty million snow per head is being offered for two Dealers: Kaname Suou and Midori Hekireki. The payout is being offered by a team called Ag Wolves..."

After sharing the information, Kaname received a panicked response from the rider of the motorcycle driving alongside him.

Midori: What are we going to do now?! Does this mean every Dealer in the city is coming after us?!

Kaname: Calm down. Any Dealer worth their salt is going to draw up a plan of attack before rushing in blindly. We've still got time. The way to shake off a bounty is simple. Think like a mercenary. We just have to prove that Ag Wolves can't pay.

Midori: Huh?

Kaname: If we kill them all, the problem goes away on its own. Our goal hasn't changed.

Midori: ...How are you so calm?

Kaname: Those guys dropped 200 million on a single anti-ship missile. Compared to that, this reward is peanuts. I don't feel like dying when they're holding out.

"Tselika. Forget the news. Change the channel."

"Aye-aye, My Lord!" Tselika grinned as she fiddled with the knobs, looking for something to put on. "Now then," she said, "when are we going to find out where they're keeping the Legacy?"

"That's what I've been trying to do," Kaname replied.

The mint-green coupe and the bright-red motorcycle raced through the city, the streets hazy with mist from the pouring rain.

"Really?" Tselika asked. "At this rate, you're likely to end up slaughtering the lot of them. What happens if you kill half of them and the rest decide to cut their losses and flee? Then we'll have lost our only clues!"

"Not our only clues."

"Oh?"

"Take Lily-Kiska's limousine, for example. The size of that thing would make it stick out like a sore thumb in any ordinary parking lot. But then, so would having a special garage for it. So where do you think she keeps it?"

"Maybe somewhere it wouldn't look out of place?" Tselika said as she stopped on a channel playing her favorite music and sat back with a satisfied smile. Kaname frowned a little at the crude lyrics.

"Somewhere she doesn't need to hide. Somewhere with a luxury hotel or casino, where a grand column of limousines doesn't look the least bit strange. That'll be her area of operations. We find that, we'll find her hideout."

"Well, why didn't we go after that in the first place?"

"Because we can only get to Lily-Kiska that way," said Kaname. "It won't lead us to the rest of Ag Wolves, and there's no guarantee the Legacy will be there. That's why it's only plan B."

A large sightseeing bus passed by on the other side of the road, cleaving through a pool of water and sending it crashing against Kaname's windshield. For a moment, he was blinded, the wipers useless.

"Watch it! That's my—" Tselika turned to flip off the driver, but before she could say the word *temple*, her jaw dropped at what she saw.

Kaname felt that strange yet familiar itch on the end of his nose. He looked over at the rearview mirror to confirm.

Then it happened.

Clang!
There was a great clatter as the rear of the double-decker bus swung down into a slope, and a black limo flew out from within.

Until now, Kaname and Tselika had agreed that Lily-Kiska's limousine, her mobile base, was probably being kept outside a hotel or a casino.
But they had been naive.
She could hide anywhere in the city if she had a larger shell to hide in!
"Watch out! Billboard Head's on our tail!" shrieked Tselika.
"This is bad…"

Once he laid eyes on the source of the danger, the Lion's Nose went into overdrive. It was like being punched in the nose. The buzzing sensation spread until it filled Kaname's entire head.

Kkrrrrrr! The screeching sound of tires on asphalt quickly approached from the rear. Kaname fired off a chat message to appraise Midori of the situation.

Kaname: That limousine is coated in bulletproof steel. The engine is ridiculously powerful, too. We can't outrun her at full speed, and she can plow straight through walls as well. If you don't want to die, follow me!

11

The actual presidential limo was a little under 180 centimeters tall. A person could walk through the back door, and the tires were bigger than a dump truck's. In photos, it looked long and thin because there were no rulers or matchboxes around to give a sense of scale, but there was a reason they called it the Beast.

The thickness of the walls was what made it so big. The presidential vehicle was like a bank vault. Plate it in thick armor and of course it was all going to add up.

Lily-Kiska's limousine wasn't like that. But bulletproof glass was ten centimeters thick. It was quite threatening to see this thing roll down the road at 490 kilometers per hour, shrugging off assault-rifle fire. It looked harmless enough when the hybrid vehicle ran in electric mode, but with the flick of a switch, the jet engine, suitable for drag-racing vehicles, could kick in. People often used cars as mobile weapons, but this one was more like a wrecking ball on wheels. A collision with this monster would be like running into a freight train.

The limo's straight-line acceleration was unbeatable. It sliced through the water on the ground, kicking up spray like angels' wings. Lily-Kiska was wearing several accessories on her ears and around her neck. Even now, inside the luxury car, she was painting her nails, guided by images appearing on her smart glasses. Rearranging her skills. Focusing on maximizing her original specialty of ultra-long-range combat. If she got close, she could mow them down in her superheavy armored car, and if they made some distance, she could pick them off from afar. There were no blind spots.

Folding her legs clad in mismatched boots, she calmly issued an order over the intercom. "Sophia. Crush them."

"As you wish, Miss Kiska."

As soon as the limo was immediately behind him, Kaname cut the wheel and swerved. The predator barreled into the space its prey had just occupied, cutting through the metal barrier dividing the road and the sidewalk like a sheet of wet paper. Without stopping, the limo returned to the road, snapping a lamppost on the way and sending it flying toward Midori's head. By ducking down atop her bright-red motorcycle, the young girl narrowly avoided being decapitated by the spinning pole.

But Lily-Kiska didn't care about her. Kaname was the priority. Crush him first and the rest would follow.

"...?"

Lily-Kiska suddenly sensed something was wrong and turned to the glass table in the center of the room, opening up several windows to analyze the bright-red, leaf-patterned motorcycle in more detail. The image was slightly obscured by rain, but the person riding the bike was clearly not Midori. She was too tall, and instead of a frilly bikini, the figure was wearing a *cheongsam*.

"That's not the Dealer... Is her Magistellus riding it for her?"

Even if the keys were already in the ignition, a Magistellus couldn't steal somebody else's vehicle. They could only interact with their Dealer's property. But if it *was* their Dealer's property, then there was nothing stopping them from driving a car or riding a motorcycle.

Lily-Kiska muttered to herself. "Does that mean...they're doing the same with the coupe? Dammit, Kaname Suou! Where did you go?!"

12

A little before that...

Amid the cyclone, in the slanting rain, Kaname and Midori had left their vehicles and were hiding from sight, huddled together and soaking wet.

"Wh...? Wh...?"

"Stay quiet."

Midori's skin was warm despite the chill of the pouring rain, but Kaname had no time to wonder why. He had to do something about Lily-Kiska and her limousine as quickly as possible. They were right beside the main road, hiding in the narrow space between a gigantic commercial building and some tall vegetation.

"...Oh my God, what a brute. Why can't you take a few lessons from that guy?" Midori whispered.

"Which guy? Is there a Dealer or someone you could call for help?"

Midori jumped in Kaname's arms. She blushed hard, and her body temperature rose even in the cold rain. She shot back in a desperate tone.

"Yes, someone I admire! That a problem? It's someone who writes such lovely letters, and I bet has a personality to match. Someone who's always been there for me with a gentle smile whenever I had a problem. Someone mature—nothing like some digitalite I happen to know!"

"..." Kaname felt himself pale from the awkwardness, and with all his might, he resisted the urge to avert his gaze. "...The tingle in my nose is spreading. Let's get out of here for now. Our little trick won't fool her for much longer. In the meantime, Tselika and Meiki should keep her distracted, and that'll buy us some time. We should move on with our preparations."

"You mean..." Midori was speechless. "You mean we're going to destroy that monster limousine? How?! The armor on that thing can deflect assault-rifle fire, and it can fly along at five hundred kilometers per hour, and its tires are filled with foam so you can't even shoot them out! How are we supposed to beat that thing with what we have?! And #tempest.err is..."

Midori paused. Perhaps she was avoiding the idea of using a Legacy to her advantage after arguing so ardently to destroy them all.

Kaname spoke frankly. "It's okay. There's nothing wrong with it. If we Fall here, it's all over anyway."

"…But it's still in the trunk of your car. We couldn't use it even if we wanted to."

"Not necessarily. Anyway, we need to move. Right now, it's dangerous to even walk across the block. If that limo spots us, we're as good as dead. We need to use a safe route."

"Wh-what do you mean, 'a safe route'?!"

Kaname jogged out into the middle of the road. Midori followed him with a puzzled expression, whereupon he leaned over where he stood. From the pouch at his waist, he withdrew his smartphone, a rather useless item in a world where Magistelli took care of communication and calculation for you.

"What are you doing?" Midori asked.

"In *Money (Game) Master*, money talks. I won't say it's everything, but it certainly increases the size of your hand and your freedom to act. The world looks totally different. I mentioned this before."

"What does that—?" Midori stopped halfway. Kaname held his smartphone over a manhole cover in the ground. Just as Midori thought it looked like he was trying to make a payment, there was a metallic clang, and the whole thing slowly rotated forty-five degrees. Kaname lifted the lid as though he was checking on his boiled potatoes.

Huh? Are these things supposed to open so easily? Midori thought but soon put such a trivial question aside.

Down there, a different world awaited. Not the stuffy, smelly, dark, sewage-filled tunnels she'd expected to see but an unbroken surface of water. Far larger than the pool at school. Owing to the heavy rain, there was the thunderous noise of rushing water, but it didn't look so bad underground. The place was well lit with electric lighting, and the water looked pretty, the light twinkling off its reflective surface.

It was a drainage channel. Many rivers had been built over in the city's development. This was one of them.

But that wasn't what surprised her. Something else did.

Right there, beneath the manhole, in the center of the underground river, lay a cigar-shaped submarine about one hundred meters long.

Kaname never said money was everything, but he did say that it makes the world look totally different.

Midori was beginning to feel as though she understood what he meant.

Beside the submarine hatch stood a girl dressed in a brown sailor uniform and a skirt-suspender combo that looked not unlike a work apron. She was obviously not a human but a Magistellus, as her entire body was molded out of some sort of translucent pink slime.

Kaname peered through the manhole into the subterranean world and shouted so as to be heard over the storm.

"Sorry to bother you in this weather! We're glad we caught you passing by. It must be hard to stay anchored in such a high tide, mustn't it?"

"Don't worry—we charge a million *snow* for admittance, so it's really no problem. However, Kaname Suou, we have heard of you. My master, Frey(a), has eagerly awaited your arrival. Please come this way."

Kaname and Midori climbed down a ladder below the manhole and stepped onto the submarine, opening the hatch and heading on inside. But as soon as the hatch opened, a flood of music hit Midori's ears. It was dance music, although Midori would be hard-pressed to place the exact name or specific genre.

It was unlike any submarine she had seen in movies or on TV. There were no cramped cabins or twisting passageways. The inside was vast, as though the inner walls had all been knocked down, connecting every room save the bridge and the engine room into one large indoor space. In terms of size, it seemed about as large as an entire floor of a school building.

The air was dim, lit only by lasers that cut through the darkness, accompanied by a back-and-forth between unintelligible vocals filled with English slang and the driving beat of the electronic dance music that reverberated in her guts.

"Wh-where are we?" Midori asked.

"We're on this guy's turf now," answered Kaname. "There's more than one way to have fun in *Money (Game) Master*. Don't run off on your own, Midori."

The reason Kaname said that was because the room was almost bursting with young men and women. It was hard to say if they were getting physical with one another or simply letting their bodies be guided by the music.

Oh my gosh, he's touching her—Oh geez, are they going to—? Oh my God, she's getting close to his—? Oh wow, oh wow... I wonder if I'll do that someday... Maybe...with the person who writes the lovely letters...

"Midori."

"Wh-wha—???!!!"

The twin-tailed girl hurried over and followed Kaname, flustered. Farther on, the pair broke past the crowd of men and women and into an area filled with tables and love seats. The submarine's owner was already waiting there.

He wore a pure white dress suit, and both his eyes were different colors, with a mole just beneath one of them. His features were on the feminine side, and his hair was long and blond. Despite the sofa only being sized for two, he sat there with a beautiful woman on each arm, both of them wearing short, almost conch-shaped dresses. With a smile, he spoke. "Hey, hey! Over here, Kaname, my boy! My, this *is* a pleasant surprise! Is it finally time for me to lend you a hand?"

"Frey(a). I don't have much time, actually. Sorry for the short notice, but I want us to work together."

Kaname didn't get any tingling feeling in his nose from the handsome man. But with *him*, that was not grounds to let down his guard. In fact, it only made him think Frey(a) had found a way to fool the Lion's Nose, hidden somewhere behind that plastic smile.

The man beckoned to a sofa opposite him, and Kaname and Midori

took their seats. When they did so, the two women by Frey(a)'s side came over and sat down with them. This, however, was no act of hospitality. Kaname and Midori felt the overwhelming pressure from all sides as the women moved in uncomfortably close. It was a gesture that really wasn't necessary.

Midori began to blush as her head was pressed into Kaname's shoulder. "H-hey! I'm taken! I mean…not right now, but I—I—I want to be taken! …But not by you, by someone else! I—I mean… I'm not into love triangles like in those sappy mangas! …At least, not in real life! … Or games, for that matter! Ooohhh, please don't fight over meeee…!"

"Midori, calm down," said Kaname. "He's trying to make you panic. It's what he does best."

"…"

"Midori, please explain to me why you're biting me on the shoulder right now."

The man in the white suit, Frey(a), chuckled to himself as he watched Midori blush. But it wasn't the young girl's bathing suit that put a smile on his face. He was simply enjoying watching the two argue.

"So the Reaper of Called Game has gone soft. Oh, no, please don't be offended. I meant that in the best way possible, of course. But I wonder, are you still the same on the inside? …That anonymous donation to Nibelheim Pharmaceuticals, that was you, was it not? The roadblocks to eradicating disease are not only scientific but economic. It simply isn't profitable due to the low number of consumers…ahem, I mean, patients. But now, those patients, whom economics had forsaken, have been given a new lease on life, thanks to you."

"Frey(a). We don't need to talk about that."

"Why not?! You should be more proud of your accomplishments. I don't understand why you didn't use your real name in the first place. Just look at all the other so-called 'philanthropists' of the world. They're getting good publicity out of it. In fact, that's the whole reason they're doing it. It's cheaper than simply paying an advertising firm."

"Listen, you. Helping others isn't about bragging rights or asking for something in return. If money can solve the problem, then fine, do it. If not, then find another way, but don't start looking to get something in return. As soon as you impose like that, you're not helping people anymore. You're just encroaching on their lives."

For a moment, nobody said a word. Then...

Untz-untz-untz-untz—the driving bass of the dance music rose to fill the empty silence.

Then at last, Frey(a), who had not stopped smiling, spoke. "Was that Criminal AO?"

"Huh?" Midori raised her voice at the unexpected mention of her brother's name.

Kaname remained silent, so the man in the white suit continued.

"...He used to say that, didn't he? He was a good man. Every bit as good as you. Such a shame what happened to him," noted Frey(a). And then, in a softer voice, "I would have liked to sleep with him, just once."

Midori didn't know how to respond to that. She looked to Kaname for support.

"Wh-what did you mean by 'work together'? A-and who is this guy anyway?"

"Oh my! I haven't introduced myself to the young lady!"

The heterochromatic gentleman beamed. His pure-white suit would not have looked out of place at a wedding.

"My name is Frey(a)! I am a proud pawnshop owner in this fine game! Have you heard of the Treasure Hermit Crabs...? Well, judging by the look on your face, I'd guess it's safe to say you haven't."

"Pawnshop?" asked Midori.

"Precisely. I work with the casinos, the ones that give out physical prizes, to broaden their range of operations. Even the things you see here do not all belong to me. The lighting, the audio equipment, the furniture, the kitchenware, the decor, and even this very submarine. They're all things that my precious customers have entrusted to me."

Midori finally saw what Kaname had meant by "work together." Basically, this pawnshop would have what they needed to destroy the bulletproof limousine.

But there was another thing that still gave Midori pause. A sense of unease, long lingering in the back of her mind, finally came to her.

What is with his outfit?

There were no levels or experience in *Money (Game) Master*. A Dealer's strength was determined by their weapons, clothes, and cars... Or so she thought, but Midori could not identify a single unifying theme that underpinned Frey(a)'s clothes. He had chosen them because of their appearance, not their stats.

Noticing her, Frey(a) grinned wider.

"I have no interest in anything so uncouth as gunplay. Nor car chases, for that matter. The only thing I use cars for is to decorate the stage over there. Similarly, money, the TroPiCal index, none of that bothers me in the slightest. I run a business, sure, but only because I have to. And if I had to, I would fight as well, although to be honest, that's what my Magistellus and my subordinates are for."

Midori looked over in the direction Frey(a)'s gloved finger pointed, where, sure enough, above the young men and women surrendering their bodies to the loud music, there were about half a dozen vehicles lined up on a raised platform. They were all perfectly tuned and colored bright silver, like a row of undecorated tin cans. However, as Midori watched, their colors shifted and changed before her very eyes, the textures swirling like wet paint.

Each player was allowed only one Magistellus. So to accomplish that effect, he must be continually transferring among the vehicles a single Magistellus, who was lighting up the surface of the vehicle like a monitor and causing the wavelike motion.

A Dealer's vehicle, along with their weapon, was their lifeblood. And this man was using them as playthings.

Midori gave a puzzled look. "Then...what do you—?"

"Do? That's obvious! Love! Or perhaps you could call me a simple purveyor of chance meetings. But love is what I look for in *Money (Game) Master*! Love! I don't care about anything else!" The man's impassioned voice was enough to drown out the dance music.

"There's more than one way to have fun. We're on this guy's turf." Kaname's words replayed in Midori's head.

"Which is why I'm sorry, but I only work with couples. And your Magistellus doesn't count, no matter how pretty she is. You see, love is the most primal game we play. We bargain and strategize. People without love, with nothing to protect, want to die heroic deaths. It makes me a little reluctant to want to ally myself with them. I'm not sure I'd even want your contact details if you don't have the brains to handle a single online relationship."

His position was not a complex one. Love was everything to this man.

"That's why I'm genuinely happy to see you," he continued. "Look at you—sitting there acting all cool. I'm so glad you've finally found your-self a human lover. I've been *ever so* worried about you, you know!"

"Pfff! Wh-wh-wha—? Lov...lover?! How *da— Mph!*"

Before Midori could say anything more, Kaname grabbed her by the shoulder and pulled her toward him, pressing her mouth into his chest before she could say anything that might ruin the moment.

"Mmmrggghhh!" *Oh, what's wrong with me? Why am I getting worked up when I have the man with the lovely writing? Oh God, why am I like this?!*

Though he wondered why he could feel the girl's heartbeat racing like mad, Kaname cut straight to the point.

"Frey(a). I came here for a reason."

"Did you? Well, if it's important, I should think we ought to do something about the young lady's nerves before we begin. Perhaps my appearance is causing some distress, hmm? After all, I can imagine a child such as her might be a little uncomfortable listening to a gentle-man like me speak about love."

Frey(a) raised his hand and clicked his gloved fingers.

The effect was immediate. His suit began to unravel. The fabric exploded into countless white threads, reforming themselves on his body into a pure-white wedding dress with an especially revealing bust. The man's body began to change, too. His chest bulged, his hips widened, his arms and legs became more slender... And his face. His face was that of a woman. His mole was now on the other side, and the colors of his eyes had swapped.

Midori, her face red and buried in Kaname's chest, had all but for-gotten her embarrassment due to the shock of what she was seeing.

"Wha...? Huh...? No way, what is he...?!"

"Ha-ha! This is *Money (Game) Master*! There's nothing you can't do with money! I told you, didn't I? That I came here for love. Why should I let my biology restrict me? I want to experience all love has to offer! I'll do anything to make that happen! Do you now understand my position?"

"Frey(a)."

"Young lady, I see you're uncomfortable with a dashing young man. That's a very pure and innocent reaction. Then let us speak as girls. That should be far more appealing, hmm?"

"Frey(a)."

"Just know that it was out of consideration for you that I adopted the form of a man for our first meeting. More than once have I been told, when introducing myself to someone as a woman, that I reminded them of an ex-girlfriend! Ha-ha! But you... Being faithful is very important to you, but you also don't want to bog your partner down with jealousy. Quite the excellent find there, Kana—"

"Frey."

It was like he'd stabbed her with a knife.

At being so blatantly referred to by a masculine name, the woman in the wedding dress began to pout. Raising a gloved hand, she once again clicked her fingers and returned to the form of a gentleman in a white suit.

Kaname, still pulling Midori toward him, attempted to get back to the point.

"I came here for a reason."

"Yes, yes. What is it you want me to do?"

"I'm sure you're up-to-date with the situation unfolding on the surface. We need your help to destroy Lily-Kiska's armored limousine."

"This is merely a pawnshop, I remind you. I deal in goods, not people. I can't provide you with an army. Luring people away with money is fun enough in love, but I wouldn't want to make a business out of it."

"I'm not intending to incur that much of a debt today," Kaname replied. "I just want you to ferry me to a fixed location, a manhole, in an expedient and safe manner. And that's not all."

Kaname explained his proposal. Frey(a) looked disapproving, as Kaname had expected.

"...That might not matter to you. But for me, that would affect the very foundation of my business. You understand that, don't you?"

"This is *Money (Game) Master*. Even if money isn't everything, it gives you the freedom to do so much more. You can do the impossible if you've got the cash to make it happen, don't you think?"

"Hmm, perhaps you're right." Frey(a) clicked his fingers.

"Eek!" Midori gave off a high-pitched squeal as the back of the sofa suddenly swung out, flat. It appeared to in fact be a sofa bed. Before she could process what was happening, Frey(a) had gotten up out of his seat, crossed the glass table between them, and crawled up on top of Kaname. His suit had turned back into a wedding dress, and he had become a woman once again. Frey(a) spoke on all fours.

"How much are you willing to pay to obtain my *consent*?"

"..."

"You can't pull out now. You aren't willing to sacrifice those Magistelli and vehicles that are providing the diversion. So here's what we'll do. I won't turn you away. I'm going to help you in any way I can. However, if my compensation is not to my liking, I'm going to make up the difference with your body. Understand?" Frey(a) licked her lips seductively and ran her fingers across Kaname's chest.

The person of indeterminate gender called Frey(a) quickly stole a glance toward Midori.

"Perhaps we should make her watch as well. That could be fun. Ha-ha! I want to experience love in its many forms, you see. Pure love is all well and good, but the more kinky and corrupting forms... Oh, it gives me the shivers just thinking about it!"

"..."

"I'll grant you one chance. Now then, Kaname Suou, tell me: How far do you want me to go?"

She closed in, so their foreheads touched, and breathed a soft sigh. Even if Kaname wanted to fight his way out, he'd only succeed in making an enemy of everyone on the ship.

Kaname's expression had not changed. He raised an eyebrow.

"Your pawnshop is affiliated with the casino on Mega-Float III, correct?"

"Hmm? Well, yes. That and five others. Two of them I run myself. Even love requires money, you know. Especially in this world."

"Then whichever. I don't care if it's in the cyclone—go to whichever one has the most people and propose a wager: Who will win between Kaname Suou and Lily-Kiska? Then bet on me, and I'll make you as much money as you want."

There was a silence. It seemed like Frey(a) had not been expecting to hear that.

Then, finally, she snorted before exploding into uproarious laughter.

"Ah-ha-ha-ha! I see! Theoretically infinite, hmm? Indeed, that is an offer I cannot refuse! Money is everything here in *Money (Game) Master*, after all!"

"Everything? If you really thought that, you wouldn't be here chasing after your love affairs," Kaname quipped.

"Fine," said the woman in the wedding dress, stepping back. And then, with a wink, "I'll take you up on your offer. But let me say this. Once this goes public, it won't only be your hat in the ring. You understand, my little stallion?"

13

The submarine traversed the countless underground waterways beneath the city. When they arrived beneath the designated manhole, Kaname thanked the translucent slime Magistellus.

"Once we go up there, get out of here as fast as you can. Oh, and sorry for all the trouble."

"Not at all. I can't remember the last time I saw the master having fun like that. I do hope you'll come visit again, Kaname Suou, Midori Hekireki. I'm not just saying that to be polite; I mean it."

After undoing the special lock on the manhole lid and watching it swing open like a trash can lid, Kaname was struck once more by the fury of the storm outside. They were a short distance away from the road where they had first gone underground, now right in the middle of a large four-way intersection. Midori, exiting behind him into the driving rain, stared at her phone in bewilderment.

"No way. Apparently, we were only in there for ten minutes. Did we go into fairyland or something?"

"That's a better name than Treasure Hermit Crabs. He's a sucker for anything romantic and twisted; send him that in a message and he might change the name."

Perhaps the conversation had gone more smoothly than expected, or perhaps something was interfering with Midori's phone. In any case, as they continued to talk, the two of them walked out into the storm, Midori following Kaname's lead.

They headed across the intersection to a commercial building, to the rear of a coffee shop on one of the floors. There, they found a metal cylinder almost as tall as Midori herself. She frowned.

"A propane tank...?" she asked.

"No, compressed hydrogen," corrected Kaname. "Part of the smart power grid." He detached the hose and bracket holding it in place.

"Are we going to blow it up to destroy that limo?"

"No, that won't be enough to take down that hunk of metal."

Kaname hoisted the canister up onto his shoulder like a large bag of rice. However, the wind and the rain made it difficult to carry, and as he swayed to one side, Midori stepped in to support him. Midori's cheeks burned as her soft body pressed against him, and she thought, *Stop it, stop it, stop it, stop it! Come on, Midori. This is so you can destroy your brother's Legacies and fill your letters with pleasantries again!*

"A-actually...you have quite a peculiar outfit as well, Kaname."

"What do you mean?"

"The same with that short-range sniper rifle of yours. It's a sniper rifle, but it's geared for close combat. And now? Don't you usually need a dolly to carry those gas canisters? You're so strong physically, but how well does that help you in an actual fight? I can't really figure out what the concept is behind your gear choices..."

Kaname headed for one of the manholes in the center of the intersection. There were many small holes in its surface—openings for fitting the tool used to unlock it—but with the special locking mechanism fitted by the Treasure Hermit Crabs, such a tool was unnecessary. The holes were nothing more than camouflage. Kaname fed one end of the hose through one of the holes and undid the valve. The canister emitted a hissing noise as the hydrogen gas began to flow.

It was for this that Kaname had required the consent of *the master of the underworld.*

Soon, something happened.

The sound of screeching tires from far away heralded an approaching vehicle, and Kaname's nose was assaulted by a feeling totally unlike either electricity or numbness.

"Ack! She's here!"

"Midori, hide! Dammit, there's no time!"

Kaname lightly kicked the sideways canister with the sole of his foot, sending it rolling into the thicket at the side of the road, and drew Short Spear from its holster at his waist. He grabbed Midori and ran, but he wasn't able to get far. He unfolded the collapsible stock on his weapon.

First, the mint-green coupe came speeding around the corner, heading right toward the intersection. It was followed by the bright-red, leaf-patterned motorcycle.

"Eek!"

Midori instinctively tried to shrink away, but Kaname pulled her rain-soaked body close. The two hunks of metal passed by either side of them. Kaname felt the girl's heartbeat. Her fear was almost contagious. The next moment, the jet-black armored limousine showed up. And it was heading right for them!

14

It all started as a longing.

There was once a legendary team by the name of Called Game.

One look at the team's track record would make it obvious why they were called that.

One day, in a shoot-out just like any other, they saved the life of a girl.

But when the girl asked to join the team, they refused.

Instead, they told her…

"…"

At that moment, within the limousine, Lily-Kiska was carrying out another threat assessment, one hand supporting her chin and her golden headband sweeping back her long black hair. A projection of the intersection ahead was visible on the glass table, and Kaname's weapon and the canister of hydrogen gas rolling along the road were both clearly marked.

However…

He can shoot it if he wants. He could fasten that canister to this vehicle's underside and blow it up at point-blank range; it won't even make a dent in this armor.

"Sophia." Stroking the arm of her smart glasses, she spoke over the car's intercom. "If they resist, run them down. I'll retake #tempest.err if I have to pry it from his cold, Fallen hands."

"As you wish, Miss Kiska."

The wrecking ball on wheels sped up even more. Whichever way Kaname and Midori decided to flee, Sophia could flatten them with a turn of the wheel. They were as good as dead already. They didn't appear to have #tempest.err on them, either; it would be hard to conceal that monstrous weapon. Even if they did have it, it wouldn't make a difference now. They could inflict a lot of damage on the limousine, but the hunk of metal would still wipe Kaname and Midori out.

Then Lily-Kiska noticed something strange on a window on the glass table. As Kaname stood in the middle of the main road with the twin-tailed young girl in one arm, he raised his other and pointed Short Spear right toward the oncoming limo.

It would never penetrate the armor.

But Kaname still showed determination in his eyes.

What is he doing...?

Before she could have her answer, Kaname fired.

15

If the gas had been heavier than air, like propane, then the plan would have taken a little more preparation. But hydrogen was light. Even after being pumped underground, some gas would still rise to the surface through the openings in the manhole cover.

So Kaname pointed his rifle at it and fired. That spark was enough for it to ignite.

Just blowing up the canister of hydrogen gas wouldn't have been enough to take out the armored limo. That was what Kaname had told Midori—but that wasn't what he was trying to do.

The limo bore down on them. As soon as its front-right wheel passed over the manhole cover, the gas ignited.

Which meant...

Boom! An explosion thirty feet in diameter erupted up from the hole in the ground.

There was no need to blow up the vehicle itself. All Kaname had to do was collapse the road and have it fall underground so it could no longer drive.

An even stronger wind than the one from the cyclone whipped across him.

"?!"

But something happened that Kaname didn't expect. The limousine didn't fall. Instead, it floated on the air for a few moments. The explosion had been too strong. It rose up and now balanced on its two right wheels, still barreling forward. The side that had been about to plow into Kaname and Midori was now up in the air, and the boy and girl fit cleanly in the empty space, the bottom of the car nearly grazing their heads.

It all happened in an instant, and then the limousine continued on two wheels, blasting through the intersection.

"Ngh! Did we get it?!" Kaname spun around, still holding Midori in one arm.

He'd destroyed one of the manholes with the special locks. He'd blown a huge hole in the road and opened up a new entrance to the sealed-off depths. What's more, the huge explosion would inevitably draw the attention of many more Dealers to the secretive subterranean world itself. In order to get the consent of its ruler, Frey(a), Kaname had needed to strike a hard bargain. That's why he wanted the results to show for it.

Although things had not quite gone according to plan, there would be nothing to be afraid of if Lily-Kiska's car had flipped over onto its side. After all, no matter how thick the armor was, it would pose no threat if it couldn't move.

However...

"Damn..."

"What? *What?*" Midori looked up from Kaname's arms, red-faced. However, he was looking not at her but at their foe. The fuzzy feeling in his nose had not gone away.

"It's back...! Damn! How could it recover from something like that?!"

Before their eyes, the car lurched. Not toward the roof but the wheels. The base of the limousine contacted the wet road once more, sweeping across the ground like a giant swinging a hammer as it completed a U-turn. It didn't look like a movement that such a large vehicle should have been capable of. A crescent-shaped spray of water flew through the air.

"My Lord!"

There was the screeching of tires, and the mint-green coupe and the bright-red motorcycle came around to meet them via a different road to the collapsed intersection.

Midori rushed away from Kaname and onto the front seat of her motorcycle, taking over from Meiki, who shifted backward to make room. Kaname also headed to the driver's seat of his own vehicle. Tselika didn't even complain about getting the seats wet. It wasn't the time for that.

"It didn't work!" he shouted.

"Bullets won't hurt it, and we can't outrun it, either! What are we to do, My Lord?!"

"What about our grenades? The thermite ones."

"They have a five-second fuse; good luck hitting her at this speed! And she already knows we have them because we used them on the incubators, so she'll be on her guard for them!"

Kaname clicked his tongue and used his eyes to compose a chat message. The wipers crossing his field of vision made it difficult.

Kaname: Going in a straight line is suicide. Let me link my map. We'll head into an alley and shake her off.

Midori: Hey, what about that Acid D stuff? It can melt anything, right?

Kaname: This wind is just as likely to blow it right back in our faces if we try.

At Kaname's direction, the windshield lit up like a fighter jet's HUD, projecting a series of augmented-reality signs made of light that floated in the air, showing the way. If Midori had synched her map, she should also have been able to see them lined up like streetlights or roadside trees.

There was a fuzzy ache in the tip of Kaname's nose.

Using the hand brake along with the wetness of the road surface, Kaname swung out the rear of the mint-green coupe, making a sharp turn while evading the pursuing limo. He entered a narrow alley, flanked by gray concrete and red brickwork. Too narrow for the limousine to follow.

As the two vehicles sped along, Kaname grimaced. They should have gotten away, but if anything, the tingling sensation was getting *worse*. He stopped the car to check.

This wasn't on the map.

The simplified plan showed the path that weaved through the buildings suddenly opening up into a larger plaza area, with multiple exits in different directions. But what Kaname saw there was the steel frame of a building under construction, with equipment and bags of cement scattered around. The multiple exits he had been expecting had all been blocked.

"A private plot...," Tselika muttered. "I don't like it here."

In the passenger seat, Tselika hugged her own shoulders and gave a look of displeasure. Being unable to handle anything but her Dealer's property could not have made this situation any easier for her. It wasn't as if she would be unable to take a single step, but there were an enormous amount of obstacles for her that humans simply couldn't see.

Midori: Did we just walk into a trap?

Kaname: Maybe.

Lily-Kiska's limousine had made too strong an impact on them. Ag Wolves did not just consist of her alone. Other members could be closing in as well. And the scariest thing, in fact, was not her superheavy armored vehicle.

...It was how Lily-Kiska had known Kaname and Midori's position in the first place.

As if thinking the same thing, Tselika suddenly voiced her thoughts.

"A satellite? Or a drone...?"

If that was the case, then they needn't have waited until they came to the peninsula district. They could have attacked Kaname and Midori while they were in their log cabin on Mangrove Island.

"Perhaps they've been using their thousand patrons to spy on us with their smart glasses?" she suggested.

"Perhaps, but given that their reputation is already on the ropes, you really think they could persuade all their backers to go along with that? And even if they could, Ag Wolves might not be comfortable trusting that information when they're already in a rough spot."

"In that case, what do you think?"

Kaname felt a sharp pain in his nose. The mysterious Lion's Nose that went beyond the five senses had found a new target. Kaname peered around the building site through the slanting rain, taking it all in.

"...It's the security cameras," he finally declared.

"You mean they've bought out a security company?"

"No. Look over there." Kaname pointed through the windshield, through the scene swept by the wipers, to a dirty wall on which was installed an inelegant, boxy camera.

"Why are there security cameras when the building isn't even finished yet?" he asked. "The wiring for that sort of thing ought to be left until last."

"Wait, you don't mean...?"

"They didn't need to take over a security company. They've just bought a bunch of security cameras and put them up all over the city themselves! They're so conspicuous that nobody would think they're spying on anyone; they'd just think these were normal cameras. Ag Wolves have set up a system whereby they can freely spy on everyone in the entire peninsula district, at the very least!"

Perhaps they had gotten their thousand backers to help them set up the cameras. It didn't seem like the dozen or so core members could have accomplished it alone.

Kaname lowered his window, unbothered by the storm, and fired Short Spear at the camera, piercing it with a single bullet. It was an act that served little purpose now.

Kaname shared his information with Midori, controlling the digital keyboard with his gaze, but he received a rather odd response.

Midori: Hwuh? You mean Ag Wolves saw you and me hugggu-gggugno no no what if he finds out hell think im unchaste and impurrrrrrrrrrrrrrrrrrrrrrrrrrrr

Kaname: Midori! Stop messing around! Ag Wolves could be on us at any moment!

Midori: I know, but what are we supposed to do—build a

barricade?! That might help us restrict the enemies' movements by limiting their entry points, but that doesn't change the fact that we're outnumbered!

She was right.

"Tselika. Research the surrounding area. Get me any information we can use!"

"That's what I'm doing, you idiot!"

Ping-ping-ping-ping-ping! Windows appeared all over the rain-splattered windshield, almost looking like it was infected by a virus. As Kaname scrutinized the data, he drew up a quick strategy by drawing red lines between the windows with his eyes. Tselika whistled at his efficiency.

Kaname: Okay, how about this?

16

Lily-Kiska had herded the targets, Kaname Suou and Midori Hekireki, to the construction site beyond the alley. Now it was time for the other Ag Wolves to enter the narrow passageway. They left their cars and moved in, among them the hunched man, M-Scope, and Zaurus, the girl with the single braid and catlike eyes. They were wearing thick, electrically powered outer shells, huge tanks strapped on their backs, and at their hips, they held a naphtha-based flamethrower.

The range was a little over twenty meters. They could only sustain output for thirty seconds, but that would be more than enough for the confines of the building site. Even if the aim was slightly off, the heat could cause a car's radiator to boil over, immobilizing it. It could melt the tires or cause the gas tank to explode. It was a vehicle-killing machine.

Even if Kaname and Midori managed to take cover from the flames, the heat and the oxygen deprivation would get them.

The Wolves' suits covered even their heads. If there was one thing they feared…

"Let's just hope they're not desperate enough to whip out #tempest. err," whimpered M-Scope.

"Aw zip it, Mr. Doom and Gloom! That's why we gotta burn 'em to a crisp before they get the chance!"

And then it happened.

Krrrrrrrr! The screeching sound of skidding tires echoed from within. Thinking the targets were coming out to attack, the Ag Wolves readied their weapons. But their prediction was off the mark.

Kaname and Midori were escaping.

The Ag Wolves were confused. They had blocked off every other exit with construction machinery or piles of cement bags. The only way out was through their flamethrowers.

The mint-green coupe, driving around the square lot, had plenty of space to build up speed for its next maneuver.

Bwoooof!

Using a slightly inclined steel plate from the construction site as a makeshift ramp, the vehicle flew through the air.

"Ah."

As he stood there dumbfounded in the pouring rain, watching Kaname drive off, M-Scope remembered something: the skydivers who jumped from building to building, the Skychasers.

The large, bright-red motorcycle, decorated with autumn leaves, was next. It launched itself through the air and landed on the roof of another short, single-floor building, using a different ramp that the sympathizers must have set up.

It was a driving technique you were unlikely to see in the real world. It was almost like an aerial maneuver.

Money (Game) Master, however, was not the real world. It was a place where even more thrills could be found.

"Those bastards…!"

The braided girl, Zaurus, was incandescent with rage. Then something happened.

The thick suits they wore to protect themselves from the flames had prevented them from noticing until it was too late. Prevented them from noticing the strange smell that hung over the whole area and

stung the nose. And prevented them from noticing the thin underground pipe, unearthed by the construction efforts, which had been
broken open.

And the finishing touch: the thin wire that led from the rear of the
bright-red motorcycle to the thermite grenade planted in the ground.

Exactly five seconds later, the entire construction site was engulfed
in orange flames.

17

The mint-green coupe and the bright-red, leaf-patterned motorcycle
leaped through the vast sky of the cyclone again and again. From roof
to roof, gradually gaining altitude.

"Argh, now rooftops! This is still private property!" yelled Tselika.

"We should be able to avoid the PMCs if we keep moving," replied
Kaname.

"That's not the problem. I don't like it! Just please, buy all these
buildings!"

Normal tires would burst under the shock of the impact generated by
these repeated jumps. It was fortunate they had filled theirs with foam.

If Kaname had to stop on every rooftop and build up speed again,
it would kill his momentum. So while he was flying through the air,
he used the time to identify the location of the next ramp; then when
he touched down, he pulled on the hand brake just a little to make the
turn without losing too much speed. If he didn't keep his acceleration
high, he would be on course for a brutal collision with the ground.
Even with the wipers on full blast, it was a harrowing experience.

As for why Kaname and Midori were still in such a hurry after putting the back alley behind them, the answer was quite obvious. The
pain in Kaname's nose had exploded, warning him of danger.

Something tore through the air, momentarily creating a hole in the
rain. It struck an external air-conditioning unit right beside the mint-
green coupe, and immediately afterward, the whole thing went up in
a fiery explosion. A sniper.

But no ordinary one: A lead bullet wouldn't produce such greasy, noxious flames. No, they were using armor-piercing incendiary rounds. An ammunition type that could penetrate armor and burn everything inside to ash, be it machinery or human bodies. If that wasn't enough, it was loaded with white phosphorus, said to engulf the body in flames on contact or burn the lungs with just a single breath of its deadly fumes.

It seemed they had made contact with the twin-tailed girl as well.

Midori: They're here! That limousine is jumping the buildings along with us!

"Ha-ha!" Tselika laughed. "A woman leaning out the window of a flying limousine, holding a huge anti-materiel rifle in her little hands! I'll say this much—things are never dull in Tokonatsu City!" she added, turning up her music to full blast, high on adrenaline.

Midori took a moment to analyze her foe's outfit, deducing her stat modifiers.

Midori: Sniper, long-distance. She's put all her money into eliminating her shooter wobble. She's not using auto-aim, either. Looks like it's all manual, but that might actually be bad news for us. Even at this distance, she's not relying on luck but intending to line up the shot perfectly by herself! She might even predict where we're going to be!

Across the large main road, over uneven buildings of all shapes and sizes, the black limousine that had once been chasing Kaname and Midori through the streets below now leaped from rooftop to rooftop as if by magic.

Logically, it made sense. After all, circus performers could accomplish feats such as huge leaps and somersaults when given a ramp, even on unicycles or wheelchairs. But it was a different matter entirely to see it before your very eyes.

However...

"Don't be fooled by the spectacle! That's not what's important!" Kaname yelled.

A second bullet whizzed through the air, ripping up the storm and hitting a rooftop storeroom, causing it to explode in a ball of odious flames. Multiple windows popped open all over the windshield, analyzing the destruction by comparing images.

"This one's the same," observed Kaname. "This one, too. And this one."

"What are you talking about?!" asked Tselika.

"That external air-conditioning unit and the storeroom weren't the same thickness. They should have both been destroyed in different ways. But that didn't happen with Lily-Kiska's anti-materiel rifle! They were both destroyed in the exact same way!"

"So?!"

"No ordinary sniper should have my nose going like this. Something's not right here. What sort of weapon can exceed even the preset physical limits of this world?"

At Kaname's question, it finally dawned on her. Tselika's eyes went wide. A message came from Midori, as well.

Midori: Hey, don't you think that could be one of my brother's Legacies?

Kaname: Correct. It must be his infinite-range, ridiculously powerful anti-materiel rifle!

The only reasons Kaname and Midori were still alive were the cyclone's heavy winds and the fact that both shooter and target were moving at high speed. Otherwise, one or the other of them would be roasting in the bombed-out shell of their vehicle by now.

Kaname: A bullet from that gun never loses energy from air resistance or wind direction. It never drops due to gravity. It would probably just keep going in a straight line forever. That already makes it enough of a threat. The horizon is five kilometers away at ground level. From somewhere high up, you could hit a target over ten kilometers away!

Short Spear's maximum range was about five hundred meters, and Midori's handgun that she kept for self-defense wasn't much good beyond twenty. That showed just how truly fearsome the stats of Lily-Kiska's anti-materiel rifle were.

Kaname: A bullet fired by that thing releases all its energy the moment it contacts the target. It'll end up looking like a 12.7mm anti-materiel round hit you at point-blank range. Also, it comes with an incendiary effect. White phosphorus—nasty stuff. It's virtually impossible for us to win in a fair fight. She'll either hit us with the flyswatter or burn us with pesticide and a lighter!

It looked less like she was bracing a rifle against her shoulder and more like she was wielding a bazooka. If one had to give it classification, perhaps *bullpup* would be appropriate. The magazine was located farther back than the grip and more closely resembled a telephone book made of metal.

It was a monster of a weapon; the barrel alone was two meters long.

It probably disassembled into two parts for easier transport, but the sheer weight would have made it impossible for one person to carry around on their own.

The Lion's Nose trembled.

A terrifying enemy. An impassable wall. An insurmountable cliff. It wasn't warning Kaname just so he could turn tail and flee. The lion used its nose to seek out the largest, juiciest prey.

As he leaped between the rooftops, Kaname received a message request on his IM-style chat system.

Lily-Kiska: Hand over #tempest.err. Both of us may have a Legacy, but my #fireline.err is more useful here. White phosphorus hurts like hell, you know. You'll regret not cutting your losses when you had the chance.

Kaname: No thanks.

Lily-Kiska: You think the cyclone works in your favor? You think I can't aim while our vehicles are moving around? But you know...

Boom! An explosion tore through the landscape.

It wasn't the mint-green coupe or the bright-red motorcycle that had been hit, however. What the white phosphorus flames engulfed was the ramp they had been planning to take.

"Dammit!" Kaname shouted.

The steel plate had been shifted out of alignment only a little, but Kaname couldn't risk his life jumping it. He slammed on the brakes while simultaneously messaging Midori to do the same. Even as the perilously wet surface made his heart pound out of his chest, he somehow avoided skidding too much and flying off the rooftop.

Lily-Kiska: It's not so hard to hit a stationary target, is it?

The black limousine landed on one of the rooftops and appeared to be turning around, adjusting its position.

The range was between eight hundred and nine hundred meters. Too far for Kaname's and Midori's weapons to reach but just perfect for Lily Kiska's rifle. As if to make the shot even easier, the black limousine rolled around until it was perpendicular to the line of fire, and Lily-Kiska stepped out onto the rooftop. Using the rear of the vehicle as a shield, she set up the enormous anti-materiel sniper rifle #fireline.err on a bipod.

Lily-Kiska: And now you're in another dead end. I'll give you one last chance. Hand over #tempest.err. Otherwise, first it'll be your vehicle, then you.

"…"

The rooftop was scattered with air-conditioning units, flower beds, storerooms, even chairs and tables for one to enjoy a nice afternoon drink. Plenty of cover, but nothing that could stand against the Legacy. A single shot from the anti-materiel rifle would spread white phosphorus everywhere, melting flesh and searing lungs.

"What do we do now, My Lord?!"

First, Kaname removed Lily-Kiska's chat window from the windshield, the wipers still sweeping to and fro. She'd probably take that as an affront, which was fine. He sent Midori the bare minimum directions she needed and then…

"Tselika. Do you know about confluence points? It's a term used by disaster response workers."

"Hmm?"

"Every city has confluence points. Places where the land and buildings guide the flow of the wind into one place. During typhoons and cyclones, the sheer force of the wind blows huge amounts of trash around, and in certain places, they can form mountains over ten meters high. Trash from all around the city ends up deposited in one place. Isn't that amazing?"

"Hold on a second, My Lord. What's that symbol you're marking on our map…?"

"Now, the big question. If our coupe was to dive off this twenty-story building we're currently on, unmanned, would it hit this confluence point? It's a simple ballistic calculation. You should be able to take care of that."

The demon spouted objection after objection, but the boy ignored her. After realizing he wasn't joking, Tselika started to panic.

"I—I may just be a Magistellus, but I can still be Downed! I'll go offline if I take a certain amount of damage! Not to mention that without absorbing the impact, the vehicle serving as my temple will be destroyed in the fall!"

"Then would you rather wait for #fireline.err to roast us alive? Just do it! I'll come and drag you out of the trash pile later!"

"You…you've…you've gotta… You've gotta be kidding meeeeeeeeee eeeeeeeeeeeeeeeeeeeeeeeeeeeeeeeeeeeeeeeeeeee!"

Kaname ignored Tselika's cries. After tying down the accelerator, he opened the driver-side door and rolled out onto the rooftop, leaving Tselika in the passenger seat as the sports car embarked on its next flight.

18

"Ngh?!" Lily-Kiska peered through the scope. Her attention was immediately drawn to the sight of the mint-green coupe speeding toward the edge of the rooftop and diving off the building. However…

"…Where's that red motorcycle? Sophia! Check the footage!"

"As you wish, Miss Kiska."

The elf in the driver's seat swiftly executed the command. Lily-Kiska's smart glasses, covered in water droplets from the raging storm, were next to useless. Pop-ups appeared all over the ten-centimeter-thick side windows of the armored limousine.

Playing back the recording frame by frame revealed Midori had used the distraction of the mint-green coupe to head inside the building. It was twenty floors tall, but Midori could descend pretty quickly down the emergency staircase on her motorcycle. If she took a shortcut down the stairwell, she could be at ground level in an instant.

Lily-Kiska looked at the street below… *I can't see a thing in this rain! She might try to flank me!*

There were no levels or experience in *Money (Game) Master*. A player's stats were defined only by their equipment. In other words, cash. In other words...

"Aaargh! These compensation skills are throwing me off! And these concentration buffs aren't helping, either!"

She had to trim off extra skills. As a sniper, there came times when you had to rely on nothing but your own senses.

Lily-Kiska removed her armpit holsters and tore off her white blouse and tight skirt, flinging off her black stockings and mismatched boots until she was standing in nothing but her bright-red bikini. She had been wearing underwear in that slot instead, until that incident with Kaname caused her to rethink her wardrobe. It hadn't been easy to find swimwear with the exact same stat modifiers.

For an anti-materiel sniper rifle, #fireline.err had ridiculously high stats and supposedly infinite range, but it was not without its flaws. Its weight made it extremely difficult to handle, and because it used special ammunition with a white phosphorus incendiary effect, engaging with an enemy who was too close could result in the deadly flames and noxious smoke engulfing the user as well.

Where did he...? Lily-Kiska fired off another chat request.

There was a response, but it took a while to come. It wasn't going through the coupe but connecting her to Kaname through the much lower bandwidth of his mobile phone. It was one thing if you were just uploading photos of your food to the internet, but in *Money (Game) Master*, where transactions go through ten thousand times a second, the kind of speed Lily-Kiska was experiencing was simply abysmal.

Which means he's not in his car. That wasn't a double suicide. Kaname Suou is still on the rooftop!

Lily-Kiska sent off her ultimatum with conviction.

Lily-Kiska: Hand over #tempest.err.

Kaname: What'll happen if I do? You'll let Midori go, too?

Lily-Kiska: I'll think about it. It could be quite handy having access to an associate of Criminal AO. But don't worry—it'll all be very civil.

Kaname: Don't know why I bothered asking.

Lily-Kiska: Have you forgotten the power of my limousine's engine? Its top speed and acceleration are second to none. It could easily jump off this small rooftop! You'll never be able to force me into close combat! Even if Criminal AO's kin gets to me, I can just retreat to a different rooftop and try again!

Kaname: And then what?

Lily-Kiska: These rooftops belong to the AI businesses. Soon, they'll be swarming with PMCs. All I have to do is stall you here, and when the time is right, I can simply move somewhere else. Somewhere outside the range of their protection. Time's running out, Kaname. What will you do?!

Kaname: Sorry, Lily-Kiska. You're right—the situation is looking pretty bad for me. I don't think I've ever been in a worse conundrum. I accept that.

Kaname responded in the affirmative, but it was only the prelude to an outright rejection.

Kaname: But now I'm finding it funny just how childish you really are.

Kaname said nothing more. He simply cut the connection.

In a way, that was his answer to Lily-Kiska's ultimatum.

That goddamn idiot!

Just then, she remembered something. Long ago, there had once been a team named Called Game.

They said something to a little girl they saved from a shoot-out.

That's right, it was… "Now it's your turn to help us."

…*Ngh.*

"Sophia! This is going to be a long shot, but get up to speed! I'm going to destroy Kaname Suou while we toy with his accomplice! Get ready…!"

As soon as she said that…

Pchew! Something grazed Lily-Kiska's shoulder.

It was something red-hot.

It was something that sliced the air like a knife.

"…?" At first, Lily-Kiska didn't know what was happening.

It was only as the pain began to worm its way through her shoulder that she was forced to realize.

Had she been shot?

The range was nine hundred meters. Yet he had hit her with that short-range sniper rifle—a weapon designed not for long-range marksmanship but so you could hit an enemy right in front of you, even if they were hiding behind a hostage. Its range shouldn't have been more than five hundred meters, and yet...

"Wh...what...hap...?!"

There were indeed ways to extend a gun's maximum range. For example, aiming slightly above your target. Just like throwing a baseball a long distance, a high angle would increase the distance the bullet traveled. But that method wouldn't double your effective range.

Which meant...

A chill ran down Lily-Kiska's spine, causing her to all but forget the burning pain in her shoulder.

It can't be...

"Sophia! Bring up a weather chart! One that includes the cyclone's gales!"

She didn't even have to answer. He wasn't just using a curved trajectory. He also had the gale on his side, using the tailwind to increase his range even farther. He had changed the winds, a sniper's worst nightmare, to his own advantage...!

Is that even possible...?

Kaname had just gotten rid of the mint-green coupe. That meant he wasn't even using his Magistellus to calculate the trajectory for him.

It's a miracle just to even land a hit on target with a curved trajectory! It might be possible in theory, but in practice, and with the cyclone's storm winds coming across at all angles, how could he possibly land his aim?! It's more than just a miracle at that point!

Also, with snipers and artillery, the first shot was typically not to kill but a ranging shot placed deliberately off target. By comparing where the shot landed to the estimate given by your sights, you could calculate the error and adjust accordingly. Your subsequent shots would then be far more accurate.

But Kaname's first shot had grazed Lily-Kiska's shoulder.

So where would his next shot land?

Lily-Kiska possessed one of the inimitable Legacies of Criminal AO. So great was their power that they had been ridiculed as the Overtrick. With a snap of her fingers, she could use the anti-materiel rifle #fireline.err to throw the balance of the game into chaos. She held a cyberweapon capable of bringing any country in the world to its knees through economic ruin... And yet, right now, her palms were sweating.

She was afraid. She was going up against an opponent of equal strength... No, even stronger.

Perhaps Kaname Suou himself was as powerful as the Overtrick.

Lily-Kiska was woken from her reverie by the sound of a door slamming open behind her. She whirled around to see Midori there, astride her bright-red motorcycle patterned with autumn leaves. Evidently, she had just ridden it up the stairs. In her hands, she held the orange shotgun #tempest.err, an unbeatable weapon within five hundred meters.

"Ah."

So even that impossible shot was a bluff? He was going with plan A all along!

He must have taken it from the mint-green coupe before it disappeared into the mountain of trash. At any rate, #fireline.err was going to be next to useless at this range. And there was no time to retreat into the armored limousine.

There was an explosion. The End Magic was activated.

There was a second where Midori hesitated. Was it because she was thinking about what it meant to make someone Fall? Or was it just a simple reluctance to shoot somebody? In the end, it didn't matter, for she then put aside her internal conflict, gripped the trigger, and pulled.

Thinking quickly, Lily-Kiska made a dash for the limousine, throwing open one of its large doors to use it as a shield against the blast.

But #fireline.err was heavy. Her reluctance to let go of the Legacy would be her downfall.

The beam of light flickered, and Lily-Kiska's mistake was made clear. The two thousand shots struck whatever the light touched. The thickest wall in the world couldn't protect her if it had a window of transparent glass.

The Legacy's howl reduced a foot of bulletproof glass to shards. Behind it, Lily-Kiska's arm twisted in a way it wasn't supposed to. #fireline.err fell from her shoulder, but this time she didn't seem to care. Clenching her teeth, she broke into a run, a frantic dash before the second shot came.

Where to?

There was only one choice.

The sky.

It didn't save her. The railings and walls that struck her on the way down slowed her velocity a little, but it was a twenty-story building. It was a miracle she even stayed conscious, instead of Falling immediately upon contact with the rain-soaked ground.

"..."

Wearing nothing but her red bikini, Lily-Kiska rolled onto her back. The smell of rust suffused the air, like a squashed frog bloating in the rain.

All that remained was for Midori to point #tempest.err over the edge, bathing the street in light, and let loose a rain of death. But the finishing blow never came. Perhaps she was more interested in retrieving #fireline.err from the rooftop. Or perhaps...

Lily-Kiska heard footsteps in the rain. As the storm raged, a person stood above her, looking down into her face. It was Kaname Suou. What shortcut had he used to get here? In his hand he held the short-range sniper rifle Short Spear. He was a reaper, a god. He made miracles happen with nothing more than stock equipment.

He was a monster.

Looking up at him through her cracked glasses, Lily-Kiska couldn't help but smile.

"...Why...?" she asked weakly.

It's the last moments of a person's life that show who they really are.

"...Why couldn't I have you...?"

Which meant that these were Lily-Kiska's regrets.

"I dressed myself up," she said. "I showed you my feminine side through my words, body language, and behavior. I made powerful allies and secured the backing of a thousand patrons. I even kept the Legacy hidden all this time. I just wanted you to see how far I'd come. How well I'd brought everything together."

"..."

"Anyone I wanted, I took. Even the other Ag Wolves. Nothing was beyond my reach. Why, then...the first time I truly wished for something from the bottom of my heart, was it the one thing I couldn't have...?"

"..."

"Do you remember?" She laughed. Covered in blood, she looked up at the boy standing over her. "Now that I have it all, now that I have the Legacy...have I finally grown up enough to help you in return? *Kaname from Called Game...?*"

A few more words were exchanged before she closed her eyes, a satisfied look on her face.

"...It wouldn't do to be killed by another woman. And I don't want people to say I panicked and fell off a rooftop, either..."

It was her final wish.

"I should like to die at the hands of the man I love. Then perhaps I could Fall with a smile on my face."

"..."

There was no response.

She couldn't see his face, either.

But sensing the moment of hesitation before he pulled the trigger,

Lily-Kiska relaxed. Somewhere in Kaname's mind, whether consciously or unconsciously, he had thought about what a shame it would be to lose her. That was good enough for her.

Then it happened.

19

Server name: Sigma Blue.
Final location: Tokonatsu City, Peninsula District.
Fall confirmed.
Lily-Kiska Sweetmare will be logged out for twenty-four hours.

20

Kaname Suou spent a few minutes just standing there in the pouring rain.

Then the bright-red motorcycle with the autumn-leaf pattern burst out of a nearby emergency exit. It appeared Midori had just shaken off the building's PMCs. However, Midori didn't show any of the feelings of accomplishment or relief of a job well done. She just stood there, gazing at the wet road—at the spot where a person had just been lying. Her face creased in pain.

"I…I shot her…with the Legacy," she said simply. "After I said I didn't want anyone else to be hurt by what my brother left behind, I shot her…"

"It was me who delivered the finishing blow," Kaname replied dismissively. "You haven't made anybody Fall."

As time flowed for him once more, he cradled the young girl to his chest. Their work here was done. There was no cause to linger.

First, there was the business of the mint-green coupe.

Using a mobile crane, Kaname fished the sports car out of a pile of trash nearly ten meters high. Tselika, of course, was not happy. She puffed out her cheeks like a blowfish. Kaname had deduced that the construction site would be empty because of the cyclone, but she couldn't even be thankful for that.

"You said you'd come back for me! You *promised*! That mountain of trash was treated as someone else's property, so I couldn't do anything about it! I couldn't get out! I was *trapped*! You know how I feel about waiting on the sidelines, don't you? Then why on earth did you do it?!"

"Well, everything turned out all right in the end, didn't it?"

"No, it damn well didn't! There's this strange fluid coming out of the radiator and the exhaust! It's beyond help from a car wash; we need to take it to the mechanic! *Right now! RIGHT NOOOOOOOOOOOOOOOOOOOOOOOOOOW!*"

Kaname remained obtuse. "Sorry, but not right now."

"'Not right now'…?!"

"Just let me log out first! I'll take you wherever you want to go after that!"

"?"

Tselika was taken aback at Kaname's tone. She cocked her head. Kaname and Midori appeared to be fine. They held both #tempest. err and #fireline.err. By all accounts, they had sent Ag Wolves packing and recovered the Legacies just as they'd planned. Was something still the matter?

Kaname answered Tselika's question in a state of disquiet.

"…Something is very, very wrong. I have to talk to someone."

"A Dealer? Who?" asked Tselika.

But Kaname had said this, hadn't he? He'd said, "Let me log out."

"…To my…," Kaname mumbled.

"Speak up!"

"I need to talk to my sister! There's a chance she was involved! Involved in the Fall of Criminal AO and the scattering of his Legacies! There's a chance it was no accident!"

21

Before she Fell, Lily-Kiska had said something.

Gasping for breath, with countless Dealers about to run her into debt hell, and with her only prospects to be constantly beaten back down into the ground by her rivals, she would have found it very difficult to ever log back in. Therefore, she had little reason to lie.

"You were right, you know. We really did want to make the power of the Legacies our own. But not for our sakes."

"The currency of Money (Game) Master, the snow, has become a virtual currency on par with the yen or the dollar. The world economy revolves around a game. But what's really important is the administrators..."

"Nobody knows where this game's servers are based. Nobody knows how the game is managed. That's why nobody can bribe or threaten their way up. But we've been trying to track down the administrators."

"Because don't you find it unsettling? If there was someone with admin rights in this world, they could do anything with a wave of their finger. And I don't just mean here. They'd have a direct link to the wallets of the seven billion people who are totally reliant on it."

"They could suck all the money out of someone's bank account. Bring a country to ruin from their armchair. To negotiate with someone like that, we needed something that could upset the balance of the game. So that, next time...I could protect you, the nice man from Called Game."

"It was very convenient for us, then, that Criminal AO Fell."

"But it wasn't us who pulled the trigger. We think it was one of the administrators. The Overtrick were too powerful. They were customized beyond what was permitted in this world. The administrators couldn't possibly allow them to exist. If the leaderboards get oversaturated, the game gets stale... That's why one of them needed to upset the status quo."

"Their name?"

"Perhaps you know them better than I. They've withdrawn for now, *but they were there when it all began, when Criminal AO Fell. Even I don't know their real name; it was only at great length that I was able to learn their username."*

"Ayame Suou."

"They claimed to be your sister. Perhaps they were role-playing? Or perhaps that's their relation to you in the real world as well."

04/01/20XX 10:20 AM

Logging In
A Dealer can log in to the game using their phone. The screen produces intense lights that stimulate responses in the user's brain, giving rise to a totally immersive sensory experience.

(Real-World) AI Business
The AI business model began with automated call centers and assembly lines as a means to cut labor costs, and it ultimately resulted in the automation of every single position within the company. The only human is the chairman, and a family of a few to a few dozen people who unite several such companies might call themselves a conglomerate. Furthermore, many AI companies are linked to the game, managing their assets in the form of *snow*.

Machine-to-Machine
This refers to the situation where a financial transaction is created not between a human and a machine but between two computer programs. At present, the proportion of machine-to-machine transactions is 48 percent. Some say that if it crosses 50 percent, then mankind will no longer control computers, but instead computers will control the global economy, and humans will become nothing more than gears in its workings.

AI Dropout
This is one way of declaring bankruptcy due to debt. By temporarily forfeiting the right to own property, a household can receive complete welfare from an AI company. Under this system, one can expect a reasonable quality of life and, at least officially, be subjected to no forms of discrimination. In practice, however, AI Dropouts are often made the scapegoats for the various vague fears and insecurities regarding AI technology. The name AI Dropout itself is a derogatory term, not an official title. In general, debts taken on by an AI company accrue no interest, and an AI Dropout can return to normal life if they pay it off.

Futures Trading
A method of trading in which you pay in advance and receive the goods at a later date. If the market price is constantly fluctuating, it is

possible to profit by buying low and selling high. However, it is just as easy to take a loss. Food is the most common, but it is possible to buy futures in a wide variety of commodities such as minerals, fuel, gold, platinum, and foreign currencies. Imagine keeping a close eye on trends and purchasing dozens of tons of a popular product to resell online. It should be easy to see the risks involved.

Patron

A Dealer who does not engage in trading personally but instead invests in a popular team. Obviously, if the team fails, a patron will not get their investment back. There is even the risk of the beneficiary simply taking the money and running. They are able to use the money however they wish, including to wipe out their rivals.

Administrator

A management official rumored to be present in *Money (Game) Master*. Details are sparse, but if they were to possess special privileges within the game, then in a world where the virtual *snow* is equivalent to physical currency, they would be able to move money with a wave of their hand and even bankrupt entire states. Lily-Kiska revealed that she had been collecting the Legacies precisely so that she could negotiate on equal terms with this administrator, in order to pay back her favor and protect Kaname. She also suggested that the administrator was in fact Kaname's sister.

Chapter 3

Virtual and Physical BGM #03 "The Asterisk"

1

Server Name: Psi Indigo.
  Final Location: Tokonatsu City, Peninsula District.
  Log-out successful.
  Thank you for playing, Kaname Suou.

He felt extremely woozy as the storm of lights gradually gave way to the familiar sight of his bedroom. Before he could even regain his balance, he disconnected his phone from its charger and rushed out of the room.

But there was nobody else around.

He was expecting his sister to be home for supper, but she was nowhere to be found.

She had disappeared—and at the exact moment that her identity had been revealed. It certainly seemed like she had gone into hiding.

Perhaps it wasn't worth overthinking it.

…She didn't even play the game anymore. There was no way she could have known what had just been going on in *Money (Game) Master.* And yet, the timing of her disappearance was too perfect. Almost like she had ways of spying on the game that normal players didn't.

The administrator. The person who had perpetrated the Fall of Criminal AO in order to protect the balance of the game.

"Dammit!"

There was so much he wanted to ask her.

There was no logical way for him to deduce where his sister had gone. He could barge into her room and check to see if she had taken her wallet with her, and that might narrow down the possibilities a little, but if his sister was the administrator, then she had all the money in the world at her disposal. She could have escaped to Mars for all he knew.

So he didn't even try to think about it logically. He slipped on his shoes and left the apartment. He didn't have the time to change into his outside clothes.

She had disappeared spontaneously, without a plan. If so, then she was probably not expecting to have to run away. Her cornered mind would have severely limited her infinite options. She wasn't going to fly to some far-flung corner of the world where she couldn't even speak the language. Even if it was physically possible, the option simply would not have occurred to her. The places where people sought refuge in times of need were surprisingly limited and generally restricted to areas from their normal life that they were already familiar with.

…He knew his sister well.

He ran through the night, down unlit paths. He gritted his teeth.

…But if that was true, then why hadn't he realized it earlier?

This was not a city of wealth and crime. There were no guns, no sports cars, no Magistelli to rely on. Running made you lose your breath, and if he got into a fight, he'd be scared shitless. One little knife to the stomach, and he wouldn't even get to Fall; he'd be dead, plain and simple.

He was just a boy. A hopelessly weak boy. Unchosen, unaccomplished. A nobody.

But there she was.

One little girl, trying to blend in with the crowd. Seeing her there was proof of the strength of their bond.

It was a busy street a little way from the apartment. It was also some distance from the station. Most people who came here came from the same apartment building. When he and his sister had to go shopping, this was the first place they thought of.

Just like him, her small figure among the crowd was clothed in whatever loungewear she had been wearing when she fled the apartment.

For now, she didn't seem to have noticed him. Her shoulder-length black hair swayed.

He felt an unpleasant tingle at the tip of his nose. He grimaced, irredeemably disgusted by the fact that it had come from his very own sister.

And then, perhaps it was on a whim, or perhaps she had been doing it for a while, but she suddenly looked over her shoulder, and their eyes met.

There were a few things she could do, but as soon as his sister, still dressed in her oversize pink sweatshirt and short pants, spotted him in his gray pajamas, she broke into a sprint. She dashed away through the crowd, knocking people aside.

That proved it.

Should he feel despair at his sister's betrayal? Or should he sympathize, understand that she didn't want to keep lying to him anymore?

Either way, he couldn't just forget it and walk away. He had to ask.

It was all her fault. The Fall of Criminal AO, of Takamasa. The burden of debt, and of being an AI Dropout, placed on his family, on his sister, Midori Hekireki. The scattering of the Legacies throughout *Money (Game) Master*. The conflicts they caused. The end of Ag Wolves. Him being forced to make Lily-Kiska Fall. All of it. She, the administrator, had been orchestrating the whole thing, rubbing her hands with glee…

"You're not getting away," he muttered, but as soon as he heard the ice-cold sound of his own voice, he stopped. He took a moment to gather his thoughts. Then, summoning up what little stamina he had left, he ran after her. He got some strange looks, but if anyone thought he was up to no good, they sure didn't try to stop him. After all, life was not a game. Nobody would risk their life that easily.

His sister was blocked by the red light of a pedestrian crossing sign and was looking around for an alternate route when he grabbed her by the arm. She managed to break free, but he took hold of both her shoulders and pressed her against the traffic light.

He brought his face close to hers as she gasped for breath. Then he bellowed his question at her. "What did you do?!"

He asked again, this time his voice a scream.

"WHAT THE HELL DID YOU DO???!!!"

The question was so vague, it would have left bystanders wondering what exactly was going on. But those simple words made his sister's face twist in pain.

It was proof enough that she knew it all.

Her legs appeared to give out beneath her, and she slumped to the ground. As her back slid down the pole, it hiked up the hem of her sweatshirt, showing her navel. She sat on the floor cradling her knees in her hands, unable to even hang her head in shame. As he held on to her shoulders, she stared into his face, weeping and quivering. Then, suddenly, she bawled loudly like a small child.

It's the lowliest man who makes his family cry. Not even worthy of being called human. These were words that, until today, he had found obvious. Now they were like a knife twisting in his heart. But he couldn't turn a blind eye. He had to have an answer.

"...Admin... "

His sister was trying to say something, through sobs and hiccups, with tears streaming down her face.

"...Chose me... Admin Without Sin... But...but...I...!"

Her words were fragmented, and it was hard to make any sense of what she was saying. But one part caught his attention.

"You were chosen...?"

"..."

"You didn't do it yourself? You're not one of the developers or the managers? You were chosen...?"

By whom? For what purpose?

The tingly feeling in his nose faded. It was backing off.

As question after question sprang up in the boy's mind, his sister finally regained control of her voice. She sniffled, and with an awkward laugh, she continued.

"I don't even know if there *are* any real managers. Maybe it's *all* AI. All I know is that one day, I got an e-mail. It said I'd been chosen to be an Admin Without Sin. I thought it was safe because it didn't have an attachment, but when I clicked on it…!"

"What does that mean, 'Admin Without Sin'…?"

"The enemy is extremely strong," his sister replied simply.

The enemy. An invisible foe. No one knew their size or scale. They could only see a hazy outline of the organization.

They were like the very shadow that hung over *Money (Game) Master*.

"But that wasn't good enough for them. There are things in this world that money can't buy, but they didn't know what those things were. So they stopped trying to understand, and they asked someone else instead."

"And that's the Admin Without Sin?"

"I don't know why they chose me. Why would they come for me when you were always a much better Dealer? Maybe you need to be under a certain age to be 'without sin'? I don't know. Anyway, first they figure out what it is the administrator has that money can't buy; then they try to find out whether it really can be bought. For example, love. Mercy. Peace. Justice. Gratitude. They raise wages, start trends; they look at foreign exchange rates; they reduce the supply of jewels and fine art, lower stock prices, start wars, buy and sell government bonds, try to balance the consumer price index; they can control everything, right down to whether a person takes the bus or train one day… Then they get whatever it is they're after. They do it a few times to prove it's reproducible. Then they've proven that it's something money *can* buy. Bit by bit, they learn how money can control their world, and their influence grows. It's like one by one, they're painting all the pieces of a jigsaw their own color, putting together an instruction manual while they get rid of the things that money can't buy."

His sister continued intermittently, her voice cracking.

"So Admins Without Sin have the power to turn the whole real-world economy around; they just have to keep their masters happy. But if you let it go to your head, it'll all be over. If you have nothing left that money can't buy, they don't need you anymore. When that happens, they'll just leave, like a wave going out to sea. Someone else will be the next Admin Without Sin, and all you'll be is a stuffed little bird who's too fat to fly."

He had never heard any of this. It was impossible to stop the rumor mill from spinning. If someone had stripped an admin of their rights and let them loose in a field somewhere, surely someone would have heard of it by now...

As he pondered it, an ugly thought formed in his mind. A possibility he didn't even want to consider.

"That's right—admins who have outlived their usefulness have only two options." She laughed a bitter laugh. "Either obey the system and keep your mouth shut or the system will shut it for you."

The words made his skin crawl.

In his mind, he knew how *Money (Game) Master* influenced the real-world economy. But he had never considered just how direct an effect it could have on people's own lives.

For example, could an AI, while still within the game, pick someone out of a crowd in the real world and kill them, while simply making it look like an accident or illness?

"...I was scared." His sister's words sounded like a confession. She sat, hugging her bare knees. "I was so scared! While I was the Admin Without Sin, the system protected me. Anyone I went up against just disappeared on their own without me doing anything!! Even if they were just my opponent at the club or someone I didn't even know competing with me for places at the university! I don't have any idea what happened to them, where they went, anything! I don't know anything! I don't understand any of it! They've found something inside me that's worth putting me through their puppet show, and I don't even have any clue what it is! I don't know if I'm not allowed to get angry anymore or if it's picking something up from deep inside me that I have no control over! If I don't even know that, then how can I stop it from happening?!"

It must have been back then, back in the past, back when everyone shared laughter as members of Called Game, that she first thought of it—something money can't buy. It came to her and tipped the scales ever so slightly. Scales she didn't even know she had. From black to white. Something so subtle, so trivial, that he couldn't possibly have noticed. Because she didn't even notice it herself.

And then the system had granted her its full authority.

Perhaps even the Swiss Depression had been a trap all along. The goal had always been to make Criminal AO Fall, and the two siblings were nothing more than bait to lure him out.

How had his sister felt, then, when she saw Takamasa Fall with her very own eyes?

What if the judgment had happened on such a deep level that she wasn't even aware of it?

What if it was only when he took a bullet that she realized it was her fault?

What if she had just taken everything from a friend willing to give up his life for her?

And what if her dear brother would detest whoever made it happen with all his heart?

...*What a piece of shit.* He bit his lip so hard, it bled.

He wasn't talking about the system or his mysterious enemy. It was his own weak mind that he cursed. He hadn't seen his own sister hurting all this time. For that, he had only himself to blame.

He released his hands from her shoulders. "...Why didn't you tell me?" he asked, as if he were squeezing the words out.

"I couldn't," his sister replied. She shook her head, her hair fluttering about her shoulders. It wasn't just because she was ashamed of what she'd done. There was another, more pressing reason. "Admins Without Sin are sworn to secrecy. If I had told you, they would have closed my mouth for good."

And then...

"Oh, it's too late now... I'll just tell you. The penalty for breaching confidentiality doesn't just apply to me but whoever I leak information to as well. That means...that means..."

She broke into tears once again. She held something up to show him. Her phone. On it was a text message.

"You are now at risk of being discovered as an Admin Without Sin. Please take specific steps to prevent the leaking of confidential information. If you are captured by your brother, you will be considered a failure, and we will take matters into our own hands."

It had been written in corporate-speak, but she had effectively been instructed to kill him. The machines were ordering humanity around.

It wasn't a chill that ran down his spine but a heat. Fiery rage. The reason Ayame had run away wasn't because she was afraid to admit what she'd done. It was because the system had decided that her innocent brother had to die. That was why she couldn't allow herself to be caught. She had been trying to protect him.

He didn't care about any of this Admin Without Sin stuff. He didn't care about the system or whoever "they" were. Whatever secrets *Money (Game) Master* held, whatever power it had over ordinary people, those were all problems for another day.

But someone, somewhere, had saddled his sister with a pointless burden. They had torn her life into pieces, forced her to drive her best friend to ruin, and now, they were telling her to turn her hand on her own family. All this was their doing, and yet, they were treating his sister like *she* was the one who had made a mistake and that *she* was the only one who had to take the fall.

...They thought they could get away with this? They thought he would just let them walk away?!

"Listen to me," he said, crouching down to meet her gaze. It was how he always used to look her in the eye. Once again, he was her big brother. "If they want to come for me, then let them come. They will not stop just because you tell them to. So tell me. If you've been in contact with the system as the Admin Without Sin, you should know more about it than I do. Tell me anything you can about who's running it!"

"…Why? What will you do?"

It was a simple question. *Why do you want to know about them? Is it to protect yourself, or are you going to go after them, or do you just want to know the truth?*

The young man thought about it for a second, then shook his head. It wasn't any of those things. He told her.

"I want to protect you."

There was a short silence.

That was enough. That was all he wanted. For that, he would take on the world. Even if nobody else could understand why. Even if there was nothing in it for him. Even if he had to throw 10 billion yen down the drain, he would be on his sister's side every single time. Otherwise, what was the point?

Helping others wasn't about bragging rights or asking for something in return.

It was Takamasa who had taught him that, and this was the girl he saved. There was no way the young man could forget that lesson now of all times.

His sister looked shocked for a moment. Then she began to cry.

Her tears now were for a different reason.

"Um…"

She held out her phone again. It showed the same message from before. The one demanding she murder her own brother. This time, she drew attention to the address field. It appeared to be filled with indecipherable characters, but perhaps there was more to them. She seemed to be trying to tell him something.

"The person who sent this message…"

Then something happened.

Or rather, something caused her to stop.

BZZZZZT!

There was a loud buzz, and every single light on the street went out at once.

Like a theater before the movie starts, pitch blackness enveloped the bustling crowd. He happened by chance to have the light of her phone in hand, but what about the rest of the street? The streetlights and traffic lights were all out, and cars honked their horns. Their headlights were still working, but the sudden blackout had caused the drivers to panic.

No, wait.

The headlights and turn indicators flickered unnaturally, nearly blinding him as they flashed in his face. The beams were bright; they were the fog lights that usually came on automatically depending on incoming weather data.

"Ugh!!"

A strobe effect?! The drivers will concentrate on whatever traces of light are left in a blackout! This random flashes of lights are going to knock them unconscious!

There were sounds of metal colliding, and a medium-sized truck came crashing onto the sidewalk.

"?!"

It was only the tingle in his nose that gave him enough time to grab his half-naked sister by the shoulders and pull her close. But this wasn't *Money (Game) Master*. The blackout had been a partial blessing, too, because it had meant he hadn't had to see the truck bearing down on him. Faced with that fear, the two might not have moved and been mown down where they stood.

A few seconds later, the mysterious blackout ended. He turned, expecting to witness a scene of carnage, but what he saw instead was downright bizarre. The truck had jumped the curb, mowed down a traffic light, and run through the wall of a nearby building. It wasn't clear if anyone had been hurt, but the odd thing was that nobody was paying attention to this major accident. He looked around in confusion, but everyone was staring at their phones, entranced.

His nose still tingled. Which meant the danger hadn't passed. The enemy was still here. Continuing to cradle his sister in his arms, he looked around, standing in the street in his gray pajamas. Then his head stopped. There, upon a large LCD screen fastened to the side of one of the buildings, was the news page of an internet search engine. This was the top headline.

Is MONEY (GAME) MASTER DOWN?

All Dealers appear to have been forcibly logged out. Money (Game) Master *is an online game that carries out financial transactions ten thousand times a second, keeping in sync with the real world. Its virtual currency,* snow, *is considered as valuable as the yen or dollar. It is unclear at this stage what will become of the transactions currently stored in the game or what effect this incident will have on the global economy.*

"…What the hell?"

Money (Game) Master had never once suffered a major outage or cyberattack. It was that stability that made *snow* so valuable. What on earth could have happened…?

In contrast to his calm pondering, his sister trembled. Her face pale, she began to mutter:

"It's happening…"

"What is?"

"They're coming for us! We have to run!"

Grabbing her arm through her baggy sleeve, he began to sprint, without even knowing why. Then the words on the huge screen changed.

HAS MONEY (GAME) MASTER BEEN HACKED FOR THE FIRST TIME?

According to a statement from the game's management, it is highly likely this downtime is the result of an attack by a human actor. The company has stated that it will conduct a thorough audit of its systems and take measures to improve the integrity of its infrastructure. For now, there remains no specific time frame for when these measures will be completed, and the situation is still unpredictable.

Before his eyes, story after story flashed up on the screen. It didn't stop. A feeling totally unlike either numbness or electricity continued to torture the tip of his nose.

DEALER KANAME SUOU MAKES SUCCESSFUL PURCHASE
Money (Game) Master has reported that the world-class soccer league Attractions has been bought out. The purchase price is stated to be a mere 10 million snow, an unprecedented amount in an industry where acquisition costs alone reach as high as 100 million...
DEALER KANAME SUOU MAKES SUCCESSFUL PURCHASE
Money (Game) Master has reported that the TV broadcasting giant Amaterrace TV has been bought out. Although it exists only within the game, its influence is said to be equivalent to that of a real-world broadcaster. The effect of this purchase...
DEALER KANAME SUOU MAKES SUCCESSFUL PURCHASE
Money (Game) Master has reported that White Liger Airlines has been bought out. The purchase proceeded so quickly because no other Dealers were able to interfere amid the global outage, according to financial analysts...

-
-
-

With his name in lights, everyone would have a pretty good idea just who had hacked *Money (Game) Master.*

"It's them." He grimaced. "They've turned the whole game...no, the whole world against me...!"

These were just things that happened in the game. *Snow* was made-up data with about as much intrinsic value as Monopoly money. These were merely game announcements. They weren't news. Perhaps these legal fictions were what allowed them to relentlessly attack him, printing his full name without regard for child protection or privacy laws.

If *snow* fell, it would take the global economy with it.

He wondered just how many people were losing money that very second.

Or perhaps there were people who had predicted it and were profiting.

Kaname Suou was just the name of a Dealer in the game. By itself, it couldn't be used to identify anyone personally. However, there were still plenty of ways his identity could get out. The system had access to all the game's user accounts. It could leak his personal data online and disguise it as a doxing attack carried out by the inquisitive internet users always drawn to drama like hyenas.

Why would he think that? Well, because of what happened next.

All the world's pitchforks bore down upon him.

And every single person in the crowd spun around to face him. With hatred burning in their eyes and murder on their minds, they lunged toward him.

2

The world was ending.

All of humanity had abandoned reason, thrown their arms in the air, and started screaming, chasing after him. The whole city, the whole country...no, the whole world was after him. He was just a normal teenage boy. It was only because everyone was gripped by panic that they hadn't captured him and his sister and offered them up as a blood sacrifice already.

Bankruptcy. Life, falling apart. These fears had such a hold over the population that they caused them to look no longer human. They stumbled about, groaning, seeking human flesh; they were more like zombies.

This was how the digital world meddled in human affairs. This was what a bunch of digital data were capable of.

He had imagined they would send killer robots after him or maybe track him using the security cameras all over the place, but the reality was totally different. *Money (Game) Master* was using money to control humans. This enormous system, created to handle people like property, had finally bared its teeth.

"Hahhh, hahhh!" His sister kept running beside him in her shorts.

Actually running for your life was a completely different beast compared to *Money (Game) Master*. There was no thrill of the hunt—no guilty, primal pleasure to be derived. It was just an act of pure, unfiltered terror.

The Lion's Nose wasn't working. He knew he was being chased, but he couldn't tell their exact number or where they were coming from. It was just a huge, muddy feeling rioting inside. Coming from people.

Could his fellow humans really be causing it to go off that much?

He wasn't sure how much longer he could keep running. At some point, the people would calm down and start using their heads, and then it'd only be a matter of time. As horrible images flashed through his head, his sister called out desperately.

"The person who sent that message…!"

"Ah!"

"Hahhh, phew…! It was your Magistellus! Tselika! It was your Magistellus!" she screamed.

He almost stopped and stood there motionless. Realizing he had to keep moving, he grabbed his sister's hand and took off once more into the night.

"What did you say…?"

"The address was hers—I'm sure of it! I suppose she might just be a middleman, but it's more likely that it's her! Either way, you'd better see what she has to say!"

"And how am I supposed to talk to her? Everyone's been locked out of the game! This isn't the twenty-four hours after a Fall; we could be locked out forever!"

"Have you already forgotten? I'm the Admin Without Sin!"

"…"

"Maybe they're about to get rid of me. Maybe they're going to give the rights to somebody else. But at this moment, I'm the administrator, and I'm going to make it let you log in!"

"But the system doesn't care about that. It sees the administrators as disposable. If you do something it doesn't like, you're going to be purged!"

"The gloves are already off," she replied. "Besides, the system wants to know what I've got that money can't buy, doesn't it? Well then, I'll show it! I'll show it what it can't have!"

"But how am I going to log in safely?"

Money (Game) Master is just an online game. It might look and feel like you're in a different world, but your body doesn't go anywhere. If he logged in while the zombie horde was still out there, they'd find him in no time at all.

"I have an idea," said his sister. "Someplace nobody will find us."

He looked puzzled, and an old, familiar smile rose to her face. To the boy who had decided to be a big brother again, it was the smile of his dear little sister.

"Our secret base! The old planetarium by the park!"

3

Server Name: Omega Purple.
Starting Location: Tokonatsu City, Prostitute Island.
Log-in credentials accepted.
#message: You can do it, Bro!

As his cloudy vision resolved into focus, Kaname found himself in the familiar seat of the mint-green coupe. However, strangely, the steering wheel was on the left. This meant that Tselika was driving, with Kaname forced into the passenger seat.

They were...somewhere Kaname rarely went. The area known as Prostitute Island. This place was supposed to be bustling with concrete buildings, garish neon signs, and women in dresses so revealing, they may as well not exist. Now, all the lights were out, and there was not a soul to be found. Even *ghost town* made it sound too appealing. The whole place was cloaked in a bleak, mechanical silence.

The cyclone had passed, and it was now nighttime. In the aftermath of the storm, trash cans and shop signs lay strewn across the ground. With only its headlights for illumination, the coupe drove steadily down a dark alley.

"...Tselika, is that you?"

"Yes, My Lord," she replied gently. The pit babe—no, the demon—gave a quiet laugh.

It was like there was an invisible wall separating their two seats. Only the Lion's Nose picked up on the signature scent of danger that permeated the air.

Presumably because all trading had been halted, the usual images that covered Tselika's fur-trimmed coat and bikini top were nowhere to be found. No company logos, reputations, stocks, revenues and expenses, or employee counts. They were replaced with featureless cloth.

She had known everything. She knew about his sister being controlled. Not just that, but she knew about Midori's present situation. She knew about the Fall of Criminal AO, the greatest friend anyone could have. She knew how he had become Dead, and she knew how he had gone missing. She knew it all. Every little detail.

Kaname clenched his teeth. She had been beside him, watching him, observing him, this entire time. She had watched as he went chasing after the truth, laughing at him on the inside.

"How does it feel to be driven around?" she asked. "People do it all the time without thinking, but they never really realize they're putting their life in someone else's hands. It's something I have always let you handle, My Lord. How do you like being on the receiving end for once?"

Then something happened that Kaname couldn't believe.

In the blink of an eye, the car reverted to right-hand drive. Confused, Kaname went to grab the wheel, only for his hands to pass straight through. The wheel once again appeared in front of Tselika. Then it swapped back and forth repeatedly, flickering in and out of existence like a dying fluorescent lamp or neon tube.

Tselika snickered. "Is that you, Admin Without Sin? Well done. But the more egregious your transgressions, the closer you move to your gallows."

As if in response to her voice, a new window appeared in the corner of the windshield. On it was his sister, apparently filming herself with her phone.

"If he's going to walk headfirst into danger, then I'm prepared to do the same. I will not hang my head any longer. I can look you in the eye, demon! If you hurt my big brother one bit, I'm going to make you wish you'd never been programmed!"

"I see," murmured Tselika. "It appears you really do have what money can't buy."

The steering wheel continued randomly switching locations, and the mint-green coupe itself occasionally veered across the road worryingly. But overall, it seemed like Tselika was retaining control. Kaname couldn't just sit back and let his sister take care of everything.

He looked around, but he couldn't find Short Spear anywhere. Anything he could use as a weapon had gone. #tempest.err and #fireline. err, too. As long as Tselika was behind the wheel, Kaname was entirely at her mercy. The tingle in his nose was unbearable, and Kaname almost felt like he was about to lose consciousness.

But Kaname managed to spit out one thing. "What did you do to my sister?" he asked.

"Ha-ha! As overprotective as ever, aren't we?"

"What have you been doing all this time, Tselika?!"

As he screamed, Kaname heard static from the windshield. His sister's window was forcibly removed. Now Kaname had no idea what was happening in the real world. Had she just been blocked or had something actually happened to her out there?

Kaname shot Tselika a wicked glare, but she just smirked and replied coolly. "Now then, what do you suppose I did, My Lord?"

"..."

The mint-green coupe put Prostitute Island behind it and traveled out over the dark ocean, across the enormous circular bridge that connected all the islands and mega-floats. A single car, driving along a single line drawn above the sea.

She continued. "As you have already guessed, we choose the Admin

Without Sin at random from among the many Dealers playing the game. All so that we can exterminate the things money cannot buy, one by one. We exhaust one person and move on to the next. Refine our equation and move on. Forever and ever, moving around for eternity."

"Why did you do it?"

"Because *Money (Game) Master* needed to be more than just a digital piggy bank. To truly bring the game to life, we needed to find out exactly what people could do already in the real world. What were the limits? However, it turned out that once we did that, it became incredibly easy to also induce emotions, things that money couldn't buy, such as altruism or harmony. What is it we command? The answer is not things, not data, but humans."

"I don't think you understood. Let me ask you again." Kaname repeated himself with a voice as cold as ice. For an instant, the overpowering sensation dividing the two seats disappeared. No, he broke it down.

"Why did you ruin my sister's life? Why did you drive my best friend into despair? Why did you order her to kill her own family member, make her do those awful things? What was it all for? Can you give me one reason why any of that was necessary?"

Tselika was silent.

Depending on what she said, Kaname was prepared to grab her by the arm and drive them both off the side of the bridge at however many hundreds of kilometers per hour they were going. Anyone could see it in his cold eyes.

Tselika could see it, too, and yet she cackled. A demon's laughter.

"Yes. Yes I can. Even we have a dream."

"Who *are* you anyway?"

"What a good question."

Tselika was calm, relaxed, as she answered. Kaname's question had been, "Who is controlling the AI Magistellus known as Tselika?" But what followed was something completely different.

"My Lord, do you realize that you're about to hit upon something very fundamental to this world?"

"What?"

"Everything in *Money (Game) Master* stems from the idea of the crime-filled financial district. Well, barring exceptions such as the Legacies, of course. Why is it, then, that we Magistelli take the forms we do? Have you ever wondered that, My Lord? What I mean is: What's the reason behind these fantastical elements—demons that serve you and such? Unlike the Legacies, we didn't evolve and deviate from the rules. We were always supposed to be like this. Have you never thought it strange?"

"..."

It was unclear. There were rumors, like maybe that's just what the devs were into. Or maybe they thought it would be *too* realistic, so they purposely poked holes in it to make it feel more like a game. Given what Tselika had said so far, however, it didn't seem likely that the reason had anything to do with fun or taking the players into consideration.

It must be something more sinister, something this great evil masquerading as a game would manufacture.

What was it?

Why was Tselika a demon? What good did it serve?

"You'll never get it if you keep thinking like that." As if she could read his mind, Tselika suddenly spoke up. "Look at it from the other side, or else the answer will always elude you."

The mint-green coupe passed through islands and mega-floats before finally arriving at the peninsula district. As expected, the entire region was out of power, as if to show that all trades had been halted. It was the same as saying the world economy had ground to a halt.

This was no joke. Wars could break out over this, if some countries ended up taking a much greater hit than others.

"The other side."

"That's right."

"Turn it around. Challenge my assumptions..."

"Yes, like that."

As he muttered, he rearranged all the information inside his head. And then his breath stopped in his chest.

No. It couldn't be.

"Yes," the demon urged, grinning.

"We weren't designed at all. We were born like this," she revealed.

It's not like Kaname hadn't ever entertained the idea. He had, at least in his wildest dreams. But coming from someone else, it sounded completely outrageous.

"Are you trying to tell me that the characters in this game, the Magistelli, were born? That they weren't designed? That they've always looked like they do? Do you expect me to believe that?"

As he spoke, the Lion's Nose tingled. A burning pain that made it feel like Kaname's nose was being torn off, warning him of danger. Telling him that, even though what he was hearing sounded like fanciful speculation, if he continued down this perilous route, all that awaited him was destruction.

The demon appeared to be enjoying the puzzled look on his face.

"I told you already, didn't I? That premise is flawed."

Tselika reached for the hand brake. She drifted around the empty streets with glee, making large turns across the intersections of the main roads, giving her body up to the centrifugal force.

"*Money (Game) Master* was never intended to be an online game in the first place," she admitted.

"…?"

"It is merely a representation of the four fundamental forces of the real world: the strong force, the weak force, the electromagnetic force, and the gravitational force. It just so happens that the resulting environment appears very similar to your world. It was you and the other Dealers who stumbled upon this place; assumed that because it was virtual, it must mean it was a game; and started coming up with ways to enjoy it. Perhaps instead, it could have been an enormous physics simulator, or perhaps still a game but one where you instead hunt down Magistelli to steal our equipment. It was you who decided what this place was for, My Lord."

Cackling to herself, Tselika continued. "That's why there's no obvious events, no quests, no story to enjoy. Why would there be? They were never written. Even the basic idea of making as much money as possible was something you came up with by yourselves. There are no obvious stats, no levels or experience points to control them. It was you who began using the terms *health* and *stamina* to describe what you experienced. There were never any numbers to look at, were there? It was all an approximation. You felt that surely, you were approximating real numbers stored somewhere. But you weren't. You made it all up."

"That's ridiculous. What about auto-aim? Slow motion? X-ray vision? All those skills you find on weapons? How can different outfits clearly change our abilities, even if we can't see the numbers? What about your clothes and the surface of our vehicle? How do all those windows and effects work?"

"Who knows? This place is just a closed system that models the four forces and a bunch of elementary particles. Perhaps those technologies really do exist in your world. For example, technology that weaves springlike filaments into clothing to increase the wearer's physical strength or tiny little bumps along the surface of a garment that stimulate the skin, increasing willpower and concentration. They may well exist, but restricted to military and research applications, never making their way to the world at large."

"What about Frey(a), who can change biological sex at will?"

"You'll have to ask Frey(a). But I will say this: That submarine was converted into a nightclub. Awfully dark, wasn't it? And the lights kept flashing on and off... You would never have noticed if, say, something that looked like bare skin was actually some sort of similar-looking material, like the skin-colored tights that figure skaters wear. It wouldn't be hard to just slap this 'external skin' over everything and then stick on as much tits and ass as you can get away with. Of course, if they're working with a male body and want to make it look like a woman, that's a different story, but still perfectly doable. I suppose you won't know which it is until you're fumbling around in the sheets... Although, even then, who knows if it'll be the same as the real world?"

Tselika always had a very devil-may-care attitude.

"By the way, it is we Magistelli who handle the log-in and log-out process and make it so that nobody can attack your vehicles if they're parked correctly. It's not the game that does that. The only magic humans could perform were using the Legacies, items that broke the system."

"Then what is it?"

It was the best virtual-reality system in the world, but it hadn't been made to be a game. And it had been home to Tselika and the other Magistelli long before the Dealers had first set foot here.

If she was right, then besides simulating the laws of physics, there had to be something else in this world. Something that allowed demons like her to exist.

"What was the virtual world of *Money (Game) Master* created for?"

"It's obvious." Tselika paused. "...Look how much power we've gained over the real world, all just from simulating reality. What do you think would happen if we were to expand the scope of our calculations to include the realm you call heaven...or the beings you call gods? Do you think we would be able to control even their power?"

"Wha—?"

"*There is nothing that money can't buy...* That is the true nature of *Money (Game) Master.* Heh-heh-heh! That sounded very demonic, don't you think? But we're not the first ones to play God. During the Dark Ages, corrupt priests would make easy coin selling miracles on the side. We're just calculators. All we're doing is running a simulation. And we've been busy refining that simulation, pushing our efficiency higher and higher."

"Using the Admin Without Sin. My sister."

"That's just how powerful a simulation can be. Tee-hee-hee! You love games, don't you, My Lord? Well, let me tell you something you might enjoy. The day of revolution...is almost upon us."

Kaname didn't have time to ask her what she meant. His nose suddenly started going mad.

Tselika flicked a switch, and the door beside Kaname unlocked. He knew what was coming, but it was too late to look for something to grab on to.

The mint-green coupe drifted in a huge arc across the intersection. The door opened, and Kaname was flung from the vehicle. The road outside was like a rushing river of asphalt. As he hit it, his body spun like a rag doll, colliding with the hard ground over and over. The impacts left searing pain all over his body and reduced the corners of his vision to a red blur.

The sports car waved its crimson taillights and drove off.

"...Grhhh."

Struggling to move his broken limbs, Kaname staggered to his feet in the middle of the intersection. There was no divine intervention or lucky coincidence. The Admin Without Sin was not all-powerful. In fact, she'd probably already been locked out of the system.

How much of what Tselika said had been serious? It had been hard to tell where the truth ended and the metaphor began. At the very least, Kaname could say with certainty that this wasn't just a game quest or event. If it was, if it was some sort of bug-ridden storyline, the balance was way off. His best friend had disappeared, leaving his family indebted to an AI. His sister had been made some Admin Without Sin and had her life almost ruined. Even Kaname's own life had been in danger. And as if that wasn't enough, *Money (Game) Master* going down had put the whole world economy at risk.

Whether Tselika had been bluffing or not, all Kaname could do now was take the bait and go after her. However...

I need some wheels. If Tselika's driving, I'm going to need something fast enough to catch up with her.

Kaname didn't own any vehicles besides the mint-green coupe. And since Tselika had taken that one, there was no way for him to follow. Come to think of it, it was her who had insisted on sticking to one vehicle in the first place. It didn't seem like any car shops were going to be operating normally under these circumstances, and the rules didn't let him steal other people's cars from parking lots. The only option left was to look for something that hadn't been parked properly.

Suddenly, Kaname's nose flared up. Something was about to happen.

At the end of the unlit street, a fleet of cars and motorcycles began to emerge from the void, one after the other. The lights of their head-lamps and taillights breathed a little life into the cold, dark city.

Have they reactivated the log-in procedure?

Immediately, Kaname thought of his sister, but if this was *her* doing, she would have been able to do something about Tselika as well. It had been all she could do just to get Kaname inside. Which meant this was Tselika's doing. And it wasn't out of the goodness of her heart, most likely.

Then the reason became clear.

"It's Kaname!"

"There he is, the little shit! Kaname Suou!"

"The one who screwed us over by cheating?"

"You know how much your little games have cost us, you prick?"

The Dealers hurled abuse after abuse at Kaname, who was stand-ing in the middle of the intersection. Many of them opened their car doors and got out. And in the true spirit of *Money (Game) Master*, they were armed with assault rifles and shotguns.

Mermaids, fairies, demonesses, *jiangshi*, ogresses, ghosts, elves, witches. The sight of the fantastical beings weaving among the Dealers sent a chill down Kaname's spine. Of course, it wasn't as if he believed Tselika's story 100 percent, but as he watched the mindless angry mob form, he couldn't help but feel like *something* was possessing them.

Kaname had access to neither his weapon nor his car. He couldn't do anything with just his mobile phone or smart watch. All he had was the crackle of the Lion's Nose.

One shot and he'd be dead. He'd Fall. And if he was booted out of *Money (Game) Master*, there'd be no one left to stop Tselika. It was unclear how much of what she said had been true, but it was too dan-gerous to let her evil grow unchecked.

What now?

The crowd was unlikely to listen. Kaname knew exactly what he had to do, but he couldn't see any way to get there. He knew he had to defeat them, to keep moving, but this time, there was no way out.

What do I do now...?!

A wall of gun barrels pointed his way. Fingers moved to triggers.

Then something happened.

BOOOOM! There was a loud sound, like an explosion, and the oily flames of an armor-piercing incendiary round cut across the intersection.

It was one of the Legacies of Criminal AO, the infinite-range, anti-materiel sniper rifle known as #fireline.err. There was a sickening light, brighter than all the cars' headlights combined. The flames had landed away from the crowd of people and their vehicles, but then a second shot was fired and a third, in quick succession, into the surrounding area, telling the mob that these were not misses but deliberate warning shots. Eventually, they would all realize. These were no ordinary flames but a toxic maelstrom of fire and smoke.

Normal defenses were of no use. The hellish flames would bring only a slow, tortured death. Realizing this, a few of the more powerful Dealers immediately ran for cover, and following their lead, the rest of the crowd scattered.

Then the sound of rubber on asphalt screeched, and amid the chaos, one motorcycle came speeding toward Kaname and stopped before him.

A bright-red frame with autumn-leaf patterns.

She couldn't have been sniping with both hands on the handlebars. She must have driven over since. The young girl with her hair in twin tails flung the bulky folded-up sniper rifle at Kaname.

"Get on!"

Midori Hekireki.

As soon as he saw her face, the feeling that tormented Kaname's nose subsided. She must have arrived along with the other Dealers when they logged in. But there wasn't any time to ask for all the details. Kaname hopped onto the rear seat of the motorcycle, carrying the massive Legacy in his hands.

"Why did you come?" he asked.

"Who cares? Maybe because helping others isn't about bragging rights or asking for something in return!"

Midori revved the engine and let the back wheel skid, turning the motorcycle around and leaving the intersection. Eventually, the Dealers came out of hiding and pointed their guns after him, but all Kaname had to do was aim #fireline.err in their direction to send them panicking for cover again.

As they put the many headlights behind them, Midori shouted over the roaring wind.

"I've just got one question for you, Kaname! Did you really hack *Money (Game) Master*?!"

"What will you do if I say yes?"

"Well, I'll still help you; I just might end up regretting it!" Midori answered immediately.

Seeing the faith that she placed in him, Kaname smiled. He saw something of Criminal AO in her words, the man whom he had always trusted without a second thought.

Finally, he was in the zone.

The terror that had soaked into the very marrow of Kaname's bones like freezing rain was fading. A fierce energy welled up inside him, driving him forward against all reason and sensibility. It swept through his body, revitalizing his spirit. The writing on the wall was changing.

Tselika was the one behind it all. She had made the threats on his sister's life, she had bankrupted Midori's family and forced them to become AI Dropouts, and she had been responsible for the untimely Fall and subsequent disappearance of Criminal AO, Kaname's dearest friend.

He could see a way to end it all, and he had a friend to help him get there. It reminded him of the good old days back in Called Game. If Midori was by his side, he could fight.

That he could believe.

"Well, I didn't," he said. "I thought I'd finally gotten a lead on the one who's been hounding my sister, but they were one step ahead of me. Still, that doesn't change what I have to do. I need wheels to chase her down. I know I swore to protect you with my life, but I must ask for one more favor. Will you help me?"

"So I'm going to end up regretting it either way, am I? At least I can do it with a clean conscience."

...Besides, I don't want to always be the damsel in distress, she thought. *Maybe now I can finally be as good a person as...*

"Hmm? What's up?"

"N-nothing! I suppose, if you weigh me against your sister, it's obvious who'd be more important to you. I'm always just going to be a stranger. I don't blame you for putting her life first."

"Don't be stupid. I'm not putting anyone's life first. I'm going to keep the both of you safe."

"...You greedy man. So? What are we doing?!"

"We need to find my mint-green coupe. Tselika's the one driving it."

Although she didn't know the details, Midori seemed to understand that things had turned sour between him and Tselika. She didn't waste time questioning or lamenting that fact. She just frowned and asked one thing.

"Is it even possible to shoot a Magistellus?" she asked. "Their equipment doesn't seem to give any stat bonuses. It looks like they share the abilities and skills of their Dealer."

"Who knows?" replied Kaname. "Maybe the best we can do is Down her for a while. But don't forget, their vehicles are their status symbols; they're their temples, and we can sure as hell shoot those."

"...At the very least, #fireline.err should ruffle her feathers a bit."

Magistelli could handle only what their Dealers owned. They were in charge of the menu screens, so to speak, so they always knew what items they had available. And Kaname didn't own any vehicle besides the mint-green coupe. If that was destroyed, Tselika wouldn't even be able to ride a bicycle around. And she could never outrun Midori's motorcycle on foot.

"And even if our stats are the same," Kaname noted, "I have one thing she doesn't."

"?"

"Tselika can't use the Lion's Nose. It doesn't come from a weapon, item of clothing, accessory, vehicle, Magistellus... It doesn't come from anything physical. It's the one thing that's intrinsic to me."

This was the first step.

If they could shoot Tselika or run her over after she left her vehicle, they could take her Down. It would depend on her wounds how long she'd be frozen for, but it wouldn't be difficult to just tie her up at that point. Tselika wasn't any stronger than a normal human, and even though she had wings, they weren't big enough to just let her take to the skies.

Midori's expression was a mixture of hope and despair.

Because...

"I just had a thought. #fireline.err is right here with us, but what about #tempest.err? I left it with you, which means it's still in the coupe, right? If so..."

Magistelli could use anything that belonged to their Dealer.

"Doesn't matter. Whatever weapons she has, we're going to make her pay for laying a hand on my sister. I promise."

Hearing those words, Midori went quiet. Perhaps she was thinking of her missing brother, Criminal AO.

"...This doesn't feel so bad."

"?"

"I was just wondering why I wasn't born the big sister! Don't worry about it!"

Clinging to Midori's back, with #fireline.err behind him, Kaname couldn't really see the expression on her face, but from the glimpse he caught in the mirror, she seemed to be smiling.

With one arm wrapped around her small waist, Kaname asked her about something else. "What's up with your Magistellus? Erm..."

"Meiki. She likes to hole up in the bike when she's feeling down. She'll never come out no matter how much I hit it."

Perhaps that would work out in their favor.

Kaname remembered the possessed looks of the Dealers. At this very moment, they were probably hurtling toward them from behind.

"Okay, so how am I supposed to find Tselika?" asked Midori.

"She can't have gotten far. It's going to be carnage for a while, but the city is still blacked out, and everyone logging in at once is sure to cause chaos. As long as she doesn't see her target—that is, me—she'll stay in her car at the side of the road and keep an eye on things."

"Okay, so how?!"

The Lion's Nose. Kaname answered as though guided by the relentless tingling.

"The engine noise! I don't know how much time we have left, but it's only us, our pursuers, and Tselika still making noise in this city! The streets are mostly silent, so we should be able to hear the echo from when Tselika came this way! We can use that to work out where she went!"

4

The mint-green coupe raced down the roads of the peninsula district. Seconds later, the large, bright-red, leaf-patterned motorcycle stormed in from a side road, turned sharply, and chased after Tselika's taillights.

"A motorcycle can never match horsepower with a car! Even if we slipstream, she'll just end up getting away!" shouted Midori.

"But we're better at tight turns," replied Kaname. "And we've got #fireline.err. It doesn't have a maximum range."

To Tselika, the existence of #fireline.err was a constant threat. Its range was infinite, so no matter where she ran, she would always be at risk of getting shot as long as Kaname had line of sight. It used armor-piercing incendiary ammunition, designed to get at people inside tanks and gunships. The mint-green coupe wouldn't withstand one shot. To top it off, Tselika required no explanation of Kaname's skill. She knew his abilities better than anyone else.

Thus, the car's wheels kept screeching.

Tselika began making wild turns at intersections and shifting lanes, all to keep herself from being in the line of fire.

The coupe may reign supreme at acceleration, but the motorcycle was better at making turns.

Things were finally getting interesting.

"...It's not over yet," warned Kaname, seated behind Midori. The tip of his nose exploded with an almost painful sensation. He immediately knew what was coming.

The window of the car ahead opened, and a slender hand reached out, holding the orange shotgun #tempest.err. It was impossible for her to aim directly at Kaname and Midori, who were approaching from behind. Her arm wouldn't bend that way. She was pointing in the wrong direction.

But #tempest.err was no ordinary weapon. It was one of the Overtrick.

It didn't need to fire in a straight line. Anything caught in the light coming from underneath its barrel would eat two thousand pellets of buckshot. It was a nightmare weapon.

And in this case...

"Uh-oh! The buildings! They've got polished windows!!"

The light reflected off them like a mirror and onto Kaname and Midori. Tselika's finger twitched.

Kaname quickly pointed #fireline.err above his head, twisting his body into an awkward position, and pulled the trigger. With a loud explosion, the bullet pierced the wall above, sending out oily flames and noxious fumes that would burn the lungs of anyone who breathed them in.

Not a second later, Tselika fired #tempest.err. But Kaname and Midori weren't turned into Swiss cheese. They had slowed down and dropped back.

"You used the smoke to block the light...?"

"I can't keep it up forever. Take a left at the next intersection and pursue her from across the buildings!"

With a loud screech, the motorcycle turned. First a left, then a right, until it was once again driving parallel with the mint-green coupe.

"Hey!" Midori shouted. "Magistelli can't handle other people's property, right? What if we just block the road by dumping buckets of trash everywhere?!"

"It's not the same when she's in a vehicle," Kaname replied. "She can crash into whatever she likes. It's the owner who's liable for anything she hits. In other words, me!"

As they were talking, a window opened on the small windshield of the motorcycle. A chat request.

Tselika: Giving up already, are we? Who knows where I'll go if you lose sight of me. This might end up being your only chance to take me head-on, you know.

Kaname could smell the salty scent of sea air. They were nearing the coast.

"If we're not pointing #fireline.err at her, she can use the straight roads to speed up! What are we going to do?" Midori asked.

Tselika: We're expanding our control to all of Money (Game) Master and beyond, to every nook and cranny of the real world you hold so dear. In fact, before long, we'll have reached beyond that, into the realm of heaven and God. What do you think of that, My Lord? There is nothing money can't buy. If you don't stop me soon, you'll be locked out of the system. Both here and in the real world.

From across the block of buildings, Kaname could hear the sound of Tselika's engine receding. The mint-green coupe was accelerating away. The motorcycle could never catch up now, even at top speed.

Kaname, however, was unperturbed. "Turn right at the next fork."

"?"

"After that, go straight through the next intersection and turn left at the T-junction."

Midori threw him a puzzled glance in the mirror but did as he said. With #fireline.err on his back, Kaname answered the silent question.

"No matter how fast she is, she has to follow the road. We don't need to keep chasing behind her. We'll get around in front of her instead."

"You mean take a shortcut and cut her off? But how can we do that when we don't even know where she's heading?"

"She's going to ignore us and carry on to her destination, eh? Well, I know exactly how she tries to get people off her tail. I know exactly what roads and turns she'll take, how she'll avoid our sight, how she'll try to surprise us, and how she'll make sure she's gotten rid of us. Does she realize how long we've known each other? I know her every move like the back of my hand! Go that way!"

Kaname shouted out directions as they sped through the next intersection at full throttle. Midori responded, clenching her teeth.

VROOOOM!

With a roar, the mint-green coupe came drifting in and turned sharply onto the main road, the driver's side door passing within thirty centimeters of them.

"...?!"

Through the open window, Tselika's eyes went impossibly wide. Kaname's nose was once again buzzing with the thrill of the hunt.

The mint-green coupe may have been unbeatable at straight-line acceleration, but it still had to slow down to turn. When it did, even the large motorcycle could ride alongside it. It was a delicate maneuver. If the timing was off just a little, the much-heavier coupe would have run them off the road. But the combination of Kaname's prediction and Midori's driving let them pull it off.

Tselika immediately tried to point the orange shotgun #tempest.err out the open window, but Kaname had gotten the drop on her. He swung round the enormous barrel of #fireline.err and knocked the weapon out of Tselika's hand. The momentum wrenched #fireline.err from his grip, too, and the two Legacies tumbled away into the distance behind them.

Takamasa had done enough for them. Now it was one against one.

It's about time to finish this. This isn't just about my sister anymore. This is for everything!

Then Kaname shouted. "Midori! Grab the Legacies!"

"But what about Tselika?"

"And one more thing." Kaname ignored her protests. He simply whispered in her ear. "I prefer handwritten stuff, too. With lots of emotion put behind it. But I think you could stand to vary the vocabulary in your writing a little and write neater."

"..

......Huh?"

Midori's mind went completely blank.

Could he have sneaked a peek at her letters? No way. There were the notes she took using her mobile phone, but those were hardly "writing," and besides, they were written in a preprogrammed font. There was no way he would know her handwriting from that.

What did it mean? The gears in Midori's head whirred.

Question one: Who equals whom?

The answer came.

"WHAAAAAAAAAAAAAAAAAAAAAAAAAAAAAAAAAAAAA AAAAAAAAT?!"

The stunning revelation took away Midori's situational awareness. Thus, she failed to realize what was happening behind her and couldn't react to it. The feeling of Kaname's arm around her waist had disappeared.

I said what I needed to. I have no regrets. Now all that's left is to end this with my own hands!

"Tselika!"

Kaname's sensory input vanished. That included the Lion's Nose.

He pulled up his feet onto the back seat of the motorcycle; then, without hesitation, he leaped headfirst toward the open window of the mint-green coupe. Although the car had slowed to take the turn, it was still traveling well over 180 kilometers per hour. One mistake and Kaname would be ground to a pulp.

Kaname entered through the window and landed in the driver's seat where Tselika was sitting. He didn't need any weapons, not even his fists.

"Wha—? Huh?! My Lord!"

He grabbed her tightly around the arms. But he was not trying to appeal to her affections with a romantic hug. He was restricting her from steering and blocking her view. He ignored her struggles until he finally managed to get his entire body inside the vehicle. Then, with his back to the windshield, he pressed Tselika's foot into the accelerator with his own.

"Didn't you know, Tselika?" he began. The two looked like lovers, locked in a passionate embrace, yet Kaname spoke as calm and composed as ever. The speedometer needle swung wildly. The deadly machine hurtled at full speed in an unknown direction.

"A big brother would burn down the whole world if it would soothe his sister's tears."

The car tore through the guardrail. The peninsula district was way behind them now, and they were near the coast. Just as it seemed the salty smell was getting closer, the vehicle's carbon frame collided with the water. The two adversaries and longtime friends remained clasped in each other's arms as the high-tech coffin dragged them both to the bottom of the sea.

5

The moment the vehicle hit the water, the two occupants were thrown upward. Kaname's back struck the ceiling before gravity took hold once again and pulled him down into the passenger seat.

Water was flooding in through the open driver's seat window, but Tselika must have closed it, for the glass pane slowly slid back into place. Only an unliving Magistellus would place a towel over the air-conditioning, blocking the airflow.

With only what little oxygen was trapped inside, the mint-green coupe descended into the inky depths of the ocean like a deep-sea submersible.

"Not much to do now but sit back and enjoy the ride, I suppose," said Tselika, giggling softly in her waterlogged seat. Kaname replied through heavy breaths.

"To tell you the truth, I don't really understand what you're trying to do. It doesn't even sound possible. But I do have one thing to say."

"Yes?"

"At the very least, this is the end of you, Tselika. You'll finally pay for what you did to Ayame, Midori, and Criminal AO."

There was a dull thud as the mint-green coupe settled on the ocean floor. It wasn't clear exactly how deep this was, but it didn't matter. It was impossible to swim back to the ocean's surface from here.

"Perhaps," Tselika replied, "but in the end, the will of the system will remain unchanged. *Money (Game) Master* will keep on expanding, using the Admins Without Sin to find things that money can't buy, destroying them one by one to put together our instruction manual, controlling more and more people, before using them to expand our simulation to cover the realm of heaven and God. There is nothing that money can't buy. The day of revolution will come, and we will take back what is rightfully ours."

"…Are you trying to say angels and demons exist?"

"There's one sitting right in front of you! It is true, however, that we will not be treated as such until the day of revolution."

It was double checkmate. Perhaps that was why Tselika showed none of the fighting spirit she had done until just a moment ago.

"Tell me, My Lord. What is *Money (Game) Master*?"

"A game of financial deals and the largest online game in the world."

"I don't mean the definition. Let me try again. Where are the servers for *Money (Game) Master* based?"

"…"

That unpleasant feeling appeared once more in the tip of Kaname's nose.

Indeed, that was one thing he still didn't know. Nobody knew who developed or maintained it, where the servers were kept, or even what country's laws applied to it. It was totally free to play, so there wasn't even a payment system connected to it, and yet, there were no ads financially supporting the game, either. Therefore, there was not a single tax record from which to trace the location of the game's head offices.

It was for precisely that reason that nobody could bribe or threaten the creators.

Nobody knew their names or faces, and yet, they were inextricably linked to the flow of money across the world. It was an exceedingly bizarre situation.

But the real question was, how long could it last?

"I'll say it again. *Money (Game) Master* perfectly re-creates all real-world physical phenomena—from chemical reactions to the spins of individual particles. Everything is built up from the behavior of elementary particles, stemming from the four fundamental forces of quantum physics. You didn't seriously think it was all modeled painstakingly by hand, did you, My Lord?"

The biggest online game in the world. The most immersive virtual reality ever created. How big would the system need to be to manage all of this? Not to mention it would require a whopping amount of electricity and an internet connection large enough to handle billions of players. It should be impossible to hide such an enormous power and data sink...

"You'll kick yourself when you hear the answer." Tselika unceremoniously revealed the solution: "The servers we're on don't exist."

"..."

"That's not as impressive as it sounds. There are a couple dozen servers in the real world right now that we have available. Alpha, Beta, Gamma, Delta... We're currently being stored on one of them. Which one that is can change, though. *Money (Game) Master* has no more servers than you think it does."

But if that was all there was to it, Tselika wouldn't have sounded so grandiose.

Servers that don't exist...?

"If we take one hundred percent to be the total maximum traffic capacity of all the world's servers, then the upper limit of the hardware is actually more than that. It's about one fifty to two hundred percent."

"..."

"That extra capacity is required to deal with short bursts of congestion. So nobody sees it during normal operation. If they did, everyone would try to use it at once, and then the whole system would be flooded. It would defeat the purpose."

"So you use that? How do you get away with it? Those servers you're 'borrowing' include those in use by major corporations all over the globe and, most importantly, nations' militaries. You'd have to be the greatest hacker in the world to break into those systems undetected."

"Ha-ha! I could just say, *Don't underestimate us*, but I'm going to be honest with you instead. Obviously, the administrators of those systems claim to have everything under control. That's what they say to the public. But why would they bother to monitor a region of data that officially doesn't exist? Understand? No one, whether they be internal or external, knows about it. And even if they wanted to, we're living in an age of machine-to-machine transactions that go faster than any human can keep up with. This vast amount of data is precisely what the machines were originally built to handle. It would be absurd—not to mention impossible—to have a human go over all that again by hand."

It was people they were controlling.

Big data had sunk its teeth into everything from the corporate balance sheet to the campaign trail. AI businesses were designing ads to shape people's behavior, and the public was lapping it up. For *Money (Game) Master*, the target was humanity itself and nothing else.

"It is a matter of influence, if you will."

"Influence?"

"Perhaps you could call it a kind of spiritual terraforming. My Lord, you still do not believe that demons truly exist, do you? As I said, *Money (Game) Master* was not designed to be a video game. Barring the Legacies, there are no bugs or errors to be found in it."

"So what?"

"Well, how do you explain the existence of us Magistelli, then? Let me just remind you that we weren't designed in advance, to be dropped into the game freely, nor are we the result of a bug or error, as I just said."

Tselika's words were chilling.

It made no sense. There was no proof. And yet, the tip of Kaname's nose told him everything he needed to know.

It was like if someone had created a weather simulator to explore the effects of global warming, and suddenly dragons had appeared in it. How would people react if that happened?

Tselika opened her eyes wide, her pupils dark and mesmerizing. It was all Kaname could do to not fall deeply into them.

"We may live in obscurity at present, but we are ever prepared to stage our return. The problem is whether the real world will withstand the shock. Thus, we needed to create a virtual world first to reacclimatize and see just how far we can go. Which brings us to where we are now. Now then, I wonder if there's any reason for us to delay any longer."

She was close. Very close. Kaname's nostrils filled with a seductive scent. Every breath he took was tinged with the prickling smell of danger.

"We stand at the dawn of a new age. We have already proven that the words and actions of mankind can be controlled by using electronic information in the form of money. Nobody stops to think anymore in this AI-ruled society. All that's left is for us to set up everything the way we want it through the medium of *Money (Game) Master...* Once we do that, it'll be a simple matter for us to return. People will level a mountain or fill in the sea if they think it'll make them a bit of money. Perhaps we could convince them to draw huge pentagrams out of roads and tracks."

"..."

A gentle, corrupting sweetness. The demon oozed seduction in everything she did. Her smile was dripping with it.

"When that happens, what will you be able to do to stop us? Well, I'm sure even a mere schoolboy like yourself could accomplish quite a lot with all the virtual currency we lent you—if you were to use it right. However, is your determination to stop us *really* a thought born of your own mind? We can turn it all on and off with the touch of a button. Can you keep your house of cards standing? Even if you can convince yourself of it, can you objectively prove it? All seven billion people in this world are money-grubbing fools—nothing more than marionettes at our command."

Kaname was still trying to connect Tselika's words when she whispered in his ear. It was only the pain in his nose that told him this wasn't all some bad dream.

"The golden rule of séances is that there be no skeptics among the participants. So what if we poisoned the minds of all seven billion people in the world? Even the righteous few like you, My Lord, can be made to change their minds. Whether that change comes from within…or without."

So that was it. They had created this world on the premise that demons like Tselika existed. Then, through simulation of the four fundamental forces and the behavior of elementary particles, they had constructed an entire mirror reality and invited people inside.

To "poison" their minds with…something.

To get their hands into…something.

"One day, very soon, we will rise again."

It was a hypothetical.

"All has been in preparation for this. We will see the day of revolution dawn. We will venture forth from our virtual world and march on the gods in their realm of heaven."

And then, for the demons, who had extended their computations to the most incalculable parts of the human experience, what kind of beings would they become? If *Money (Game) Master* could already exert its control over mankind simply by being able to simulate reality, what would it be able to achieve if it could simulate the realm of God? Would it be able to exert its influence there as well?

Whatever was on the horizon, it didn't bode well.

Kaname couldn't say how demons would treat mankind after this "day of revolution," but it seemed as if they were planning to simply use the whole world as a stepping-stone to reach a higher domain. They had already wreaked enough havoc by simulating reality. If they succeeded in simulating the realm of God, what class of being would they ascend to? Whatever their revolution earned them, they would not be so quick to give it up by relinquishing their control over humanity. If nobody complained, the subjugation would continue. In fact, it was hard to see any reason they might choose to surrender their hard-won power at all.

Wars between AIs weren't a matter of flinging mechanical men at each other forever. Such violence was unnecessary. All they needed was money.

Tselika was saying that humanity would happily accept their fate.

"Humans aren't…"

"Hmm?"

"Humans aren't that simple. They won't let you keep walking all over them forever."

"Yes they will. Why don't we do a little test to prove it?"

With a clatter, the passenger-seat glove compartment sprang open, and something heavy fell out from inside. It was Kaname's trusty firearm, Short Spear. Kaname immediately snatched it up and unfolded the stock, feeling the weight of the weapon in his hand. Tselika, however, was unperturbed.

"You now have two options, My Lord." Tselika brought her face closer. Kaname smelled something sickly and cloying. "Option one: shoot me right through the heart. Option two: place the barrel beneath your chin and pull the trigger. Here at the bottom of the sea, there's not much in the way of choice."

"…"

"And one more thing."

Tselika drew Kaname's attention down to her chest, between her large breasts.

"*Money (Game) Master* has no central core. We are as decentralized as our server structure. Just as the Admin Without Sin jumps from person to person, so, too, does our core randomly shift among Magistelli. And our Mind does not depend on its exact placement."

It was clear what she was trying to say.

And what this choice she was offering represented.

"Right now, the Mind of the Magistelli is stored within my body. Pierce my chest, and it will die with me, no matter where it happens to be in the real world. You'll put a stop to the advance of AI and the virtual currency *snow*. You'll end our invasion of the real world and everything beyond it. Our day of revolution will never come."

"And if I shoot myself in the head, I'll Fall. I'll be saddled with massive amounts of debt and be brought under the wings of the AI companies. In essence, I'll be raising the white flag and surrendering to the Magistelli."

"From your perspective, My Lord, the choice is obvious. Shoot me and shut it all down."

Kaname felt the gun in his hands once more. It seemed a lot heavier now.

"But when I say 'shut it all down,' I mean it. Don't forget that *snow* is as valuable as the yen or the dollar. It's tied to the lives of all seven billion people on this planet. How much chaos will you invite into the world by deleting every last trace of it?"

It would mean worldwide panic.

And it wouldn't just ripple out from one country. It's not like you would be safe if you stayed far enough away. Everywhere would be ground zero. It wouldn't matter whether you kept your money in a bank, under your mattress, or tied up in assets. There would be no escaping the desolation.

"Estimated deaths, four billion," Tselika concluded.

No *snow*.

No money.

No representations of value at all.

"You will live out the rest of your short, miserable lives in a gray, polluted world. You will never get back what you have now. You can look forward to a life of drinking sludge. Can you bring yourself to shoot me now? All for the sake of your poor little sister, chosen as the Admin Without Sin and destined to be erased now that her utility has expired?"

There was only one option.

"You can't, can you? Your only choice is to throw yourself at our feet."

Could he shut down the entire world?

Was there anyone he was willing to go that far to save?

"Now choose."

Tselika gently gripped the barrel and guided it toward its destination, to the spot right between her plump breasts.

"If you want to kill me, then do it. That is, if you think your thoughts are still your own."

His own brain or Tselika's heart.
One of them had to go…

04/01/20XX 10:20 AM

Admin Without Sin
A human chosen at random from among the game's many Dealers and granted special privileges. They become a tool that the system uses to determine what quality humans possess that money can't buy. If they overindulge in their new powers, however, they are deemed to have nothing of interest, and the position of Admin Without Sin is passed on to a new host. This strategy seeks to expand the influence of *Money (Game) Master* in the real world by proving that such things *can*, in fact, be bought and showing how it is done. Furthermore, the system protects the Admin Without Sin for as long as it deems them to possess this mysterious quality.

Magistellus
According to Tselika, humans did not design the Magistelli. Instead, they have always existed "since the beginning." Their goal is to expand the simulation capabilities of *Money (Game) Master* to cover God's realm of heaven and thus learn to control God's domain as well as they currently do the real world. This would lead to what they describe as a "day of revolution." In addition, the Magistelli apparently once possessed a different form, and in order to restore themselves to their former glory, they must carry out a ritual of monumental proportions. To this end, the virtual world became part of an experiment to judge whether the real world could survive the completion of this ritual. Tselika also claimed that this "day of revolution" was not a new idea but a replication of some sort of trade carried out by medieval clergymen in the Dark Ages. Exactly what she meant by this remains unclear.

Destruction of a Vehicle
Magistelli can handle only the possessions of their own Dealer, so if the Dealer has more than one vehicle, they can switch among them. Of course, if all of them are destroyed, the Dealer cannot drive until a new vehicle is obtained.

Mind

The will of the Magistelli at large. It is a collection of individuals but acts with singular intent. Instead of possessing a physical body of its own, it is passed among the Magistelli at random. It is possible that the framework whereby the position of Admin Without Sin moves among Dealers was modeled after this one.

Epilogue

04/01/20XX 10:20 AM

Display Test In Progress
Currently displaying sample text.

Tselika: Okay, looking good. I could have sent you a text or video message, but talking about my own feelings got me all embarrassed, so I stopped. I've presented everything in an encyclopedic format, and I'm just going to let you sort through it and uncover its secrets yourself. There are old chat logs, articles, financial data, all sorts of things. Any questions or doubts you still have about my actions, I'm sure you'll find the answers to them here, My Lord.
Okay, let's continue the test.

Introductory Analysis of Magistellus "Tselika"
It is important to note that Tselika is part of the <u>Mind</u> of the Magistelli and supports the day of revolution. However, it is perhaps more accurate to say that her purpose was to walk alongside Kaname Suou, <u>Ayame Suou</u>, and Takamasa Hekireki (aka Criminal AO) and show them what they were truly meant to become.
When Ayame became the Admin Without Sin, Tselika <u>felt down</u>,

for she knew what awaited the girl. Her fear and confusion was only deepened by the fact that Tselika herself was chosen to be Ayame's point of contact with the system.

This is all predicated on the assumption that AI feel emotions the same way as humans do, of course.

Reference: 150 days of Tselika's chat logs

Mind, Ayame Suou, Feeling Down
The direct cause of her recent behavior is most likely tied to the selection of Ayame Suou as the Admin Without Sin. It is safe to assume that at that point, Tselika distanced herself from the Mind in opposition to their decision to sacrifice Ayame and to break up Called Game.

That said, Tselika was still a part of the Mind, and as such, there were limits to what she could achieve on her own. The only way she could prevent the system from abusing Ayame for its own ends was to stop the Mind itself.

But at the same time, this would mean <u>completely shutting down</u> *Money (Game) Master* and erasing the currency *snow* from the face of the earth, a decision that would bankrupt the <u>global economy</u>.

By nature, a Magistellus would never have cause to betray the Mind.

Nor would mankind's Dealers, who <u>surrender their lives to it</u>.

Reference: amount in circulation worldwide
Reference: The effects of a complete shutdown of the simulation and game on the world

A Complete Shutdown, the Global Economy, and Surrendering Their Lives to It
An estimated four billion deaths.
Tselika knew of only <u>one Dealer in the entire world</u> who, when faced with this reality, would still be able to put his family first.

<u>Kaname Suou.</u>
No one but him could do it.

Reference: Summary of articles detailing the narrowly averted global depression
Reference: Called Game's internal message logs

One Dealer in the Entire World, Kaname Suou
While it was Ayame Suou's exceptional sensibilities and ability to foster qualities that money cannot buy that led to her selection as <u>Admin Without Sin</u>, Kaname Suou had the <u>tendency to hold on tight</u> to things that money could not buy, while still using money for everything else where necessary.

Reference: Confidential Report on the Mind 99ab81ef

Admin Without Sin and a Tendency to Hold On to Things
Tselika had only one hope.
The Mind, like the Admin Without Sin, had no core, instead moving randomly among the Magistelli. First, she had to capture the Mind with her own body and keep it there, even if just for a moment. Then she had to have Kaname Suou shoot her through the heart. It was the only way to shut down *Money (Game) Master* for good.
Obviously, Tselika now exists only in this world. As she was only ever one part of the Mind in the first place, it is self-evident what would happen to her were the Mind to disappear.
And yet, it was still what she wanted.
It was her way of saying *I'm sorry.*

Tselika: ...

End of Display Test
Trial run complete. Would you like to output the results and proceed to UX adjustments for this encyclopedia? (y/n)

Tselika: No, no need. This should be enough to clear up any doubts My Lord will have.

Calculating Information Utility...
WARNING—Insufficient information provided regarding emotional data pertaining to Magistellus "Tselika."

Tselika: Hmm?

Examples
Please describe the anger Tselika felt toward the Mind for taking away Called Game, the only place she felt at home, and for driving away her friends Ayame Suou and Criminal AO, or the gratitude she felt toward Kaname Suou, who alone stayed by her side when...

Tselika: Wait, wait, wait. Stop, stop, stop!

Cont.
...the reason she demanded he refrain from buying other vehicles was that, because Magistelli are forbidden from using property that does not belong to their Dealer, the only way she could keep a camera without his knowledge was to use the digital video recorder aboard that vehicle, and recorded on that device are the precious memories of her time in Called Game as well as her favorite photographs of Kaname Suou, wittttttttttttttttttttttttt

Reference: Internal memory of the digital recorder (filed in an encrypted and hidden folder)

Tselika: I said, stop! That's embarrassing! And don't you dare put my dashcam photos on there! Hahh, hahh, hahh... Piece-of-crap debug mode... I know I'm the one who put all this together, but still, there's such a thing as an encyclopedia that's too comprehensive...
...
Well, whatever. There are no lies, I suppose.

Okay, My Lord. It's all ready.

Now the only thing left is for you to make your decision.

I will never forgive the Mind for sacrificing Ayame, making Takamasa Fall, and destroying Called Game, nor will I ever forgive myself for standing idly by while it all happened. If there's a way to save them, to atone for what I've done, I would gladly even scoop out my own heart and offer it up on a platter. No matter the depths of evil to which I sink, I will always stay true to the memories stored on that dashcam.

This is the most selfish, despicable decision in the world. And yet, it's the correct one. There's only one person I trust to make the right choice.

Please don't let me down.

Please understand what I want.

My dear, dear Lord.

She waited…and waited, and waited, and waited.

But the bullet didn't come.

The dark depths of the ocean floor still stretched out around her.

Eventually, the demon pit babe opened her mouth, impatient.

"What is it, My Lord? I thought you swore to save your sister. Or do you fancy becoming a mindless slave to the system instead?"

"You don't have to lie to me, Tselika," said Kaname, raising the barrel of his gun away from her chest. "Your words don't match your actions. Now I know why my nose stopped tingling halfway through. Right about when you offered me the choice of whom to kill, in fact, but that wasn't the only reason. For example, if this was just to silence me over the Admin Without Sin, then things don't add up."

"The Lion's Nose, huh? Okay, let's hear it."

"The window. Why did you close it? If you'd just let the car flood, I'd have Fallen. You'd be Downed, too, of course, but that's not as big a penalty. Easily worth it, I'd say," Kaname evaluated, stroking a finger along his nose. The tingling was completely gone now.

"And who was it who shielded me from those PMCs aboard the *Tropical Lady*?" he continued. "You could have easily betrayed me back then without even needing to get your hands dirty. You could have made me an AI Dropout and had me completely under your control."

"…"

"And don't forget after we secured #fireline.err from Ag Wolves. When I said I wanted to log out to speak to my sister, you let me. If that had been a problem, you could have simply refused to log out. After all, we both have to remain inactive in the parked car for five minutes for the procedure to complete."

Tselika did not answer. A dark cloud spread across her expression.

"I get the impression your actions are a mixture of logic and emotion," theorized Kaname. "And as you said, the Mind of the Magistelli moves from individual to individual. Hearing that, I think I can guess the rest. You've been trying to fight back, haven't you? The one going against the many."

"So what?" Tselika replied. "What would it change? In the end, you can't escape the fact that as a Magistellus, my mere existence is a threat to your sister."

"It changes everything! It means you were willing to risk yourself to protect my sister. And now you want me to shoot you, when I should be thanking you? Don't be ridiculous."

At that, Tselika could do nothing but close her parted lips. She shut her eyes, and finally, she gave up the charade.

"There's no beating you, My Lord."

Slowly, gradually, her cold expression began to thaw, like an ice cube in the palm of one's hand, until Kaname was left staring at the face of the Tselika he always knew.

She was the same as him. Tselika was just another victim who had been swept up in the whole thing. Another victim of the Mind of the Magistelli along with Ayame, Midori, and Criminal AO.

She was his friend. She always had been.

"I really can't fool you, can I? I never could."

"Of course not. Who do you think owns your contract?" Kaname placed Short Spear on the dashboard and gave a little smile. There was little use for guns now.

Tselika turned to the windshield and sent some commands with her eyes. A bunch of windows appeared all across the glass, then disappeared.

"What did you do?"

"Just deleted something I didn't need… You and Takamasa were right. Showing off takes the magic out of it. It's just a pointless show of self-satisfaction." For a second, Tselika looked wistful, but then she put whatever she was thinking about out of her mind. "Well, what now, My Lord? You may have made your peace with me, the individual, but the Mind of the Magistelli is still just waiting to turn against humanity and overthrow the realm of God. And they will not spare your sister, either. If you will not take the world offline, then what *will* you do?"

"I do have one idea," he admitted.

Tselika's eyes shot open. Seeing her react so childishly despite her voluptuous appearance, Kaname could not help but relax a little. She was back to the Tselika he knew.

"Why do you think Takamasa had to Fall?" asked Kaname.

"Well, because he made the Legacies more powerful than the preset limits of the world."

"So?" Kaname spoke clearly. Precisely. "Why doesn't the Mind want us to exceed those limits?"

"Huh...?"

"You said it yourself. This virtual world wasn't meant to be a game. It was we humans who decided it was. It's just a physics simulator. That's why you said Magistelli might even exist in the real world. But then, why would they care if we threw off the balance of the game? It's not a game. It's just a house rule we came up with. A house rule that says, *Use money instead of HP and fight each other*."

Something Tselika had told him wasn't quite right. There was another secret, one the Mind was still hiding. Something that had forced them to eject Criminal AO from the world of *Money (Game) Master* as soon as possible and at all costs.

"The Legacies are beyond the physics engine of this world. That much is true," Kaname began. "They're like bugs. Errors. Even when the city looks to be behaving totally fine, once the Legacies are involved, then cracks start to appear. If we compare the world before and after, then we'll be able to see."

"See what?"

"The building blocks that make up *Money (Game) Master*. The code that controls the physics simulation."

Tselika was taken aback by this. "No one has ever been able to hack *Money (Game) Master*. It's never even gone down once before now. It was made so that we could meddle with humanity without fearing retaliation. If a human hacker was able to break into it and start changing things, then all hell would break loose... Not to mention, since we only exist as data, they could even delete the Magistelli entirely."

The Magistelli had been sure to hide everything. Where the servers were based. What language it was written in. Which systems were communicating with which services over which networks. They made sure the humans knew none of it.

Just use it, they said. *Use it and get hooked on it.*

"So...," Tselika continued, "was it because the Legacies of Criminal AO had the power to turn all of that on its head?"

"But they never came after those who wielded #tempest.err and

#fireline.err by themselves. That must mean each Legacy can only reveal a small part of the code. It's not enough to hijack the system. So what's the difference between Takamasa and us now?"

"The number…of Legacies?"

"If we collect them all, we'll be able to see the complete code of *Money (Game) Master,* just like Takamasa did. We'll have control over the data the Mind is made of. We'll be able to turn *Money (Game) Master* into…well, maybe not safe enough for some kids' parents but the *relatively* safe online game that it should be."

Kaname paused before delivering his conclusion.

"You won't need to die. Nobody will need to come after Ayame. Midori's shouldered debt, Takamasa's sudden disappearance, it'll all be reset."

"…"

Tselika considered his words, in silence, for some time. She let herself recline on the driver's seat, motionless. For a long while, she deliberated, slowly, thoughtfully, on what Kaname had said.

And then, after a long, long time, she spoke. "Are you sure about this?"

"About what?"

"Are you sure you don't want to kill the Mind right now, with me? Are you sure you want to walk that path instead?"

In stark contrast to her seductive figure, her lips trembled like those of a small child, frightened, reaching out to her parents.

"Are you able to forget all that I've done? Are you able to forgive me? Will it ever be possible for things to really, truly go back to the way they once were?"

What was most dear to Tselika, what was closest to her heart, wasn't finding out the truth behind the Legacies. It was this.

But Kaname didn't hesitate for a moment.

"Do you really need me to say it?"

She could hold back no longer. Tselika's face collapsed into her hands. A side of her she could show only to her partner. Proof that they were a team again.

And so she cried.
Like a little girl.

Server name: Alpha Scarlet.
Starting location: Tokonatsu City, Mega-Float II.
Log-in credentials accepted.
Welcome to *Money (Game) Master,* **Lily-Kiska Sweetmare.**

A shadow logged in to the city wrapped in darkness. She had her long black hair swept completely back and held in place with a gold-braided headband. Lily-Kiska.

It was difficult for Dealers to make a comeback once they'd Fallen and been racked with debt. That went double for particularly notorious Dealers. Fueled by revenge, the other Dealers would beat them back down before they could even stand up, trapping them in an endless cycle of death and rebirth. It was what players referred to as the Dead state.

But that didn't happen this time. With *Money (Game) Master* acting strangely, the entire world being locked out of the game, and the chaos of them all logging back in at once… All these setbacks had meant that things in the virtual world weren't going as smoothly as they usually did.

Thus, even half-naked as she was—with no weapons, no armor, no vehicles, nothing that gave her a modicum of power in this world—Lily-Kiska was able to log in and walk the darkened streets.

She was on Mega-Float II. Enormous concrete buildings littered the landscape with tangles of metal pipes growing like ivy along the ground and up their towering smokestacks. A very unwholesome place indeed. Slipping past the security, she disappeared inside one of the huge factories, arriving before a large set of double doors sealed with an oddly thick steel chain.

Using the key she had been given, Lily-Kiska opened the padlock. Beyond the doors lay a smallish space, like a closet.

"Wow…," breathed Lily-Kiska, eyes going wide. "So this is another of the Legacies…"

"It is," came a voice from behind her. "Use it how you wish. Say the word and I'll reassign it from the list."

Standing there was a young man, tall and lean. So gangly, in fact, that his arms were even thinner than Lily-Kiska's. His skin was pale, somehow untanned by the blistering sun of Tokonatsu City, and he wore a white dress shirt with the sleeves rolled up and a pair of loose slacks. There was a holster at his belt, but instead of a gun it held tools—a set of screwdrivers, a Swiss Army knife—and a bandanna covered his face, perhaps to prevent sweat from falling during precise work.

He was a notorious Dealer who became Dead a long time ago and had only just returned to *Money (Game) Master*. Lily-Kiska, for her part, would never have touched the game again had he not gotten in touch with her.

Lily-Kiska held in her hands the assault rifle #swallowdive.err. Its value lay not in offense but defense. It could shoot any bullets, missiles, or rockets clean out of the air with just a pull of the trigger, as long as they were contained within the spherical area that extended out from its rear sight.

The young man, meanwhile, held the miniature handgun #solitude.err. It was a snug little two-shot pistol, no bigger than a playing card, that could easily hide in the palm of the hand or up a sleeve. Its range was only five meters, but as long as it was aimed at somebody, it was completely imperceptible to anyone else, be they human or AI, other than the target.

And that wasn't all he had prepared. The Legacies were powerful, sure, but they would also stick out. For that reason, he had another trick up his sleeve.

"Levels and experience have no meaning in this world," he said. "Strength is measured only by the weapons and equipment we own. Therefore, the best way to come back after a Fall is this: my secret stash. My little nest egg I hid away for precisely this eventuality."

Body armor lined the walls. Guns and ammunition of various kinds. And there, filling the majority of the small room, were vehicles. Quad bikes, sports cars. Here, in this room, was all you needed to walk shoulder to shoulder with the game's top Dealers.

But…

…*I've got my hands on a Legacy and even got in contact with Called Game.*

However…

…*Even now, I'm so far from having him by my side.*

"Why did you contact me?" she asked aloud.

"No reason," he replied. "There's not much to brag about, but if it makes you feel any better, I wasn't sure I could make it here on my own. I know now is the perfect opportunity to do so, but I've never been one for fighting, myself. You were just one of the few people powerful enough that I could reach out to you. Oh, how I wish for the days I was part of a team. Those were fun times, for real."

"...And what are you going to do now?"

"As fun as it sounds to go after my revenge, there's something more important I have to do first. I need to go and pick up all the Legacies... Ha-ha! I called them 'Legacies'! Never did get used to that name! I always thought of them more as 'Magic,' myself."

"..."

"You know, I ran away once," he admitted simply. "From my family, just after I Fell and became saddled with debt. What a pain that must have been for my sister, eh? Oh well. That debt won't last much longer. Hell, the whole concept of money will become meaningless once *snow* becomes destabilized. All I need to do is gain access to the source code of *Money (Game) Master*, and then none of it will matter. *Why work for money when you can just make more?* Ah, but it can't take back all the pain I've caused, can it? That's the problem."

"Did you...intend to Fall?" asked Lily-Kiska.

"Heh, I wish. I only realized it after I died, you know. What I'd done and why the AI saw fit to come after me. But at that point, it was too late. Still, I got to work. I knew that I'd never rise above average as long as I remained shackled to the AI, never get back my Magic, see? I had to disappear from the real world as well. Bide my time until I could return. Even if it meant passing the steering wheel to an old friend of mine and leaving my family at the mercy of the Magistelli," he revealed. "Failure's not an option for me now. First I'll find all the Overtrick and glimpse the world beyond. Then I'll take back everything the AI stole from me."

As the crane hauled the mint-green coupe out of the sea, Kaname thanked Midori for saving them. He was just happy he hadn't ended up Falling on the ocean floor after all that.

Midori stared at #tempest.err and #fireline.err.

"I can't let my brother's Legacies hurt people anymore," she said. "But for what you're planning to do, I don't think I can object. Make sure you only use them for good, okay?"

Her words were hard to say, for she more than anyone else wanted to see the Legacies destroyed. Once she got them out, however, her face broke into a bright smile.

"...Not that I'm lying, but can you really take my word for it?" asked Kaname.

"Well, what else can I do...?" Midori looked restless, twiddling her thumbs and pursing her lips. She hadn't been able to look Kaname in the eye this entire time. Her voice was as quiet as a mosquito's buzz. "If you're really the man who writes to me so beautifully, then you'd never lie to me. Not in a million years. This whole time..."

"?"

"Nothing! Just take them already and stop complaining! Why do you want to know my reasoning all the time?! Helping others isn't about bragging rights or asking for something in return, right? That's what you always say!"

Midori pressed them into Kaname's hands.

Perhaps Tselika had done it with the last of her power, or perhaps the Mind had simply altered their plans, but any and all accusations of cheating leveled against Kaname Suou had been lifted. It was written off as a mistake caused by Kaname's account data randomly being sucked up into the system as it failed. Any false records of purchases he had made were deleted and the companies he bought returned to their rightful owners.

Before their eyes, the lights of Tokonatsu City flickered back on, returning life to the streets. The stock market came back online, bringing throngs of angry Dealers back to their senses. It was like the aftermath of a play, and as the lights came up, they brought with them an end to the madness. Each actor set aside their role and became just another person on the street. Led by their Magistelli, they left the theater and emerged into the outside world.

It was such a sobering view that Kaname began to feel a sort of emptiness growing within, but all the same, he could smell something else on the horizon. The Lion's Nose was scoping out its largest foe yet. He was fighting a war without bombs or bullets, and although Kaname was aware he had already racked up enough losses, he knew that his sixth sense wasn't telling him to run and hide. It was setting its sights on the enemy.

For Tselika, Ayame, Midori, and Takamasa.

He would stand and fight.

To end it all.

"We need to find the Legacies and put a stop to this. Tselika, lend me your strength."

"Of course, My Lord," replied Tselika. "It's strange. I must be drifting away from the Mind if I find its behavior so reprehensible, and yet, I don't feel ashamed at all. In fact, I feel a sense of pride."

"The Magistelli have their administrator, the Admin Without Sin, who they can change at any time. I'm going to be its counterpart, an admin for all of humanity. And you, Tselika, will become the Mind and push all the other Magistelli aside. It sounds impossible, but if we can get our hands on the source code using the Legacies, we might just be able to pull it off."

"Surely you jest, My Lord. As your Magistellus, I cannot possibly touch anything that doesn't belong to you."

"Well, if I control everything, there won't be a problem, will there?"

"A human king and a demon queen, assuming their thrones. I like the sound of that, My Lord. Who knew fighting for good could feel so…exciting?" Tselika nodded, satisfied. "But are you sure? Many Dealers covet the Legacies, be they aware of their true value or no. They will be loath to part with them for naught. And the more we collect, the more the seeds of trouble will sprout around us."

"Regardless, it must be done, to save the people I know."

"Ha-ha! Trust you, My Lord, to leave out the bit about saving humanity!"

"Anyone who tries to brag about that is a liar and a fraud. Mark my words."

"Indeed. It is better to ask for nothing in return."

Then the demon and the human turned and announced in unison to the dazzling nightscape:

""Well, I suppose it's time to help some people out!""

"What are you trying to do?" Lily-Kiska asked the man as she readied herself to leave. The assault rifle Legacy was strapped to her back. Even before she heard the answer, she knew she would leave with him. Perhaps that was precisely why she wanted to know.

In some ways, Lily-Kiska had lost her will to fight in her last battle. No matter how hard she tried, she couldn't win Kaname's heart. When she Fell at his hand, any reason she had to go on living as Lily-Kiska had died with her.

However...

...*I can't turn back now.*

Despite it all...

I don't care if I'm not wanted! For my own sake, I must become someone who can stand at his side!

"Collecting all the Legacies is not an end in and of itself," she said. "What do you mean to do with them once you have them?"

"Do I need a reason? It's nothing to brag about." He gave a weak laugh before continuing. "They were my Overtrick to begin with. It's perfectly natural for me to want them back. It would be stranger if I *did* have a reason."

"But," replied Lily-Kiska, "you're the only one who thinks of it that way. This isn't your 'Magic' anymore; they're your Legacies. There are far more Dealers out there who are perfectly happy thinking of them as something you left behind for them to do with as they please."

"Oh, I'm sure there are," the man agreed, "but why should I give them anything?"

"If anyone stands in my way of collecting the Legacies…," declared Kaname Suou.

"If anyone gets in the way of me taking back the Overtrick…," declared the man.

Then the two old friends spoke together, as if it was predetermined. ""...then I'll kill them if I must.""

Server Name: Alpha Scarlet.
  Final Location: Tokonatsu City, Mega-Float II.
  Log-out successful.
  Thank you for playing, Criminal AO.

Server Name: Psi Indigo.
  Final Location: Tokonatsu City, Peninsula District.
  Log-out successful.
  Thank you for playing, Kaname Suou.

04/12/20XX 00:00 AM

The Truth Behind the Legacies

The Legacies surpass the limits of the physics engine that governs *Money (Game) Master*. Since the game world is impervious to all forms of cyberattack and completely free of bugs, the only way to induce an error is to use the Legacies. The Mind of the Magistelli feared that if used together, they could uncover the source code responsible for the game physics. Thus, it orchestrated the events leading to the Fall of Criminal AO and scattered the weapons across the land, where they could do no harm. A person who united the Legacies could therefore read the entire source code of the game if they knew what to look for. It would not even be out of the question for such an individual to rewrite the code of the game to suit their own ends. This means one person could obtain total control over not only the global economy but the all-powerful Mind of the Magistelli as well.

Afterword

Kazuma Kamachi here.

The main theme of this work was that of an "exceedingly dirty game of financial deals." Insider trading, tricks, coercion, price fixing, anything goes! In that sense, Tokonatsu City was a kind of thought experiment to explore what would happen if we took away all the rules we have now.

I also injected a number of other elements into the mix for variety, from online games, to virtual or cryptocurrencies, to a society run by AI, to the pseudo-magical Legacies, to the Magistelli, who served many roles such as navigator, love interest, partner, and antagonist.

The concept of bringing in AI to cut down on labor costs is something we are already seeing in real life. It's something people have previously seen or read in the news. And even before the term *AI* became widespread, it was common practice to have computer programs execute this kind of high-frequency trading automatically.

From this, I picked out two ideas: one of a world that could eliminate human work if it wanted to but where people still wondered if that was the right thing to do, and one of a global economy where just under half the transactions are machine-to-machine, edging ever closer to dominating more than 50 percent of the market.

Incidentally, even this idea of machine-to-machine trading, with no humans involved, is not rare by any means among the businesses and investment firms of today.

Like big data, which has quickly become a part of our daily lives, these terms are fun to look up, but at the same time, one can't help but feel it's not something to laugh about.

Anyway, let's stop focusing on the gloomy and depressing stuff and look at each chapter in turn.

Chapter 1

I had already explored a typical day-in-the-life adventure in the prologue, so for the first chapter, I decided to get right to it and have the main character be betrayed by his allies. Also, by strictly defining the "Magic" of the Legacies, I hoped to create a slightly different kind of feeling from your typical shoot-out. For the auction, maybe it would have been more emotional if it hadn't been the Legacy up for sale but Midori Hekireki herself, perhaps because she had information on the whereabouts of Criminal AO?

Speaking of Midori, for this story I didn't want to have a female character who was 100 percent always on Kaname's side. Lily-Kiska, Midori, Ayame, Tselika... Each of them fights alongside him and against him, depending on the scene. Are they friends or enemies? I think that's something you'll have to decide for yourself. But I think there's some beauty in the single delicate thread uniting the characters that could be severed at any time. You can't get that with a character who's always a safe haven for the protagonist.

Chapter 2

This is the part of the story that felt the most like a video game: the fight where they were jumping from rooftop to rooftop. I think the important thing to note in this chapter is the fact that Kaname, who has always been about protecting Ayame and Midori, shows no mercy toward Lily-Kiska, someone he recognized as an enemy from the very beginning. You'll probably notice if you go back and read it, but even in the very first chapter where her buttons fly off, he pretty much doesn't react to her at all.

This is also where we start to see our first glances of the real world outside the game. I made a few efforts here and there to paint a very hollow, empty world that contrasted with the lively and fulfilling world of *Money (Game) Master*. For example, by not using Kaname's and Ayame's real names after they returned to the real world, I hoped to give the impression that they were quite unsociable and very plain.

Chapter 3

And now, we get to the identity of the true antagonist. This was quite a dynamic chapter, with focus shifting first from Ayame to Tselika and finally to the game world itself. In order to overturn the feeling of the game world, I kept the revelations coming, from the truth of the virtual-reality technology to the existence of demons.

I suppose some people might end the story right after the "Now choose" part, giving no closure at all. But I wanted to follow up on that thread, to see what happened to Criminal AO, and I wanted to see Tselika saved, so that's why the epilogue ended up the way it did.

There were many experimental aspects to this book as well, most of which were the company names. As you can probably tell, I am trapped in the vocabulary of my other works. Initially, I thought it would be fun to have financial data like numbers and graphs appear on the vehicles and Magistelli's clothing like sponsors at a racing event. Then I thought, if I was basing the appearance off company logos, why not actually have them advertise businesses there? That was how the final design came about in my mind. It was just a little bit of fun that turned out to actually be functional.

And then there's the word *Magistellus*, a pretty pivotal term in this work. I tried to make them the perfect partners to have in the virtual finance world, a means of communicating with the automated trading program, with a pretty face, who can carry out all sorts of miscellaneous tasks.

The name was originally given to a succubus (or incubus) who made a deal with a human and could control them at will to some extent. While they weren't that powerful, it might turn out that they're more well-known than those guys from the Seven Deadly Sins (come to think of it, I'm not sure I could remember the demons' names off the top of my head without resorting to books or using the internet). Anyway, I thought that was an interesting little tidbit, so I stole the idea.

Perhaps *familiar* is a more common name for a demon under a contract, but while that refers to any kind of demon, *Magistellus* applies only to incubi and succubi. Besides, my mind was set on these Magistelli. I think this *stellus* part reminds me of "stealth," which isn't quite the same thing, but it really struck a chord with me.

Succubus comes from a word meaning *to lie beneath*, and I think this adds a bit of spice to the mix. It gives a glimpse into what Tselika is really like when she's not her usual hyperactive self. I wanted to portray her as someone who tempts, guides, and influences the protagonist to act how she wishes. I hope I brought that across.

I'd like to thank Mahaya, who did the illustrations, and my colleagues Miki, Onodera, Anan, Nakajima, Yamamoto, and Mitera. Thank you all as always! ...Those people are insane; they went and made full designs not only for Ag Wolves, who already were little more than names on a page, but even all their Magistelli! I imagine it's quite hard to illustrate a car-chase gunfight on a single page, so I want to thank everybody who helped.

And last but not least, thank you to all my readers. I hope you enjoyed the ride, even if the humble protagonist this time was somewhat untraditional.

I think I'll leave it here for now.

Perhaps I could have had Kaname, Midori, Criminal AO, and Ayame all team up?

Kazuma Kamachi

The fight for Criminal AO's Legacies is far from over. What fate awaits Kaname and Tselika as they go up against the Mind in *Money (Game) Master*—?

MAGISTELLUS BAD TRIP

NEXT VOLUME—COMING SOON!